M000317322

no way but through

An American Refugee Story

A Novel By
Emily Anne Brown

ISBN 978-0-578-41699-1

Front cover photo credit: Debbie McCale
Back cover photo credit: Jose Antonio Sanchez Reyes

www.emilyannebr.com

Dedicated to the 60+ million displaced people in the world who have survived all this and much worse. I pray you find hope and encounter kindness.

Author's Note //

I've never been a refugee. I'll just go ahead and name the elephant in the room. At the outset, I knew this project was bigger than me, and I'm likely not the right person to take on such a book. But I was compelled and inspired through the whole process.

I'm an American, my family dates back to the Mayflower on both sides. Our history is marked with the blood of slaves, and probably the mistreatment of natives, but also rich stories of involvement in the Underground Railroad (different sides of the family). None in my family have fought for their country, most choosing conscientious objection over the killing of foreign brothers and sisters. All this family history, and all my privileged life, is due to the freedoms we enjoy in this country.

I didn't write this book from a place of experience, or even much knowledge, but from deep empathy. From a desire to love others better, and to help others love better. I wrote this book hoping to open my eyes, and yours, to a fraction of what over 60 million people are living through today. I wanted to breathe the deprivation and danger. I wanted to rub shoulders with loss. I wanted to live in the "otherness" that so many displaced people experience. But this is just a book. This is a product of my imagination.

A book may give a brief voice to the voiceless, but it can't change the lives of real displaced people who in fact aren't voiceless. Are they? Or have we merely turned deaf ears to their cries and their worth? I did set out to write this book to make a difference, but I've learned that all I can do with my words is stand in solidarity with displaced people for just a moment. To use my voice to reach out an olive branch of peace from a closed country who will no longer take "your tired, your poor, your huddled masses yearning to breathe free."

I don't mean to bring politics into this project, but I do mean to open our eyes to love people better. So much gets in the way of loving people. Fear most of all. My deepest fear in setting this book free is exploiting or in some way mocking the experiences and lives of refugees. That's the opposite of my goal.

The attention of the world was brought to refugees in 2015 when an image of a drowned toddler went viral. After that, resources and volunteers poured into Greece to assuage the refugee crisis. The outpouring was swift and massive, and much too short-lived. It's been three years and due to instant media updates online, much of the world's attention is focused elsewhere. But there are still hundreds of thousands of refugees in the world, and there always will be as long as war and persecution are part of our story.

My hope is that every average Tom, Dick, and Janey going about their lives in America will read this story and feel a shift inside themselves. A move, however small, toward compassion and understanding. If enough heart-change happens, maybe we can salvage what this country was intended to be. Maybe we can change lives beyond our borders for the good.

I believe in a Kingdom where there will be peace. Where no one will feel displaced because there will be no borders, no countries, no nationalism. I believe in a Kingdom where we are one and we are all free. Where tears won't fall, and poverty and illness won't be part of the vocabulary. I believe in trying, even in small ways, to bring that Kingdom here and now.

Writing these pages broke me down in so many ways. I hope they break down your walls too.

"By the rivers of Babylon we sat and wept
when we remembered Zion.
There on the poplars
we hung our harps,
for there our captors asked us for songs,
our tormentors demanded songs of joy;
they said, "Sing us one of the songs of Zion!"
How can we sing the songs of the LORD
while in a foreign land?
If I forget you, Jerusalem,
may my right hand forget its skill.
May my tongue cling to the roof of my mouth
if I do not remember you,
if I do not consider Jerusalem
my highest joy." – Psalm 137:1-6 (Of the Israelites' exile to
Babylon)

Foreword //

In the winter of 2017, I found myself on Zack and Emily's couch pouring my heart out. Many circumstances had brought us to this moment: summers working at camp with Zack, leading me to know his wife, a season of working in a primarily Syrian refugee camp in Thessaloniki Greece, then preparing to move to Europe long term in order to be a good neighbor to immigrants and refugees. Emily had caught on to what I was doing and felt a stirring in her spirit to partner in some way.

So there we were, exchanging passions and asking God for a way to collaborate. I wanted them to understand the complicated nuances of the crisis, especially for Syrians: many of them professionals, driven from their homes, forced to flee, and subsequently getting stuck in a country far more impoverished and disorganized than their own; waiting to be sorted. "It would be like if Americans had to flee to Mexico and wait for the Mexican government to resettle them." The more I delved into this metaphor, the more Emily lit up. "I have to tell that story."

She has done a masterful job. What would have been a daunting--nearly impossible--task, perhaps too close to my PTSD, came bursting out of Emily's heart in a matter of months. She truly was the one anointed for this project.

I've appreciated her attention to detail and extensive research to do it justice. I love that she makes Emma a business owner, since many of my Syrian friends were. It is clever she makes the Smiths Texans, since they have an American reputation of being pretty rooted. My friends can trace their families living in one city back to Biblical times. Mark my words, many refugees never dreamed of leaving home.

So why did they leave? An unrest, which came to a head in Spring of 2011 pitted some Syrians against their own government when it responded violently to what they called a peaceful protest.

As tensions and retaliations increased, world powers began taking an interest and capitalizing on the chaos. Soon the protestors were joined by extremists, but also the United States, Saudi Arabia, Turkey, and Qatar. They were gaining ground until Syrian President Bashar Assad called reinforcements of his own. Soon the scales were tipped in the opposite direction by Russia, Iran and Hezbullah (an extremist group based out of Lebanon). Meanwhile the chaos also attracted the attention of the Islamic State of Iraq. They marched West and soon became the Islamic State of Iraq and Syria, more famously known as ISIS.

While most parties claimed they were there to fight ISIS, bombs were being dropped everywhere on everyone. I naively asked one of my friends which side they were "rooting for", to which they graciously replied, "No one. If I'm on this side of town, Russia bombs me, if another, ISIS, if another, the Free Syrian army. We, in Aleppo, never wanted to be involved, but the war was brought to our doorstep. It's the same war that always exists between the United States and Russia or Iran and Saudi Arabia, but here, they can fight on someone else's land, with minimal personal cost." It's true. While over 500,000 souls have perished in this war, none have been Russian, American, Iranian or Saudi.

Homes and businesses, schools and hospitals, reduced to rubble. With many days turning civilians into first responders, no one has been without great personal loss.

To make matters worse, the government was forcefully searching for men to draft into Assad's army. Those who had previously been excused for the freedom to pursue education were now being hunted to join a battle no one was winning. This is the main reason many refugees are young men. They have been marked as deserters and it will never be safe for them to return. A country whose population used to be 23 million, now has over 7 million of its people internally displaced, and over 5 million registered as refugees abroad.

I admire Emily for sticking to this idea long after it was trendy to care about refugees, Syrian or otherwise. I hope her compassion is contagious and more people are able to walk in the tired shoes of these 60+ million people. Maybe the inspiration which led me to Greece, and Emily to write, will be passed on, and you will find your place in the story.

This issue is deep in the heart of our Creator. His trifecta of concern is for the orphan, widow and foreigner. Since joining the cause, I have seen Him move in powerful ways and open impossible doors. He is eager to empower the people who care about this. It's not up to governments to do the work of His Kingdom, it's up to His Spirit alive in you and me.   – Bethany Cetti

Prologue //

A stalemate rose between two of the world's most powerful nations. Nuclear weapons were researched, built, and flaunted. Treaties were signed to halt potential nuclear wars. A writer, George Orwell, called it a Cold War. It caught on. Almost forty-five years of tension and distrust. Everything was laced with the strain, from ballet and the arts, to politics and strategic military maneuvers.

At the close of the Cold War, the United States signed a treaty with the USSR. Known as the Intermediate-Range Nuclear Forces Treaty, it required the destruction of each party's ground-launched ballistic and cruise missiles with ranges from 500 to 5,500 feet within three years of the signing. It was the most detailed treaty in the history of nuclear arms control.

When the USSR disbanded in 1991, the US pursued the implementation of the treaty with the former Soviet republics. For more than thirty years, the treaty has held, but over the last several, Russia and the United States have taken their turns in accusing each other of violating this treaty. Tensions are rising again.

White House, Oval Office
Sunday, June 3rd 20—
8:32PM //

Chairman of the Joint Chief of Staff, Eric Richardson, paced around the Oval Office. He checked his watch.

The President of the United States sat at the historic desk, scrolling on his cell phone. "Is this meeting completely necessary, Richardson?"

"Afraid so, Sir." Richardson set his lips in a thin line. Perhaps it was Richardson's tone that made the president look up from his phone. Their eyes locked. The president swore under his breath.

The door opened, and the Chief of Staff entered, followed by the Communications Director, the Press Secretary, the National Security Advisor, and the Secretary of Defense. They all filled the couches in the center of the office.

Richardson stood in front of the president's desk. "I called this emergency meeting because the Russians are threatening to break the INF treaty."

The room was silent. No one was surprised at this announcement. Some appeared annoyed.

"We've been back and forth with these so-called threats for years. What makes you think there's a real threat now?" The impatience in the President's voice was palpable.

Blood boiled in Richardson's veins. "This is no idle threat. We've confirmed that those unmanned submarines they were boasting about, that can aim a nuclear missile anywhere in the world, are parked not far from the east coast. And active."

"You're suggesting they would actually go through with firing a nuclear missile at us?" The Communications Director started jotting notes.

"Yes. I suggest we raise the Terror Alert to orange." Richardson leaned against the desk, with his back to the president.

A loud thump sounded on the wood behind him. "I see no reason to raise the alarm and spread unnecessary fear. Vaselik swore up and down that those submarines are there for protection."

Richardson faced the President. *You're the one who swore up and down in front of the whole nation. Now you're just trying to cover your own ass.* "Protection from what? We aren't planning to use nuclear force against anyone."

"That's the official party line, yes." The president glared at Richardson from under bushy eyebrows.

"Richardson, I'm going to need more reason to crank up the terror alert to orange. Yellow, maybe." The Communications Director met his eyes, her hand still.

Richardson inhaled. "We got a reliable tip-off that they're planning to strike on Friday."

Monday, June 4th

5:31AM   //

An eerie, dark hush settled over the coffee shop in the pre-dawn hour. Emma stood just inside the door and could see the dull gleam of the spotless espresso machine, presiding over the long counter. She walked across the café and switched on a light behind the bar.

Her coffee shop materialized around her. It's hard-wood floors and white cinder block walls decorated with tin Texan stars and industrial bookshelves were all she had dreamt it would be. And was even better than her dreams.

Emma cranked the music, Adam Larson and Co, from the back room and left her purse on the break table. She poured a measured amount of whole beans into the grinder and set a filter in the funnel. A slow smile spread over her face as she went through the familiar motions.

She heard the front door open and turned. "Hey Rick."

The local baker's arms were laden with boxes of the day's fresh pastries. "Hey. Today's special is strawberry fritters." Rick set the stack on the counter.

"You know my weakness for fritters." Emma eyed the boxes.

"I know. The small box on top is yours." Rick thumped a fist on the wide, rough-hewn wood counter and turned to leave.

"Thanks. Have a good day." Emma pulled the top box off the stack and peeked inside.

Four sugar-crusted fritters beckoned her with their sweet aroma. She hurried to arrange the other pastries in the glass case. She made a latte and took her fritters to the back room.

Rick's pastries were the last word in buttery, melt-in-your-mouth flakiness, and the perfect balance of sweetness and tartness from the strawberries. She savored every bite and took a sip of her latte. She jumped when her employee, Amy, came around the corner.

Her cheeks warmed, and she held up her hands. "You can have one. Rick gave me extras."

"You're the boss. You can do what you want." Amy hung her purse on a hook in the wall.

"Well, take one if you want." Emma wiped her hands on a napkin and stood.

"Thanks." Amy tied a black apron around her waist. "Maybe later."

Emma turned the music down to a reasonable volume and went out to turn on the rest of the lights and flip the "Open" sign on the front door.

7:01AM //

Emma twisted the knob on the espresso machine to turn on the steam wand. She glanced around, taking in the din of conversation filling her coffee house.

The fragrant, dripping espresso permeated the air, the steam rose to meet her warm cheeks, and the chaos of a full café was imbued with the early-morning sun's golden rays. Common Grounds had been open for just over a year, and the morning rush always rekindled the excitement she'd had in the very beginning.

As Amy took orders, Emma looked out over the sea of faces lined up on the other side of the espresso machine. Most were stopping by on their way to work. Moms stopped in before or after taking their kids to school. The city of Houston was awake and bustling, everyone entrenched in the normalcy of routine.

When the initial rush faded, the students and entrepreneurs would fill the tables and stay for hours. Small meetings and coffee dates would take place throughout the day. This is what Emma had anticipated when she'd opened Common Grounds. A place for everyone to stay and feel at home.

"No early morning meeting today, Tom?" Emma looked up at a regular customer as she passed his caramel latte across the counter.

She noticed the news headline on his tablet. The terrorist alert was flashing orange. A frown creased her brow. She smoothed her features as she focused on Tom's response.

"Not today. I might sit and read the news for a minute. Seems like a cheerful start to my day, doesn't it?" Tom walked to a nearby table with a grim chuckle.

Emma's mind wandered as she made the next several drinks, moving on autopilot. Heat had been escalating between the United States and Russia for some time, but Emma didn't think there was anything to it.

The president had been explicit in calming the national fear. He had spoken with the Russian president and there was nothing in the threats.

Whatever that means. Maybe it's not Russia. Maybe it's the Middle East again. Emma's hands went clammy. *Don't think about it.* She shook her head. She handed out the last drink in the line with a smile.

"I'll be right back, then you can take a break." She walked passed Amy, who was rearranging the pastry case, to the back room.

In a side pocket of her purse Emma found her phone and saw she had texts from her mom and her fiancé, Jack.

DON'T FORGET, FAMILY DINNER FRIDAY NIGHT. Mom's was a group text including Dad, Emma's brothers, Aaron and Matt, as well as Aaron's wife, Claire, and Jack.

Emma replied with emojis of an excited face and a bowl of ice cream. Her dad loved chocolate peanut butter.

She pulled up Jack's text. I LOVE YOU.

Emma pushed the green call button under the picture of Jack's face and brought the phone to her ear.

"Hey Em."

"Good, you answered. I was afraid you'd already be at work." Emma looked through the open doorway leading to the workspace behind the counter and watched Amy interact with a customer.

"I am at work." "Oh, sorry. I have to make this quick anyway. Are we still on for tonight?"

"Yep, I'll stop by the coffee shop after work. You get off at four?"

"Yeah. Can't wait. Hey, Jack?"

"Yeah?"

"I saw a headline this morning showing the terrorist alert at orange. Why's it orange?"

"You know not to trust the hype of the news. They use pointless fear tactics to control our perceptions of what's going on in the world."

Emma laughed at Jack's mocking intense tone.

"I don't know, Em. For some reason, they're hell-bent on demonizing Russia right now. I wouldn't worry about it. Go do what you do."

"Okay, thanks. I love you."

"Love you too. Later."

"Bye." Emma set her phone on the desk and went to relieve Amy.

The day flew by in a steady stream of latte and smoothie making. At two 'o clock, Amy left and was replaced by Andrew. Emma was walking to the back room with a bin full of dirty dishes when a familiar voice stopped her.

"Hey Emma." Her fourteen-year-old brother, Matt, moved his bicycle helmet from one arm to the other, his backpack sagging low. His face a mask of sullen boredom.

"Hi Mattie. I'll just put these down real quick. Tell Andrew what you want." Emma nodded her head at her employee standing at the cash register.

"How was your day?" Emma returned and dropped chunks of peeled banana into a blender to make smoothies for her and Matt.

Matt shrugged. "Fine."

"Yeah? Freshman year not all it's cracked up to be? Still bored?"

"Has the school system changed?" He raised an eyebrow.

Emma chuckled, started the blender, then grabbed two plastic cups.

With smoothies in hand, they went to a nearby table. "Do you have any homework?"

"Not much." Matt pulled a book and binder out of his backpack. His brown hair swung over his eyes.

The last time Emma had joked about a broken neck due to all the hair flipping Matt did, he hadn't spoken to her for a week. But he also hadn't cut his hair.

"That's good. I'd better get back to it. I get off soon, though. I can give you a ride home when I'm off."

"Thanks."

The final hour of Emma's shift was busy with students on their way home from school, and more moms picking their kids up or carting them around town to different practices and clubs.

At the tail end of the rush, Aaron showed up. "Hey, I'm running home for a bit and thought I'd stop by. We're taking dinner to a family Claire doesn't exactly love, so I thought I'd grab her favorite drink. Better make it decaf though." He was two years older than Emma and lived in an apartment downtown with his wife.

"That's sweet." Emma squirted chocolate sauce into a cup for Claire's cinnamon mocha. "Will you guys be at family dinner on Friday?"

"Yep. Looking forward to that."

"Oh good. We're not one of the families Claire doesn't exactly love?" Emma winked at her brother as she handed the mocha over.

Aaron let out his deep belly laugh, drawing the attention of everyone in the café.

Emma couldn't suppress her own laughter. "Tell Claire that what you guys do in this city is important."

"Thanks. I'll pass it along." Aaron took the cup from Emma.

"And don't forgot there's still construction off the feeder road."

"Always." Aaron lifted his cup to her and left.

At four 'o clock, the employee who would be closing with Andrew arrived, and Jack sauntered in after her.

"Hey." Emma surveyed Jack as he approached the counter in his slacks and button-down shirt. His dark hair was disheveled, and shadows were forming under his deep brown eyes.

He undid the top button and pulled on the collar, sticking his tongue out. "Hey yourself. Are you done?"

"Yep. I'll go grab my stuff. Matt's coming with me." Emma untied her apron and looked in Matt's direction.

"Cool." Jack leaned forward to kiss her cheek before turning toward Matt's table.

Jack helped Emma load Matt's bicycle onto the back of her Jeep. "I'll see you at your house." He dropped another kiss on her cheek.

"Emma, did you always want to own a coffee shop?" Matt spoke over the music during the car ride to their parent's house.

Emma glanced at Matt. "No, I guess not. I didn't know what I wanted to do until the end of college. Luckily, I majored in business because it seemed like the most practical degree for someone who didn't really know what to do. Then I realized how much I loved the environment a coffee shop creates. And the rest is history."

"Yeah right. I know how hard you worked to build that place from nothing. Nobody ever saw you for almost a year." Matt gazed out the window.

Several moments passed before he spoke up again. "I want to be a detective."

Emma raised her eyebrows. "A detective? Really? That's cool."

Any comment from Matt was rare, let alone a divulging of his deepest wishes. "Yeah, I want to be one of the guys who solves the crimes. Aaron is trying to get rid of poverty in this city, and I want to get rid of crime."

Emma gazed at her little brother as he looked out the window. "You're smart enough. You could do it."

Matt didn't meet her eyes. When they pulled into the driveway of their parent's house at the end of a cul-de-sac in the suburbs of Houston, Jack was already waiting at the curb.

Emma helped Matt take his bike out of the Jeep. "Tell Mom and Dad hi for me. I would come in, but it's date night. I'll talk to Mom tomorrow."

"Okay. Well, thanks for the ride." Matt opened the car door.

"Anytime." Emma waved and walked to Jack's car.

When she had slid into the passenger's seat, he tugged on the ends of her caramel brown hair and leaned over to kiss her lips.

Emma's cheeks warmed under the tender, but firm pressure of his. She took a moment to catch her breath when he pulled away. "Where are we going?"

"I have an idea." Jack steered the car around the cul-de-sac. He took Emma's hand as he drove, stroking her thumb with his, and they listened to the radio, caught in a sweet silence.

A jarring voice interrupted the stillness. "Breaking news— the president has been moved from Washington DC to an unknown location. This is a confirmed leak from within the White House. The president has retreated from Washington. . ."

Emma squeezed Jack's hand.

Monday 5:37PM //

After laying the third plate on the dining room table, Carol hurried back into the kitchen where dinner was likely burning. She stirred the contents of the pot and peered at the recipe Joe had printed off for her. It was a "healthy" recipe. Something new she was trying. She only hoped Matt would like it.

Joe had been thrilled when she announced she wanted to start making healthier meals, determined to lose the weight that seemed to have hung on, and grown, since Matt's birth, fourteen years ago. If she was being honest with herself, it was another attempt to bridge the chasm that was opening between her and Joe.

She looked down at her distended midriff, her pudgy hands. Sighing, she tucked her short blonde hair behind her ears. The smell coming from the pot on the stove was not enticing.

It will be worth it, no matter what it tastes like. I've tried everything, this has to work. If Matt hates it, he can make a peanut butter and jelly sandwich for all I care.

The pantry door was open, revealing a large box of cheesy fish crackers. Her stomach rumbled.

Just a couple won't hurt. This will be the last box. Mattie doesn't eat them anymore.

She heard the front door open and jumped, backing away from the pantry. "Hi honey. Did you have a nice day?" Carol picked up a wooden spoon and stirred dinner as Matt entered the kitchen.

"Yeah. Emma gave me a ride home. Emma said she would've come in, but it's date night." Matt rolled his eyes. "What's that smell?"

"That smell is dinner. Get used to it." Carol waved the wooden spoon in Matt's face. "So, it's just the three of us, then. Maybe that's best. You and Dad can be my guinea pigs."

"Can't wait." Matt opened the fridge.

"Stay out of there. You'll ruin your appetite."

"If anything ruins my appetite, it'll be that smell." Matt pointed at the pot.

"Don't judge before you've tasted it." Carol placed a fist on her hip, hoping she looked intimidating.

"Okay, okay." Matt raised his hands in surrender.

Carol bit her lower lip. "Do you have homework to do?"

"No, I got it all done at the coffee shop."

"Good. Could you finish setting the table for me? It needs silverware."

As Matt collected the cutlery, the front door opened again.

"Hello!" Joe's voice boomed from the entryway.

Matt didn't respond but walked around the kitchen island into the dining room.

"How was your day?" Carol turned away from the stove as Joe entered the kitchen.

"Fine. How was yours?" Joe followed in Matt's footsteps to the fridge and peered inside.

"Fine. Dinner's almost ready, so don't eat too much." Carol stared down into the contents of the pot, dubious.

Matt marched out of the dining room, heading toward the stairs.

Joe shut the fridge door with a few baby carrots in his hand. "What's cooking?"

"That recipe you printed for me. I hope it's good. It doesn't smell very good. Has some weird ingredients. We'll see." Carol lifted the lid of the pot and stuck her wooden spoon in.

When they were seated around the table, Carol's eyes darted from her husband to her son, and back again. Joe brought his fork to his mouth without hesitating.

Matt eyed his food and shuffled it around his plate.

"This is good." Joe raised his eyebrows and took another bite.

"Really?" Carol and Matt spoke together, with differing tones of hope and skepticism.

Joe grinned. "Yes, really. Try it. Both of you." He stared at Matt before returning to his own food.

Carol brought a bite to her mouth. The flavors were different than she was used to, but much better than expected. "It is good. Wow."

Maybe losing weight will be easier than I thought. Carol glanced up to see Matt's face contorted in disgust.

The urge to whip up Matt's favorite meal was strong. *Matt's always loved my cooking. But this is worth it, for all of us.* "Mattie, we all need to eat healthier. This will be good for the whole family. You'll get used to it."

Matt cleared his throat but didn't say anything.

"I've decided I want to be a detective and solve crimes." Matt's voice startled Carol out of her study of her food.

She stared at her youngest, her baby who'd grown so sullen lately.

"Yeah? What made you decide that?" Joe stuck another large bite into his mouth.

"Well, I like the idea of learning about forensics and the process of narrowing down clues."

"Sounds dangerous." Carol looked from Matt to her husband.

Joe swallowed. "I think it's a cool idea. You've got a lot of time to learn more about it and make sure it's a good fit." He reached out and ruffled Matt's hair.

Matt sighed and smoothed his hair down.

While Carol did the dishes, Matt retreated to his room and Joe turned on the TV. Carol thought about what she could do to break through their evening routine. Soon, Joe was on the floor doing sit-ups. He did one hundred every night, and one hundred push-ups.

When Carol finished the dishes, she left her blue and white kitchen sparkling and joined Joe on the floor.

His eyebrows rose. "Are you going to do sit-ups with me?" Joe got up on his knees.

Carol nodded, ignoring the note of incredulity in his voice. She lay on her back with her knees up.

"Okay, I'll hold your feet and count. Remember to keep your back as straight as possible." Joe put a hand on each of Carol's feet.

"You're cute." Carol stalled, admiring his salt and pepper hair, and the laugh lines around his eye. Blue like faded denim.

I'm getting shameless trying to get his attention again. I can't remember the last time I did anything like a sit up.

"Don't try to distract me. If you can do ten in a row, I'll do that thing you love so much." Carol rolled her eyes, but her heart was light.

"You mean clean the bathroom?"

Joe chuckled. "Come on, you can do it. Cross your arms over your chest. There you go. One, two . . ."

It was much harder than Joe made it look. Carol couldn't even get past two. *I'm in worse shape than I thought. I'm going to have to stick with—*

A shriek of laughter pierced the air. *Did that come out of my mouth?*

Joe tickled her without mercy. Something he hadn't done in a long time.

"Stop, please. Stop, I'm going to pee my pants." Carol tried in vain to calm down.

Joe crawled forward to hover over her. "I'll race you to the bedroom." His breath was warm against her ear.

He was up like a shot and running to the stairs. Carol stood and followed at a slower pace. This attention from him was unusual. *It's like he's overcompensating for something he doesn't want me to know.*

"What's going on?" Carol stood before Joe who sat on the bed stripped down to his boxers.

"Nothing. I'm just proud of you for cooking such a good meal and trying to be healthier." The lie flickered in Joe's eyes.

Carol put a hand on her hip. "We've been married for twenty-eight years. I know when you're lying."

"Alright, alright, alright. Well, I wasn't lying. I am proud of you. But, that isn't the whole truth. On my way home, some breaking news came over the radio." Joe scanned Carol's face before continuing. "They moved the president from Washington DC."

Carol stared at her husband. Her throat dried out. "What does that mean?"

Joe sighed and rubbed the back of his neck. "It means there must be something behind all this hype about the Russian threats."

Carol lowered herself onto the bed beside Joe. The air was sucked out of her lungs. Her thoughts flitted from Emma to Aaron to Matt. A hot flash came on and she lay back onto the down comforter.

"Honey, don't worry about it." Joe turned to face her. "There's nothing we can do about it at this point. Worrying is only going to make things worse. Everything's going to be fine."

"You don't know that. What if it's not fine." She could only just get the words out. Her throat constricted like someone had a vice grip around her airways.

"This is why I didn't want to tell you. Just take a few deep breaths. It's going to be fine. Breathe with me." Joe slowed his breathing for her to follow, but Carol couldn't fight the panic taking over.

Darkness enveloped her vision.

Tuesday, June 5th
9:17AM //

"Hey, Emma!" Aaron's voice boomed through the near-empty coffee shop.

"Hi, what's up?" Emma glanced up from straightening the pastry display. Her brow was furrowed in concentration unfitting the mundane task.

"The usual. What's on your mind?"

"Oh, you know—war, terror, nuclear bombs." Emma didn't meet his gaze.

"Hey." His tone demanded her attention. "There are real things happening right now. People in this city who we can actually help. Whether or not a war is building, let's focus on the present moment."

Emma exhaled and gave Aaron a withering glare.

"Remember when we talked about giving out vouchers to the homeless for a free cup of coffee?"

"Yes, I printed some out a few days ago. I also had Jack laminate them at his office so they would last longer. I decided to offer a free cup once a week. So, I listed the next several weeks on them and we can mark them with a permanent marker when someone comes in each week. I was hoping you'd come by today." Emma reached under the counter and pulled out a drawer where a stack of slim, shiny cards sat.

"No way. This is better than I was expecting. These are perfect. Thanks so much. And tell Jack thanks. You have no idea how excited I am to give these out." Aaron took the stack from Emma.

"I think I everyone in the shop can guess how excited you are." Emma laughed and threw an apologetic look toward the customer receiving his latte.

"Sorry. My volume runs away with me."

"I'm excited too. We'll get some people in here who we wouldn't normally see."

"That's the spirit." Aaron thrust his index finger at his little sister. "I'll take my usual, and I'll get a mocha for my friend."

Aaron checked his watch, then drummed his fingers on the counter.

"Are you sure you need coffee?" Emma rang in his order, giving him a substantial family discount.

"Yep."

Emma shook her head.

Armed with a drink carrier, and a pocket full of coffee vouchers and invitations to a dinner, Aaron set out for his appointment.

A man lounged in a doorway a few blocks away, the most inconspicuous shade he could find. Aaron walked this route to see this man, and others like him, claiming what space they could on the side streets of Houston as their home.

Aaron waved as he approached. "Hey, Chuck. How are ya?"

Chuck's belongings weren't spread out as usual but tucked into the backpack he was leaning against.

"Going for a job interview today?"

"Hoping this will be the one that sticks."

Aaron crouched at Chuck's level. "You've worked hard to get to where you are now, I'm sure it will. Here, Claire and I want you and everyone to come to a nice dinner at the old Armory on Thursday night. We'll have a feast."

Taking the paper Aaron offered him, Chuck gave the invitation a cursory glance. "I'll see what I can do. No promises."

"Well, we hope you can make it." Aaron was used to these non-committal answers. "Also, my sister owns a coffee shop a few blocks down and she wanted me to give out these vouchers for a free coffee every week. You should take her up on it. They have great coffee."

"Thanks, man." Chuck pocketed the invitation and the voucher.

"What time is the interview?"

Chuck consulted a second-hand watch. "In about an hour. Suppose I should clean up and head out. Thanks for the coffee."

"Let me know how it goes today. Good luck." Aaron stood and continued down the street.

The humidity of the day already settled onto him like a hot, damp blanket. He handed out five more coffee vouchers, along with the invitations. Most people showed excitement and said they'd be there.

Several blocks later, Aaron found himself in front of the dilapidated house of the friend he had scheduled a meeting with. He knocked on the door and noticed the white paint of the house was dingy and peeling. *Maybe we should see about repainting this for her.*

His family said Aaron took his concern for the people of the community to unnecessary levels, but he wanted to do all he could to make Houston better for everyone.

The door before him opened a crack and a young woman peered out.

"Hola, Marie. Como te va?"

"Hi, Aaron. Come in." Marie continued their conversation in Spanish and held the door open just enough to let Aaron through.

Two distinct baby cries sailed in from a back room.

"One minute." Marie disappeared for several minutes before coming back with a baby in each arm. "Sorry, they both needed changing."

"No problem. May I?" Aaron held out his arms for one of the babies.

Marie lay a tiny girl in the crook of his elbow. Aaron sat on the ragged, sagging couch against the front window.

"Claire was disappointed she couldn't come with me today. She loves seeing the girls." Aaron looked down at the bundle in his arms.

Hopefully in the next year, we'll have a little one of our own. Shouldn't say that to Marie, though. She's up to her eyes with five kids under age six.

Aaron attempted to master the swooning look he was sure had taken over his face. "Do you have a list of things you need this week?"

"Yes." Marie was still standing, swaying the other twin from side to side. She took a crumpled piece of paper out of the back pocket of her jeans and handed it to Aaron.

Aaron unfolded the note and scanned it. There were plenty of food items listed, but no other essentials like diapers and wipes. "Are you sure there isn't more you need? We're happy to provide anything and everything."

"I know. That's really all I need." Marie kept her eyes on the baby in her arms. Her cheeks glowed with warmth.

"Claire will be happy to come by tomorrow after school to help out while you get some work done. Trust me, refusing her would only be robbing her of the thing she most looks forward to every week."

"Oh, I love having Claire around. She's so good with the babies."

Aaron flashed her a smile. "How is Bobby liking his new job?"

"It's a good job. Pays pretty well. I think he's happy there. Better than his last job, so he hasn't complained. Thank you for helping him get it. We should be able to get on our feet soon. I just hope what I hear on the news about Russia isn't true. Everyone's so afraid. What are we supposed to do?"

"Keep living our lives, Marie." Aaron gave what he hoped was a reassuring smile.

The back door opened with a bang as Marie and Bobby's other three kids charged in from the alley behind their house.

"Aaron!" A chorus of three voices rose and they all jumped onto the couch.

Marie chastised them in rapid Spanish for disturbing their sister who wailed in Aaron's arms. She took the baby back and the three older kids climbed onto Aaron's lap. The oldest boy scaled the back of the couch and sat on Aaron's shoulders. A tickle and tumble fight broke out.

"I'll have Claire bring all these with her tomorrow." Aaron extricated himself and held up the list before putting it into his pocket. "Please, don't hesitate to call if you need anything."

"Thanks, Aaron." Marie gave him her first genuine smile since he'd arrived.

5:42PM //

"How was your day, shaping impressionable minds?" Aaron drew his wife into a hug right as she walked through the door that evening.

"Chaotic and wonderful. I started teaching them cursive today." Claire released Aaron and headed for the tiny kitchen. She placed two brown paper bags on the card table where they ate their meals.

"Is that even part of the curriculum anymore?" Aaron opened one bag and inhaled the fresh smells of authentic Mexican food.

"No, and it's ridiculous. I have to sneak in little lessons. I don't want cursive to die with this generation." Claire filled two glasses with water from the sink and placed them on the table.

Aaron grabbed plates from their meager collection of dishes. They sat down to their feast of tacos, tortilla chips, and salsa.

"The kids were great today. How was your day?" Claire popped a chip into her mouth and flipped her long brown hair over her shoulder.

Aaron gave into the urge to lean over and kiss her lips. "My day was good. Emma printed out a bunch of coffee vouchers. They're good for a free coffee every week."

"That was generous of her."

"I know. I handed all of them out. There were probably fifty, or more. I also handed out all our invitations. A lot of people seemed excited."

"Awesome. I can't wait for Thursday." Claire's face lit up.

"Me too. I saw Marie today. She's looking forward to having you over tomorrow."

"Is she doing okay with the new babies?"

"I think so. Bobby's new job is a really good change for them."

"It was nice of your dad to arrange that interview for him with the oil field manager."

"Yeah." Aaron's phone flashed, and he clicked the side button to make it go black again. "I spent too much time in the office today, there was a lot to do. I was able to get out in the afternoon and check on some people though. Chuck had an interview. I saw him before and afterward, and he thought it went well. Always with the self-deprecating tone."

Claire laughed through a mouthful of taco. She swallowed. "Poor Chuck. Always down on his luck."

Aaron let out his belly laugh. "I know! I don't understand. He has it more together than most of the houseless people we help. I always try to tell him he's doing a great job and he'll get out of it soon. He's one of the few who's actually trying to change his circumstances."

"Yeah, I wish we could make him the guest of honor at our feast, but he would hate that. He would just leave."

Aaron's mind spun around Claire's idea as they finished dinner.

After dinner they curled up on the couch to watch their favorite show. A luxury they only indulged in one night a week. Claire nestled her head against Aaron's shoulder.

"Hey." Aaron swallowed a lump in his throat.

Claire looked up at him, her golden-brown eyes penetrating as ever.

"Are you ovulating?" A radiant grin spread over his wife's face and she nodded.

"Just, being with Marie's kids today made me excited about having a kid with you. You know?"

Claire nodded again, her grin widening. Before they could move from the couch, Claire's phone buzzed and flashed red. A presidential alert.

Aaron's went off the next second. They gave their screens cursory glances.

TERROR ALERT APPROACHING RED.

Wednesday, June 6th
8:39AM //

"Last on the agenda, we've made a decision as to who will replace Jerry in the position of Director of Operations. You all know Jerry's last day is Friday, and after many interviews and tests, we've decided to promote Joe Smith."

All eyes turned to Joe as the Vice President, Mr. Hooper, finished his announcement.

Joe almost hadn't heard him. All morning, thoughts of the red terrorist alert filled his mind. He forced a smile. This promotion was what he'd been hoping for all year.

"We'll have a little party in the break room during lunch on Friday to send Jerry off well and celebrate Joe's promotion. Let's get back to it." Mr. Hooper rose from his seat at the head of the oval conference table and everyone followed behind him.

"Congrats, Joe." The man next to Joe held out a hand to him.

Another smacked him on the shoulder. "You've earned it."

"Thanks. It hasn't been an easy year, but it was all worth it."

Some of the men and women who had sat around the large table left without a glance at him. It had been a competitive race to the position. Joe had known he'd make some enemies along the way.

"They chose the right man for the job." Phil, a man who would now be working under Joe, watched the people filing out of the room.

"Glad you think so." Joe extricated himself from the small cluster around him and approached Mr. Hooper.

"Sir, thank you again for this opportunity." Joe held out his hand to the older man.

"Well, I'm confident you'll steer your team in a good direction." Mr. Hooper flashed a smile and shook Joe's hand.

Back in his office, Joe pulled out his cell phone.

I GOT THE PROMOTION! GET READY FOR EASY LIVING, HONEY. MAYBE WE CAN TAKE THAT VACATION TO EUROPE YOU'VE ALWAYS WANTED.

Joe sent the text off to Carol, then composed one for all his kids, including Jack and Claire.

GOT THE PROMOTION. WOOHOO!! CELEBRATION, FRIDAY NIGHT. OUR HOUSE!

The smile he couldn't wipe off his lips made Joe feel foolish. Two minutes later, his phone chimed with a new text message. It was from Carol.

I'M SO PROUD OF YOU! YOU DESERVE IT FOR ALL YOUR HARD WORK. WE'LL HAVE TO MAKE FRIDAY NIGHT EXTRA SPECIAL.

THANKS, HONEY. LOOKING FORWARD TO IT. I CAN'T BELIEVE I GOT IT OVER SOME OF THOSE OTHERS. I WAS SWEATING IT DURING THE MEETING.

I KNEW YOU COULD DO IT.

Ten minutes later Joe's phone went off again. He was having a hard time focusing on all the reports he had to finish by the end of the day. This text was from Emma, within the group text to all the kids.

DAD! CONGRATULATIONS! I'M SO EXCITED FOR YOU! AND I CAN'T WAIT FOR FRIDAY NIGHT. WE CAN EAT ALL THE CHOCOLATE PEANUT BUTTER ICE CREAM YOU WANT, AND WE CAN WATCH *FATHER OF THE BRIDE*, RIGHT?

WOULDN'T WANT IT ANY OTHER WAY. Joe tapped out his reply, then put his phone in the top drawer of his desk.

I really need to get this report done before they regret promoting me. I hate report days.

Joe heard incessant chimes from the top drawer. His kids were texting back and forth. He set his mind to his work and pressed on.

Wednesday 8:05AM //

Pulling her long ponytail tight, Emma turned out of the driveway and jogged along the cul-de-sac, to the neighborhoods beyond. The day was bright, but not yet too hot.

As she ran, she shed the dark thoughts which had plagued her over the past few days. The music singing out of her ear buds and the rhythm of her feet against the pavement lulled Emma into a running stupor.

She ran on for three miles before circling back toward home. A refreshing breeze tugged at her ponytail and a free day lay before her. Emma showered and dressed, then hurried downstairs to eat breakfast.

Her phone flashed with several texts. Dad got the promotion. Jack loved her. Aaron thanked her for the coffee vouchers, they would change lives. Emma's lips turned up. She sent replies to each of them.

"Good morning, Honey." Mom didn't look up from the cookbook she was studying at the kitchen table.

"Morning." Emma set to work making an omelet.

"How was your run?"

"Good. It's a great day out there." Emma chopped a mushroom.

The morning sun gleamed over the granite countertops. She looked out at the backyard, kept lush and green by the expensive sprinkler system, to the above-ground swimming pool filled with the sun throwing diamonds over the water, to the creek where she and Aaron played as kids.

"Did you get a text from Dad?" Mom's voice pulled her back from sun-kissed days of catching crawdads and coming home covered in mud.

"Yeah. I'm so excited for him. He definitely deserves it."

"I know." A tenderness laced Mom's voice. "What's your plan for your day off?"

"Kate and I are going to indulge in some retail therapy. I have a wad of tips burning a hole in my pocket."

"Sounds fun." Mom closed the cookbook and sighed.

"What are you up to today?" Emma carried her plate of omelet to the table.

"Oh, probably just the usual. I'm meeting up with Fay later, though."

A half hour later, Emma met her best friend, and maid of honor, at Houston's downtown shopping area.

"I need a new summer dress . . . or two." Kate opened the door to a boutique and let Emma walk in first.

They ogled the dresses and blouses and ignored price tags. They piled their favorite picks into a dressing room. Emma pulled the first dress off the hanger and slid the silky fabric over her bare skin. She didn't own anything like it.

"I have to have this one." Emma examined herself in the mirror and saw the way the dress hugged her form in all the right places.

"Let me see." Emma turned from the mirror to face Kate who was halfway undressed.

Her friend gave all the responses Emma wanted to hear. They continued trying on clothes and modeling for each other. A half an hour later, they left the store burdened with one large bag each.

They went into one more store where they found some cute bikinis, then settled in for lunch at a deli.

"Their coffee isn't as good as yours." Kate chose a table by the window, latte in hand.

Emma sat across from her with her own mug full of caramel macchiato and took a sip. "It's not bad. I've heard their sandwiches are amazing."

"Look, there's a bridal consignment shop right over there." Kate pointed to a store kitty corner to the deli. "Have you been in there?"

"No, we should check it out. That dress in the window is gorgeous." Emma looked up as a server placed a large plate in front of her, laden with a grilled turkey club and a bag of gourmet potato chips. "Thank you. This looks so good."

"Have you guys even settled on a date yet?" Kate took a bite of her roast beef sandwich.

"No, but we need to narrow it down and send out save-the-date cards. We want to get married in the fall which is only about five months away. My only worry is that fall is a busy time for us at the coffee shop. I feel bad about taking a honeymoon." Emma crunched down on a chip.

Kate pulled up the calendar on her phone. "I'm sure they can manage without you for a week or so. You deserve this. You haven't taken any real time off since you opened Common Grounds. Let's see. Why don't you get married the first weekend in October?"

Emma looked at her own calendar. "That could work. I know we'll be able to book the barn whenever we decide to get married."

"Perfect. See? I'm putting your wedding down for the first Saturday in October. You guys want an evening wedding, right?" Kate tapped the event into her phone.

Emma exhaled. "It would be so romantic to have an evening wedding, but I don't want to be exhausted by the time we leave for the hotel, or wherever we might stay."

Kate looked up from her phone, her eyebrows disappearing beneath her strawberry-blond bangs. "Oh yeah, you guys are waiting for your wedding night. I forgot. How's that going?" She leaned back and crossed her arms.

"It's hard." Emma let out a nervous chuckle. This was one topic her and her best friend didn't see eye to eye on, but Emma still wanted to be honest with Kate. "But I know it's worth it. Aaron and Claire waited, and they said it was the best decision they made for their relationship."

"I don't know how that could be, but more power to you." Kate's tone was laced with sarcasm, her turquoise eyes amused.

Something under Emma's skin flared. "Kate, we've had this conversation before. I'm not changing my mind."

"I know, I know." Kate raised her hands in surrender. "I didn't mean to try to talk you out of anything. I just can't imagine—but never mind. Let's drop it."

"You ready to go to the bridal shop?" Emma gave her friend a sweet smile, hoping to convey there were no hard feelings.

"Let's go. Maybe you'll find the dress." Kate piled her dirty dishes and grabbed her purse.

Emma followed her out of the deli and sent a call through to her mom. "I want my mom to be here in case I do find the dress." She answered Kate's curious look as the phone rang in her ear.

"I'll be right there. I'm just a few blocks away finishing up with Fay." Mom sounded excited when Emma invited her to join them.

As they entered the store, all the excitement and anticipation of the wedding settled on Emma. *I'm getting married on October sixth. It's actually happening. And I might find a dress today!*

White, lush fabric met her eyes at every glance. Elegant chandeliers hung from a creamy, white ceiling. Thick, soft rugs covered the dark wood floor. Soft music fit the soothing ambiance. Emma closed her eyes and drew in a breath.

"Can I get married here?" She leaned into Kate's ear as a well-dressed woman approached them.

"Hello, girls. Welcome. My name is Stella. Can I get you anything to drink? We have water, wine, or perhaps a mimosa?" The woman exuded grace and hospitality.

"I'd love a mimosa." Kate found her words first.

"I'll take one too." Emma tried to reflect Stella's graceful smile.

"Excellent. May I take a peek at your IDs?" Stella glanced at the driver's licenses the girls held out to her, then turned to a woman behind an ornate desk that stood on one side of the store. "Two mimosas, Haley. Now, you may leave your things here."

Stella pointed to a plush, ivory fainting couch. Everything about her was fluid, from the movement of her arm to the liquid gold of her voice.

Emma and Kate set their shopping bags and purses on the floor. They stood entranced by Stella.

"Which one of you is getting married? Or are you both?"

"She is." Kate pointed to Emma.

"Oh, lovely dear. And when's the big day?"

Emma's cheeks warmed. This was the moment she had been dreading. Five months was not long to find a dress and get it fitted just right. She had already been laughed out of two stores for suggesting the coming fall.

She cleared her throat. "This fall. Probably October sixth."

"The perfect time of year, in my opinion. I have no doubt we will be able to find just the dress to suit all your wishes. I would estimate you're a size four?"

Emma nodded as she took her mimosa from Haley.

Stella pulled a measuring tape from around her neck. "May I?"

"Please." Emma held her arms out, ready to do whatever this woman asked of her.

As Stella measured Emma's hips, a delicate sound of tiny bells rang out through the store. Emma turned to see her mom entering, a surprised expression on her face, red from the day's heat, as she took in the stylish shop.

"Hi Mom." Emma waved with her free hand.

Stella took some notes in a small notepad she had retrieved from the desk and studied Emma's face. "What time of day will the ceremony be?"

"Evening." Emma shared a look with Kate.

"Yes, good. Well, I'll let you take a look around while I dig out a few dresses I think would suit you."

"Thank you." Emma turned to a huddle with Kate and Mom. "I don't even know where to start."

"Let's start . . . over there." Kate pointed to the back of the room.

Stella was busy near the front.

Kate led the way to the back wall where hundreds of wedding dresses hung. "Do you know what you're looking for?" Kate looked back at Emma.

"I have an idea, I guess. I was hoping I'd know it when I saw it."

"You will." Mom looked near tears.

Emma's heart swelled.

"These are all used?" Mom held a particularly dazzling dress up, her eyes wide. She checked the price tag. "Why that's so reasonable. We'll find your dress here, honey. This place is a God-send."

Before Emma could respond, Stella's voice called from the fainting couch. Next to her stood a hanging rack on wheels filled with exquisite gowns. Emma hurried over, followed by Mom and Kate, both of whom had abandoned all other dresses.

"You can look through these and try on any one you'd like." Stella motioned toward the fitting room to the right of the couch. A beautifully framed full-length mirror stood just outside the fitting room.

"Can I try all of them on?" Emma ran her fingers over the first dress, a cacophony of tiny glinting beads and broad-patterned lace.

"You may." A wide smile graced Stella's features.

Mom followed Emma into the fitting room with the first dress. After slipping into five dresses of greater and greater beauty with increasing anxiety, Emma melted into a chair in the corner of the fitting room in her underthings, while Mom went to get the sixth.

"All this changing is exhaust—" Emma's voice faded as Mom carried in a gown that took Emma's breath away.

"You like it." Mom raised her eyebrows as she scrutinized Emma's face.

"Yeah. Well, let's put it on. It isn't anything like what I thought I'd pick. But it's—help me get it on."

Mom slipped the slim dress over Emma's head. Emma stared at her reflection. Over a long, blush-colored slip was a delicate mesh of intricate, off-white lace.

"It's like something Belgian nuns would take months tatting." Emma's hushed tone brought a girlish laugh from her mom.

The boat neckline shone with clusters of small pearls and incredible lace detail. The opening swooped low down Emma's back. The last adorable touch was the lace-capped sleeves.

"Look at your face." Tears traced their way down Mom's cheeks.

Emma looked up from the cascading dress and into the mirror again. A soft glow emanated from her face. Her cornflower blue eyes were radiant and sparkling.

"This is the dress, isn't it?" Mom brought her hands to her mouth and shook her head. "Oh, honey. I'm so glad you called me so I could be here for this moment."

"Me too." Emma flattened her hands over the striking fabric hugging her to perfection.

"How's it going in there?" Kate's voice sailed through the thick curtain door of the fitting room.

Mom pushed the curtain open and stepped aside for Emma.

"Oh wow. That's amazing. It looks incredible on you." Kate stood from the couch as her eyes roamed over the dress.

"Yes. That's the one. Lovely." Stella crossed her arms over her middle and cocked her head. "I know just what it's missing." Stella marched away.

Kate approached Emma and took her hand. "You are going to floor Jack."

Butterflies flitted around in Emma's stomach as she imagined Jack's reaction to seeing her in this dress.

Stella returned and placed a tiara of pearls on Emma's head. She narrowed her eyes studying the full effect. "Yes, that finishes the look perfectly."

Emma turned to look in the mirror again. A lump formed in her throat. *It's really happening. We're getting married. I can't believe I get to spend my life with Jack. And I can't wait to see the look on his face when he sees me in this.*

On either side of the mirror, Mom and Kate snapped pictures with their phones, eyes glinting with unshed tears.

Wednesday 12:03PM //

Joe tapped his hands on the steering wheel as he drove into town for his weekly lunch with Aaron. Fewer people were out as the temperatures rose. He passed the hardware store where he and Aaron used to go on Saturdays to get supplies for their latest project.

He's always been a visionary.

Joe pulled into the parking lot of the Panaderia. He found their usual table empty by the front window and sat down.

"Hola, Rosa." Joe greeted the young woman who brought fresh tortilla chips and homemade salsa.

"Hola. The usual for you and Aaron?"

"Yes please." Joe rubbed his hands together, producing a sweet smile from Rosa.

Aaron locked eyes with Joe as soon as he walked in the door. "Dad, did you hear the terror alert is at red? And they moved the president." He sat across from Joe and leaned on his forearms.

"Hello to you too." Joe gave his son a sardonic look.

"Hi. It's been quite a week, hasn't it? Any murmurings at the refinery?" Aaron grinned up at Rosa as she placed full plates in front of them.

"Well, now you mention it, the higher ups have seemed a little edgy."

Aaron's eyebrows rose. "Really? I was being facetious." Aaron's features etched with concern, before smoothing out again. "Congrats on the promotion, by the way."

"Thanks." Joe took a bite out of his chicken burrito.

Aaron chewed on a piece of his taco. "But you heard they moved the president out of Washington, right?"

Joe nodded, his mouth still full.

"So, there's got to be a real threat, right? But they haven't said why he's been moved. Do you know where they moved him to?" Aaron dipped a chip in the salsa and held it over his plate.

"It's probably a miracle, or more likely a horrible mistake, that we know as much as we do. I agree, it doesn't sound good. I haven't heard where he is."

"What should we do?"

Joe studied his oldest son's face. Aaron had more compassion than anyone else he knew. "I wouldn't worry about it too much. We have a strong military, and they'd be breaking the treaty made after the Cold War." Joe took a tortilla chip.

"Yeah. Maybe."

"They would be asking for World War III."

Aaron narrowed his eyes at his near-empty plate of tacos.

"How's Claire?" Joe succeeded in wiping the anxiety from his son's face.

"She's good. Ready for summer break. About two more weeks."

"Wow, does summer start that soon?" Joe shook his head. "Matt will be a sophomore in high school next year. Do you two have any plans for the summer?"

"We might get away to the gulf coast for a few days." Aaron looked down at his hands before meeting Joe's gaze again. "We've started trying."

Joe's crumpled napkin fell from his hands. His pulse quickened. "Are you serious? Don't kid an old man."

"I am serious, old man. The school district has a great maternity leave policy, and when Claire goes back to work, the baby can hang out with me all day." Aaron's grin was wide and bright.

"That's great. I've been waiting my whole adult life to be a grandpa. Have you told your mom?"

Aaron tossed his head back and laughed. The sound filled the restaurant and Joe couldn't contain his own excitement.

"No, we're waiting to tell everyone on Friday night at family dinner."

"You know your mom. She'll see right through me."

"Keep a lid on it, Grandpa." Aaron's widest smile spread over his face.

It was the same one he'd worn when he proposed to Claire. The same one that had appeared on his wedding day.

A strange ache of joy and pride filled Joe. And some kind of old sadness over the swift and merciless passage of time.

Ten years earlier //

"Ah, the princess." Mike smirked as Emma Smith walked by on her way to class.

She didn't look at them. She never noticed them. Jack rolled his eyes and pushed off from the wall.

"You going to class, man?" Ryan tagged his arm.

Jack shrugged. "Nothing better to do."

Without another glance at his buddies, Jack followed "The Princess" into Mrs. Dunn's English class. He sat down in the back of the room as Mrs. Dunn glared in his direction. *And they wonder why I choose to skip class all the time.*

"Alright everyone, take out your books and answer the questions on the board based on the reading assigned last night." Mrs. Dunn sat at her desk in the front corner of the room and scrutinized her students.

Jack pulled out his copy of To Kill A Mockingbird and thumbed through it. Opening his binder, he fished a pen from the inside pocket and turned to a blank piece of lined paper. He wrote out the questions from the white board. None of them made sense, he hadn't even read the first chapter of the book. He tapped his pen against the paper and glanced around the room.

In the second row, Emma wrote at an intense pace with her honey-brown hair touching her bare knees as she bent over the desk. Her page looked already half-filled. Jack's stomach growled, and he shifted to cover the noise.

Mrs. Dunn let the class work on the questions for the first half hour. Jack nodded off a few times, and read a few pages, but got nothing written. When she finally stood up from behind her desk, Mrs. Dunn erased the questions from the board and wrote PARTNER PROJECT in big letters. Jack suppressed a groan. Others didn't.

"Yes, I'm assigning a partner project, and I will be pairing you up. You are to finish reading your books and together come up with a way to present what you learned from the book. Please be creative. I don't need to hear twelve lectures on a book I've read a hundred times. At least. Now I'll list off the partners." Mrs. Dunn read off a piece of paper in her hand.

Jack zoned out until he heard his own name.

"Jack Davidson. So nice of you to join us today. You'll be working with Emma Smith." Mrs. Dunn grinned like a cat.

Jack's stomach dropped.

Emma's hand shot up. She didn't wait to be called on. "Mrs. Dunn, you can't seriously expect—"

"Emma, you're one of our brightest. I'm sure Mr. Davidson won't harm your GPA too much. Though you should all know this project counts for twenty-five percent of your grade for the term. You have the remaining two weeks of school to finish it. Now, to move on to our favorite part of the day, grammar."

Jack watched the back of Emma's head through the rest of class. She barely moved at all, but kept her gaze focused on the board. *How can anyone care so much? She's right to argue with Dunnce, I'm only going to drag her down.*

When the bell rang, Jack took his time cramming his book and binder into his bag. As he leaned forward to zip the backpack up, a pair of strappy white sandal-clad feet appeared in his line of vision. Jack raised his head, lingering over the long, tan legs, white shorts, and flowy pink top before meeting Emma Smith's blue eyes. He leaned back under her scowl.

I never noticed how blue her eyes were. Jack shook the thought from his head.

"My house or yours?" Emma placed a hand on the perfect curve of her hip. "Jack?"

"Um, yours I guess."

"Okay, let's go." Emma turned toward the door.

"What, now?" Jack stood, shouldering his backpack.

"Yes, now. We only have two weeks to do this project and I'm on track for Valedictorian next year. Judging by your history of completing homework, I'd say we need to start now." Emma led him out of the classroom.

He soaked in the view of her the whole way to the parking lot, noticing for the first time the way her body moved as she walked.

They went the opposite direction his buddies would be headed. *Good. There's no reason for them to see us together.*

Emma pushed a button on her keychain to unlock the red Jeep Wrangler her parents were rumored to have gotten her for her sixteenth birthday. Before climbing into the car, which emitted heat waves when the doors were open, Emma pulled the soft top off and shoved it into the back seat. Jack dropped his backpack behind the passenger's seat.

They drove in silence to the nicest suburbs around Houston. Neither said anything. Jack kept his eyes on the ever-more impressive houses along the road. Emma drove fast, weaving her way through traffic and road construction.

Maybe she's not the princess we make her out to be. Jack's thoughts halted as Emma pulled into the driveway of a large, house in a cul-de-sac full of even larger houses.

"My mom and little brother are home. Try to act like you have some manners." Emma climbed out of the car and grabbed her messenger bag without looking at Jack.

Anxiety roiled in his stomach. *What am I doing? I don't belong here.*

Emma stared across the kitchen table at the strange guy with dark hair hanging low over his forehead. A plate of sandwiches, cookies, and a pitcher of sweet tea provided by Mom sat between them. Jack grabbed a sandwich and took a huge bite out of it. She'd never thought of Jack Davidson as shy, but he wouldn't meet her eyes and he hadn't said anything the whole ride home.

You'd think he's never had a decent meal. Maybe he hasn't. Her curiosity was piqued. Jack didn't hold enough importance at school to be part of the rumor mill.

"Do you have any brothers or sisters?" Emma started with an innocent question while pouring sweet tea for Jack and herself. She took a cookie.

For the first time, Jack looked her in the eye. Emma held the cookie still between the plate and her mouth.

His eyes were dark and penetrating. How much of her could he perceive with that look?

She shifted in her chair. *Take the grease out of his hair and the sullen look out of his eyes, and he'd be really good-looking.*

"No. Just me. And sometimes my mom." Jack shrugged. "Your mom's nice."

Emma stared at him, bewildered. "Yeah, she is. What do you mean by 'sometimes my mom?' Do you live with your dad sometimes?"

"No. Never knew my dad. My mom just—look, are we going to work on the project or not?" Jack gave her a black look.

Emma shrank back. "Of course. So, how far have you read?"

"Let's see." Jack pretended to think hard. "About two pages in class today."

"What? You've only read two pages? How are we supposed to even start when you haven't read the book?" Emma crossed her arms and leaned back in her chair.

"You tell me, Miss Valedictorian."

"Look, I didn't ask for this. I'm not going to hold your hand through this project and do all the work for you. I'm sure as heck not going to let you bring my GPA down. So, you'd better start reading." Emma shot daggers at him, but Jack's features had softened. *Now what?*

"I can't—I have a hard time reading. I think I'm dyslexic. I've never been tested, but I just can't read."

Emma narrowed her eyes at him. "You expect me to believe that? I know your track record. This is just your excuse for never doing any homework."

"Thanks for the support. Oprah would be proud. You have to believe me. Have you ever had a math class with me?"

"I don't know." Emma shrugged, fighting her amusement at his sarcasm.

"I ace every math test. Once I figured out I sometimes switch numbers, math was easy. Reading and English are hard for me. I'm sorry you got paired with me. I really am." His apology seemed genuine.

Emma stared at the uneaten cookie on her plate. "Okay, I have an idea. Let's go." She stood and walked toward the front door. She didn't look back to make sure he followed her but heard his footsteps after a few moments of silence.

"What does your mom do?" Emma weaved her way into downtown Houston.

She glanced at Jack without turning her head. He was staring at her. A thrill of goosebumps traveled up Emma's spine. She was surprised at her reaction to his attention.

"You don't want to know. I don't see her much anymore, but she makes just enough money to keep paying rent, so I at least have a place to live." Jack's tone was resigned.

Emma had a sudden urge to reach for his hand. *She probably doesn't make enough money to feed him, which would explain why he devoured those sandwiches. Have I been misjudging this guy all along? Me and the whole school. Or is he lying to get my sympathy?* Emma's instinct told her he was being honest.

When they pulled in at the Public Library, Jack looked at her, questioning. "I already have the book."

"I know. But here you can get the audiobook and listen to it. You can use my library card." Emma's smile was met with an odd expression from Jack. A timid mixture of gratitude and . . . admiration?

"Thanks. I never would have thought of that." Jack's face flushed, and he turned toward the front door of the large stone building.

He opened the door and stepped aside to let her in.

Wednesday, June 6th
6:13PM //

Her face was radiant when he opened the door to let her in. Jack hadn't seen Emma look so beautiful since the night he'd proposed. He gathered her in his arms. His breath caught in his throat when she lay a lingering kiss on his lips. She would be his, forever. He couldn't believe his own good luck.

"You had a good day?" Jack didn't want to pull away from Emma, so he kept an arm around her shoulders as they walked into the living room.

By the smell issuing from the paper bag in her hands, Emma had brought tacos.

"Yes, actually. It was perfect. I found my dress." Emma couldn't contain her joy as she sat cross-legged on the couch and opened the take-out bag.

"Your dress?" Jack held her gaze as he pulled out a Styrofoam container and handed it to her.

"You know, the dress." Emma's eyebrows rose, her brilliant smile still in place.

"No way. That's awesome."

"I know. I wish I could show you pictures." Emma took a small bite of her taco.

Jack shook his head. "I don't want to see it yet. I can wait."

"Well, you'll have to. So, what do you think about getting married the first weekend in October? Kate and I were talking about it today and thought that was as good a weekend as any."

"Let me see. Nope, I don't think there's anything going on that weekend." Jack laughed at the affronted look on Emma's face. "You know I would marry you tomorrow if you'd let me. Just name the day, and I'll be there." Jack smoothed a hand over Emma's cheek.

"October sixth it is then. That's only about five months away." Emma licked some runaway salsa off her finger. "Are you going to invite your mom?"

Jack set his taco down on his plate and stared into his lap for a moment before meeting Emma's eyes again. "Yeah, we can send her an invitation, assuming she's still at the address I have. I doubt she'll come, so don't get your hopes up."

"Why wouldn't she come to her own son's wedding?" Emma tilted her head to the side.

Jack exhaled. "She hasn't wanted to be in my life since I was nine. That's when she disappeared for hours, sometimes days at a time."

"I know, you had to take care of yourself." Emma kissed his cheek. "But you don't think she'll come?"

"I'm just saying, don't expect much." Jack shrugged.

Emma didn't say anything for a while but ate slowly.

"Want to talk about other details?" She met his eyes again.

"Yeah, I'm all in. But I'm planning the honeymoon, so don't worry about that. Now that we have a date, I can start booking stuff."

"You want to plan the honeymoon?" Emma's gaze was soft and tender.

Jack swallowed. "Yeah. I want it to be a surprise. My wedding gift to you." "Jack. That's so sweet." Emma reached out to put a hand on his cheek. He leaned forward and kissed her, running a hand down her back. "I'm thinking about getting a tattoo." Emma moved away from Jack, leaving a few inches between them.

"You are?" Jack pivoted to face her with one arm along the back of the couch.

"Yeah."

"Why? You're perfect. Why would you want to mar your perfect skin with a tattoo?" Jack took Emma's hand.

She rolled her eyes and shook her head, but an adorable, slow grin was growing up her cheeks. "This is an epoch in our lives, and I guess I want to celebrate it somehow."

"An epoch, huh? Can't we just celebrate it with a ridiculously expensive wedding?" Jack squeezed her hand.

Emma leaned her head against the back of the couch and giggled. Jack's heart flipped.

"Maybe I'm just trying not to freak out over this huge change in our lives. Don't get me wrong, I'm so, so excited to marry you. It's just a huge change, you know?"

"I know. I'm so ready." Jack brought Emma's hand up and kissed her palm. "What would you get a tattoo of?"

Emma exhaled and looked at the ceiling. "I don't know. I have a few ideas. I shouldn't even be spending money on it anyway. Forget it."

Jack looked deep into Emma's blue eyes and shook his head. They spent the next few hours talking through every imaginable detail of the wedding. Jack took notes in a notebook he kept handy on the coffee table.

When they had cleared the dinner things, Emma lay with her head on Jack's lap. Within minutes she was asleep.

"Do my ideas bore you that much?" Jack stroked Emma's long hair and chuckled.

As he watched her, the same feeling came over him as when he had first opened the door that evening. And when he had first realized he was falling for her in high school.

Who knew I would ever be so lucky, coming from nothing, and falling in love with a girl like this. Jack leaned down and kissed her lips.

Emma's eyes fluttered open. She met his intense gaze with a soft smile.

"I never thought anyone would love me."

"What are you talking about?" Emma sat up and put a hand on his knee.

Jack closed his eyes for a moment. "The only family I ever had was my mom, and she worked all the time. She never gave me much attention when she was home, besides providing for me. I never thought any girl would be able to love me. I thought something must be wrong with me, if my own mom couldn't love me."

Tears gleamed in Emma's eyes. "Jack." Her voice was thick. "I love you so much, and I'm so honored that I get to love you for the rest of our lives."

Goose bumps erupted all over Jack's skin as Emma leaned into him and their lips met. She kissed him with more passion than she ever had before. Her lips firm against his, her tongue probing his mouth, sending electric shocks through his whole body.

She grabbed the collar of his shirt and pulled him back to lay next to her. Emma's hands roved over his back, and into his hair. His hands found the skin of her side, sliding up and down. Things had never been this heated, and Jack didn't know how far she would want to take it. He kept a step behind her, letting her take the lead, though blood pumped through him at a furious pace.

Then she was up, off the couch, hauling in deep breaths of air.

She turned away from him, then faced him again. "I'm sorry. I love you, but I have to go now." Emma grabbed her purse and left.

Jack blinked and let out the breath he'd been holding in.

Thursday, June 7th
7:47AM //

He pedaled faster, letting the cool morning air clear his thoughts. He couldn't let his mind wander to his evening with Emma the night before. Jack had a long list of things to do at work and recalling the feeling of Emma's bare skin under his fingers wouldn't help his productivity.

Jack locked his bike outside the front doors of his accounting firm's office. He reached his desk five minutes early and grinned. His joy was short-lived.

"Jack!" His boss's voice boomed over the near-empty room of desks that would soon be filled with accountants like him. "Can I have a word with you in my office?"

Jack left his bag in his chair and followed his boss into the only enclosed office on the floor.

The older man sat behind his desk and squinted at Jack, his way of communicating displeasure. Jack had seen this tactic before and wasn't worried.

"I saw how efficient you were with your last few clients. Finish these by the end of the day and I'll consider giving you the Hopewell account." The man pushed a pile of papers across the desk toward Jack.

"The—the Hopewell account?" All thoughts of Emma faded as his mind was taken over with the idea of working with the company's biggest client.

"Yes. I've been thinking about handing it off to someone, and I've been watching you." The man beamed, proud to pull off his "angry boss" ruse.

"Thank you, sir. I'll get these done." Jack took the stack of papers and returned to his desk.

On further inspection of the work given to him, Jack's stomach plummeted. *How could I possibly get all this information confirmed by clients and entered into the database by the end of the day? I doubt anyone could.*

Jack took a deep breath and plunged ahead. He worked through lunch and ignored the pings and buzzes of his cell phone. He even ignored the calls to his desk phone. By four o'clock the numbers on the pages blurred before his watering eyes. He leaned back in his chair and rubbed them.

I can't let this defeat me. I need this account. It would set me and Emma up for life. I could take her anywhere in the world for our honeymoon. We could put a down payment on a nice house. With these bolstering thoughts, Jack trudged on.

He lost track of time again and didn't notice his colleagues eyeing him as they left for home. When someone turned out the lights, Jack looked up. It was seven o'clock. His eyes were watering, but he had one more sheet of data to enter.

Pulling out his phone, he tapped out a text to a group of his friends. MEET ME AT THE WHISTLE STOP IN A HALF HOUR. WORK WAS HELL.

Jack finished his work, slammed his laptop shut, and left. He rode the few blocks to the pub, almost hitting a parked car. His vision was still blurred from staring at a screen all day. The tension which had built in his shoulders, began to melt when he entered the pub and saw a table filled with most of the guys he had texted.

"Jackie!" Dan called out, lifting his pint up. "Whoa, rough day? Can we get another pint over here? Or two?"

Jack slumped into the open chair and rubbed his eyes again.

"You do look like you've been through hell, man." Charlie pushed a pint of Shiner in front of him.

Raising the glass to his lips, Jack downed it in one go. His friends laughed and patted him on the back. Another pint appeared in front of him. Jack grabbed the basket of fries from the middle of the table and shoved a few in his mouth.

With his friends and a good beer on the table, Jack's mind cleared. "Can I get a burger?" He looked around without focusing on any one face. "How could he do that to me? Making me do chump work to 'prove' myself. He was going to give me the account all along." Jack thumped a fist onto the table.

His friends went silent.

Jack ate and drank. The beer kept coming. "I should just quit. That would show him. I deserve better treatment for all I do for that company."

He had lost track of how many beers he'd had. He'd lost track of what his friends were doing.

"Hey, man. Call Emma. Have her pick you guys up. Come on." It was Sam, the owner of the bar.

He handed a mug of coffee to Jack. Jack fumbled for his phone. Hours had passed.

His sipped the coffee as he pushed on the icon of Emma's pretty face. "Hey baby. We're at Whistle Stop. Come pick us up?"

"Jack? Are you drunk? What happened?"

Shame shot through Jack at her tone of voice. He hadn't gotten drunk in a very long time. "Not drunk, exactly. It was stupid work. I think I might quit. They can't take advantage of me like that."

"I'll be right there." Emma hung up before Jack could say anymore.

Then Emma was there, standing in front of him, arms crossed. She had never looked at him like that before—her eyes narrowed, and her lips pursed together. "Come on, let's go."

Her hand gripped him hard under the elbow and she helped him stand.

"I'm fine, I'm fine." Jack was surprised, but pleased, with how steady he felt on his feet.

"Thanks, Sam. There's a cab outside for the rest of these guys. They're more drunk than Jack, I'm not letting them get in my car. I already paid the fee." Emma narrowed her eyes at Charlie, Dan, and Greg.

"Thanks, Emma. Take care." Sam waved as Emma stalked out the door.

Jack followed on her heels. The fresh air awoke Jack's senses even more. He took Emma's hand. "Emmy, please. I'm sorry. I'm not even really drunk."

Emma pulled away from him and went to the driver's side of her Jeep. She started the car before Jack was settled in his seat.

"So, what happened? How bad could your day have really been?" She was mad, but he was grateful she was willing to listen.

Why won't this seat belt go in?

The weight of the day, and Emma's reaction, compounded into a ball of frustration in his chest. "Work sucked—"

"So you said." Emma sped through town.

Jack had a crazy urge to laugh. "My boss gave me an unreal amount of work to do. I worked through lunch until after seven, and I just wanted to blow off some steam with the guys."

"You sound like a child."

"I'm just tired. That's all." Jack's cheeks warmed as his voice broke.

Emma didn't say anything for the rest of the night. She made sure he got into his apartment, then turned to leave after one long look, riddled with confusion, and maybe a little sadness.

"Em, please. Say something." Jack grabbed her arm. Emma's disappointed look cut him deeper than if she had yelled at him.

An ache opened inside.

Emma squeezed his hand. "I'll talk to you tomorrow. Go to bed."

Thursday 7:03PM //

Claire grabbed Aaron's elbow and squeezed. "It's happening."

"I know. You did an amazing job in here." Aaron admired the work Claire and some other volunteers had put into decorating the armory.

It seemed like all the homeless people Aaron had met in Houston were filing in through the front doors, mouths agape, many of them with hair slicked back, trying to look their best. Volunteers ushered the guests sit at round tables. Each table had a glowing candle, a white tablecloth, pitchers of cold water and sweet tea, and baskets full of hot breadsticks.

Aaron took it all in, watching his friends' reactions as they were treated like royalty. Some took careful bites of bread as soon as they sat down, holding back the hunger he knew gnawed in many of their stomachs.

He walked around with Claire on his arm, greeting their guests.

"Diego, I'm glad you came." Aaron stopped at the last table. "And Chuck. Have you heard about the job yet?"

"Yeah, I got it." Chuck struggled to hide his smile.

"No way. Congrats." Aaron patted the man on the shoulder.

Claire gave him a sweet smile. "Good for you, Chuck."

"Thanks. Should be good, should be good."

By seven fifteen the tables were full, and the doors were closed. A volunteer stood at each table ready to serve food and get whatever the guests might need.

Aaron shivered as he and Claire stood to the side. He looked at Claire and shared a smile with her, before surveying the tables again.

He cleared his throat. "Can I have your attention?"

The room grew quiet.

"I'm so happy to see you all here. Claire and I, and your servers, wanted to have a good dinner with our friends. The food is provided by a local chef who pulled out all the stops to spoil us. Please enjoy yourselves and let us know if you need anything at all."

Aaron's heart threatened to burst. Clasping Claire's hand, he led her to the table where Chuck and Diego sat. The table settings matched the elegance of the food brought by an upscale restaurant in downtown Houston. Aaron couldn't wipe the grin off his face.

"This is really good. How did you pull this off?" Claire took a bite of her French onion soup. The first course.

"I went to college with the chef and he owed me a favor."

"A big favor." Claire's eyes widened. Aaron shrugged.

"Well, yeah. I'm glad I could cash it in for this. Look at everyone. These people have come off the street today, to this. Their best meals are probably the mediocre mess the shelters give out. They're all acting like they go to fancy dinners all the time because they know they're honored here."

"You did this." Claire put a hand on Aaron's thigh. "You make them feel honored every day. You pull them back from the margins. I'm proud to be your wife and your partner in this."

Aaron took a long, deep breath. "I'm really happy you're my wife." He took her hand and squeezed it.

Chuck's voice rose from across the table. "It's all crazy suspicion. I can't believe you put so much stock in what the news says."

Diego faced Chuck with a glare. "You're in trouble if you don't think there's any truth to what's being said. Why would they raise the terror alert to red? To spread panic for no reason?"

"Yes." Chuck thumped a hand on the table, jostling his silverware. "They raised it to red but didn't tell us where the threat is coming from. Is it the Middle East? North Korea? Russia? We don't know. They're spreading panic to exercise their control over us."

Diego turned away and rolled his eyes.

"UFOs!" A man at the next table interjected his opinion.

"Gentlemen, let's just enjoy this meal together. Let's pretend the world out there doesn't exist and we'll have a great time, and a great meal. Trust me, the next course is brisket and it's to die for." Aaron kept his tone light.

"The soup's excellent too." Claire lifted her spoon into the air.

When everyone had finished the main course, they started in on dessert, cheesecake with strawberry coulis, and coffee.

Aaron stood. "We've arrived at the best part of the evening. Besides the amazing dessert you're all enjoying right now, I want to give an award to each of you, my friends. It may seem a little cheesy, but this is a night for honoring who you are." Aaron looked down at the notes in his hand and cleared his throat.

No need to get emotional.

Claire stepped up beside him. Her smile was dazzling and bolstering.

"My wife will help me pass out the awards. I know most of you don't need more things to cart around, so I had personalized t-shirts made for each of you, with your own 'award' printed on them. So, when I call your name, please stand. I'll try to go quickly because there are a lot of you."

Murmurs rose around the room as everyone looked at each other bewildered and curious.

"Without further ado, we'll start with Shelly. Are you here?"

A black woman on the far side of the room stood, grimacing around the pain in her trick knee.

"Shelly gets the award for the quickest smile. Every time I see her she has a huge smile on her face, and no matter how much pain she's in she has a smile for everyone."

Shelly swiped at her cheeks even as her signature smile bloomed out.

Claire hurried over to hand her the t-shirt that read "Quickest Smile."

As Claire hugged Shelly, Aaron continued amid the dying claps. "Next award goes to Artie for most entertaining."

Several chuckles rose around the room as Artie stood and waved.

"Artie is the class clown, turning every frown upside down, whether you want him to or not." Aaron handed Claire the shirt saying, "Most Entertaining."

Artie gave a deep bow before sitting down.

"Our next award is for most tenacity. This one goes to Chuck who has weathered life's storms and fought his way out of dark places, and now has landed himself a job. I'm proud of you, man." Aaron tossed Chuck's t-shirt into his lap.

Chuck refused to stand, which was no surprise, and he didn't meet Aaron's eyes. Aaron let the applause go on longer for Chuck.

In all, they distributed fifty-two "awards."

Aaron left the armory late, hand in hand with Claire, and looked up into the black sky above the city lights. "I don't think I've ever felt happier in all my work with these people."

"Tonight was incredible." Claire laid her head on his shoulder as they sauntered back to their apartment.

"I wouldn't be able to do any of this without you and your support." Aaron placed a kiss on Claire's forehead. He inhaled the coconut scent of her hair.

From far off a deep rumble sounded. It grew louder as they neared home. Aaron tilted his face to the sky as a jet flew low overhead.

A small earthquake rattled the windows around them. Even the light posts swayed.

"I wonder what that was about." Claire tightened her grip on Aaron's hand.

"Strange. Let's get up to bed, I'm beat." Aaron opened the front door of their apartment building for Claire.

He glanced at the sky again before the door closed behind him. A few lights came on in the apartments across the street.

Friday, June 8th
11:56AM //

TGIF. Matt added the letters to the doodles in his notebook as the teacher covered material from the book he had already read. He didn't have to look up at the board to know what she'd written there. Following the syllabus, Matt had finished all the homework assigned for the next week. A totally free weekend lay ahead.

"Matt. Are you listening to me?"

Matt looked up. Everyone was staring at him.

Mrs. Stratton's glare could've bore holes right through any student. "This is the umpteenth time in so many days I've caught you not paying attention in class. I'm tired of it. I work hard to teach you thankless lot, and you don't even have the decency to pretend to listen. Go to the principal's office. Now." Mrs. Stratton looked near tears.

Matt almost felt sorry for her. Almost. The last thing he needed was another trip to the principal. Mom would come unglued.

Matt gathered his books into his backpack and roamed the empty halls toward the administration offices. The smells of body odor and stale French fries lingered in the air. Matt sighed, trying to breathe through his mouth. *I hate this place.*

"Ah, Matt. So nice to see you again. You must have missed me. It's only been, what, a week since our last visit?" The principal's administrative assistant greeted Matt with her usual scathing sarcasm. "I'll let Mr. Hayes know you're here. The principal is busy in meetings all day."

Matt sat in one of the hard, plastic chairs to wait for the vice principal. There was a sticky spot under his left leg and he tried to avoid it.

"Matt Smith!" Mr. Hayes poked his head out his office door and smiled.

"I'm sorry, sir. I didn't mean to disrupt class." Matt sat in the soft chair across the desk from Mr. Hayes. This wasn't his normal routine with the principal, but Matt knew Mr. Hayes might be more understanding.

"Tell me what happened."

"Maybe this is a bad excuse, but I already finished all the homework for the next week. Mrs. Stratton was repeating everything from the book. I was bored, I guess." Matt stared into his lap. His shoulders tensed as he waited for the words defending Mrs. Stratton.

"Are you bored often?" Mr. Hayes met Matt's look of surprise.

Matt nodded.

"And you always get your homework done early? Your test scores are near perfect every time." Mr. Hayes glanced at the laptop in front of him.

"Yes, sir. Everything's so easy." Matt shrugged.

"That's what I suspected. Well, let me call your mom and we'll see what we can do."

Matt watched with curiosity as Mr. Hayes punched his mom's number into the landline phone. This was unprecedented.

What's going to happen now?

"Mrs. Smith, hello. It's Mr. Hayes, the vice principal at the high school. No, no, Matt's not in trouble again." Mr. Hayes rolled his eyes for Matt's benefit.

Matt bit the inside of his cheeks.

"I called to talk about the option of moving Matt up a grade, maybe even two. He's bored, Mrs. Smith, and that's why we keep seeing him here in the office. I want to make sure we're not the reason he hates school."

Matt's eyes grew wider with each amazing sentence Mr. Hayes dropped through the phone. As he continued to talk with Mom, Matt thought of family dinner that night, about Aaron and Claire, and Emma and Jack being there. All of them together.

A swoop of excitement turned his stomach. *I can't wait to tell everyone about this. I could be a junior next year.*

Friday 1:35PM //

"Ugh!" Emma smacked the coffee grinder in frustration. She knew Amy was staring at her. The after-school rush was about to start, and the grinder had stopped working. None of her little tricks were making any difference this time.

Emma grabbed the shop's phone and called her fix-it man. The dark mood during the morning rush had been palpable. News reports had come out about the escalating tension between the US and Russia.

This, added to Emma's already distracting thoughts about Jack's behavior the night before, had her on the verge of tears all day. The grinder was the last straw. A lump stuck in her throat. José promised to be there in ten minutes to work on the grinder.

As she hung up, Emma clung to the image of her and Dad eating chocolate peanut butter ice cream and watching *Father of the Bride* that evening. She could cry on his shoulder over her fiancés stupid choices, then laugh at the gentle humor of a classic.

Emma took a steadying breath and joined Amy in helping the growing line of customers.

5:44PM //

Emma dropped her purse on the bench inside the front door. A delicious smell wafted from the kitchen. She took a deep breath, trying to let all the darkness of the day melt away. Something still loomed ominous in the back of her mind. A strange tension.

Mom's off-key hums met her ears.

"Hi mom!" Emma kicked her shoes off and stretched her sore toes as she walked to the kitchen. "Anything I can help with?"

An orange glow of late afternoon sunlight filled the room, shining on every sparkling surface.

"Hi sweetie. You can set the table." Mom looked happy—her cheeks were rosy, and her eyes danced. It had been too long since the last family dinner.

Emma reached for the forks and released a sigh, absorbing the excitement in the air. Her eyes met Mom's and they smiled. "I can show Claire my dress—"

A deafening boom filled the house and drowned Emma's words. Every little part of her body shook from the inside out. An old picture of the family fell off the wall. It landed face down on the wood floor, the glass shattering to pieces.

Emma grabbed the counter to steady herself. "An earthquake?" She looked at her mom.

The light in her mom's eyes had clouded over. "Let's turn on the news and find out."

Emma followed Mom through the dining room into the family room, her hands still full of silverware. Mom switched on the TV.

"Breaking news, Houston has been bombed. This is not a drill—Houston has been bombed. The Russians are suspected to be behind the attack—"

A loud clatter echoed through the silent house as forks and spoons rained out of Emma's hands.

The TV filled with a live feed of a decimated city. "Washington DC has been levelled by nothing less than a nuclear bomb." An announcer's broken voice penetrated Emma's disbelieving ears. "New York is obliterated too. The entire west coast is gone. Everyone is encouraged to flee. Go south. Get out. Now!"

Emma watched Mom move toward her as if a movie was playing out in slow motion. Was Mom running? Mom's hand was around hers then, pulling her to the door.

Emma's feet were like lead. A tingling numbness spread over her body. Shock made it impossible for her to gather a thought. Another thunderous boom rent the air. They staggered on their feet. Mom grabbed both their purses at the front door and called up the stairs to Matt, her voice was panicked.

Emma saw and heard all this as if through a long tunnel. The fear on Matt's face as he raced down the stairs had a clearing effect on her mind. She grabbed her shoes. She put an arm around her brother as they hurried to the car.

Emma stopped and looked up at the clear blue sky above her. She squinted. There was no sign of anything unusual. Emma pivoted on her heel and saw a plane flying low, right toward them.

Hysterical tears choked her as Matt reached out and pulled her into the car. The cries coming from her lips sounded foreign. A bomb dropped just a few miles away. A blinding explosion. Emma covered her face. A scream came from the back seat. The car lurched out of the driveway.

"Where are we going?" Emma took a deep, shaky breath. Her voice came out high-pitched.

"To your dad." Mom's face was set and determined.

"Jack! What about Jack!" Emma couldn't control her screaming as her chest tightened in fear. She pulled her cell phone out of her pocket. "No service. Mom, there's no service."

Mom didn't answer. She was driving faster than Emma had ever seen, dodging around debris in the road.

Emma's phone dropped into her lap as she peered out the window. Whole buildings were caved in on themselves. Rubble and glass lay everywhere, and still fell from the ruins. People ran around in sheer panic. Military vehicles rumbled over the streets, causing other drivers to jump the curbs. The ruined city flashed by.

Matt put a hand on Emma's shoulder. Tears streamed over her cheeks, her heart pounding.

Mom swung into the parking lot at Dad's work, which was lacking its usual guards. The parking lot was always full of Humvees.

"Those aren't American vehicles." Matt opened his door.

Emma blinked and looked at Mom. "What is happening?"

"Let's go." Mom jumped out of the car.

They all ran into the building.

"Joe! Joe!" Mom ran down hallway after hallway, deeper into the labyrinth of the compound.

Emma kept pace with her, dragging Matt along by the hand. The hallways were deserted. Tears continued to flow down Emma's cheeks. As they rounded another corner, Mom ran into the back of a guard with a large gun.

A gun?

"Where's my husband, Joe Smith?" Mom didn't wait for the man to turn around.

When he did, he looked down at them with a harsh frown. "Come with me." He had a thick Russian accent.

Emma shook, and her sweaty hand almost slipped out of Matt's.

I can't believe this is happening. The Russians are here. What's going on?

"We need to find my husband, Joe Smith. He works here. Where is everybody?" Mom's voice grew more shrill with each sentence.

The man didn't say anything but continued down the hall. After several turns, the man stopped at a door and entered a code into a pin pad to unlock it. Dozens of people surrounded a large, oval table.

"Carol!" Across the room, Dad stood, eyes wide, face pale.

Mom gave into her tears as she ran to Dad. Emma pulled Matt along right behind her. She breathed in the comforting, familiar scent of Dad's shirt as he wrapped his arms around all of them.

"I'll do whatever you ask. Just keep my family safe." Dad made eye contact with the man sitting at the head of the table.

He was thick and short and had no neck. Emma suspected he would also have a Russian accent when he spoke. His eyes narrowed at Dad. Emma tightened her grip around him.

The guard standing behind the man in charge raised his gun.

Friday 7:03PM //

Heat burned behind Jack's eyes and a thick lump blocked his throat. Everyone in the office fled when the bombs hit. Jack had driven his car to work that morning, so he could get to family dinner on time, and now he sped to the Smith's house. His only aim was to get to Emma, but his mom's face intruded on his thoughts.

He rounded the last corner, into the cul-de-sac, and hit the brakes. Everything was destroyed. Only a few walls from the outlying houses stood.

A cry wrenched from deep inside him, sounding strange and far away. "No!"

Jack lowered his forehead against the steering wheel. He fought the bile rising in his throat. As though moving of its own accord, his body climbed out of the car. In a dark corner of his mind, Jack thought getting out of the car would expose him to death. That would surely be better than living.

He stumbled and leaned against the open door of the car, giving way to heaving sobs. In his back pocket, his cell phone vibrated. Jack reached for it, and his whole body shook when he saw Emma's beautiful face staring up at him from the screen.

"Hello?" Jack could only manage the word around a grunt.

"Jack! Jack, you're alive. Thank God. Oh my God." Emma's cries came through the phone.

Jack closed his eyes as tears fell down his cheeks. He cradled the phone against his ear as if it were Emma's own hand. Her weeping was music to his ears. Several minutes passed.

"Where are you? I thought—" The sick feeling rose again, and Jack cleared his throat.

"I couldn't call you. This is the first time I've had service since—We're at Dad's work. We came to find him and it's full of Russians. They've taken over the oil plant." Emma took a few shallow breaths. "They're holding us hostage. I think because of the work Dad does. Come. Please, come." Emma's tears choked her words.

"I'm on my way." Jack slid into the car again but didn't want to hang up the call. "Are you all okay?" His silent tears continued to flow.

"We're okay. I don't know what's going to happen. We're in an empty office that Dad said his co-worker was using this morning. I think they want to keep us here. Mom's trying to call Aaron right now." Emma spoke fast and high.

"What do the Russians want?"

"Dad says they want control of the oil. Oil equals money, and money equals power. Jack, this is why they moved the president. They knew this would happen." Emma's tears evaporated as her tone grew angry.

Jack swerved and corrected. There was almost no one on the roads. "I hadn't thought of that."

A bomb fell, miles away, shaking the city.

Jack accelerated. "Emma, I keep thinking about my mom. She's all by herself. She has no one."

More cries came through the phone. "She's so far away. You can't leave me."

Jack set the phone on his lap and let another sob escape. He took a deep breath and picked up the phone again. "I won't. I won't leave you, Em."

He turned a corner and slammed on the brakes. Before him stood a blockade of military vehicles, including one that appeared to have rockets loaded on the back.

"Em, no matter what happens, I love you more than I could ever say."

"Jack?"

Friday 7:48PM //

Aaron clung to Claire's hand as they walked the cratered streets. By this time, everything was quiet, except for the occasional plane flying low overhead, or the sighting of a Humvee.

Where is everyone?

Many houses and buildings in the center of Houston had been taken out by the bombs. Aaron and Claire had been home when they started to fall, getting ready to leave for his parents' house.

Without a word, they had run to the basement of their apartment building, in a crowd of other tenets. It wouldn't really have saved them from the kind of bombs being dropped, but instinct drove them all down.

When the worst seemed to be over, they crept out to find their street had been spared. Aaron's first impulse was to walk his usual routes and check on his friends. As he and Claire set out, he didn't have to explain anything to her, and his heart swelled with love for his wife.

His phone buzzed in his back pocket and Aaron reached for it. "Mom! Are you okay? Is everyone okay?"

"Oh honey, it's so good to hear your voice. We're alive." Mom was crying. "Are you two okay? Where are you?"

"We're fine. Our apartment didn't get hit." Aaron evaded her second question. "Where are you?"

"Well, we're at your dad's work, but the Russians have taken over. They're holding us here. I don't know for how long."

"But they let you call me?" Aaron shared a glance with Claire.

"They don't seem to care what we do as long as we don't leave."

Aaron rubbed the back of his neck. "Well, maybe that's the safest place for you to be. I'll try to come by and see you. Tell everyone hi for me. I love you, Mom." Aaron hung up, his hands shaking.

Claire looked up at him, brows furrowed.

"Russians have taken over the oil plant." Aaron swallowed. "Let's go."

A lump grew in his throat as they traversed the rubble littered over familiar sidewalks. He focused on what was around him, not letting his mind wander to the repercussions of the Russians infiltrating US oil.

Most of the nooks and crannies where his homeless friends once took up residence were gone. The first dead body they came on brought Aaron's heart to his throat. He stared at the man for a long time, while Claire buried her face in his shoulder.

"This is a war. Our country hasn't seen war on our turf since the Civil War. What does this mean for America?" Aaron wrapped his arms around his wife and kissed the top of her head. He steered them on.

Where the bombings had been worst, bodies were strewn around, always catching Aaron off guard. A lump burned in his throat.

Dull light from the setting sun filtered through the haze stirred up by the bombs. The air hung heavier than usual.

Claire lifted her head and put an arm around his waist. Tears pooled, ready to fall from her eyes. Aaron held her close to his side. They walked slower.

Aaron guided them through the streets, unaware of where he was going. They checked in on one family whose house was still standing.

"Miguel, is everyone okay?" Aaron grasped the man's shoulder.

A little girl clung to Miguel's leg.

"Yes, everyone is fine." Miguel's dark brown eyes were bloodshot. "Not everyone has been so lucky. Many are fleeing to Mexico. We're leaving as soon as Alicia feeds the baby. We have connections at the border. You can come with us."

Aaron shared a look with Claire and knew they understood each other. "Thanks man, but we're staying."

"Alright, well, thanks for everything you've done for us." Miguel held out his hand.

Aaron shook it. "Take care."

"Can we see Alicia?" Claire put a maternal hand on the little girl's head.

Miguel stepped aside for them to enter.

They continued on their journey through the city after a tearful goodbye with Miguel and Alicia. Rounding another corner, Aaron drew a sharp breath. The place where Marie's house full of kids once stood was now just a foundation.

He jumped away as Claire threw up. Looking at the ground in front of them, he understood why. A child's hand lay dismembered and singed nearby.

Aaron put an arm around Claire's shaking shoulders and turned back toward their apartment. "I think we've seen enough for today."

Saturday, June 9th
5:55AM //

A loud, metallic banging on the door woke Emma. She shot up, off the cold linoleum floor. Next to her, Matt raised his head. His eyes were puffy.

"Mr. Smith!" A voice boomed from the other side of the door.

Dad stood, moving as though every muscle hurt, just like he had after his first marathon. He opened the door a sliver.

The voice in the hallway spoke just as loud. "Breakfast is in the cafeteria. Report to the conference room in fifteen minutes. Bring your family."

Dad turned back to Mom, Matt, and Emma, then dropped his head against the closed door. They all stood to leave.

Jack. What happened to him? A fresh lump formed in Emma's throat and silent tears fell.

It was incomprehensible to not know when she might see him again, or if she ever would. Her mind blocked those thoughts. He had been such a staple in her daily life since high school.

And Kate? And Amy? What's happened to everyone? Where is everyone? Emma closed her eyes and steadied her frantic breathing. *I just can't think of them. I have to focus on finding Jack again.*

She had tried calling him right back, after they'd been cut off, but the signal was dead. Mom had reassured her that the call had probably just been cut off. Jack was fine. Emma lay awake most of the night wondering what had happened, where he might be.

Her stomach churned. She didn't know when she had last eaten, but the idea of putting anything in her mouth made her feel sick. A few of Dad's co-workers shuffled through a line in the cafeteria, loading bowls with cold cereal. There was no milk.

Emma slumped onto a bench at the nearest table.

"Sweetie, you need to eat something." Mom leaned forward to look into Emma's eyes.

Emma shook her head. "I can't. I want Jack." Her voice broke.

Mom smoothed a hand over Emma's hair, then followed Matt to the food line. When they came back, Mom set a bowl of cereal in front of Emma. It was her favorite.

Fresh tears welled up in Emma's eyes. "They have cinnamon toast squares? What the hell's going on?" She looked from Mom to her dad.

Dad's eyes were rimmed with red. He looked defeated.

Anger roiled in Emma's gut. "How could the US let all this happen? Where are our defenses? Where's the army or the National Guard?"

Dad looked around with furtive glances and kept his voice low. "They were bombed. We didn't stand a chance against Russia's underwater missiles. We never saw them coming. I'm sure there are military divisions out there trying to help, but who knows what the rest of the country is like."

Emma stared straight ahead as they walked the stark white hallways to the conference room. Her cheeks burned, and her heart pounded as she thought of the Russians waiting for them. She met Matt's eye and a flicker of a smile passed over his face. He took Emma's hand. She squeezed his.

As Emma had anticipated, they were met with a group of large, Slavic men. A few of Dad's co-workers also sat scattered around the conference table.

What happened to their families?

"Mr. Smith. I hear you are in charge." The man who appeared to actually be in charge scrutinized Dad.

"Where's Hooper?" Dad looked around at his coworkers.

Bobby's slight shake of the head almost went unnoticed by Emma. He worked directly under Dad since the promotion, out in the oil field.

"Your family is still with us, I see." The man at the head of the table gave a cursory glance over Mom, Emma, and Matt. "I will send them with a guard to get a few things from your home, then they must come back." The man waved a guard forward without taking his eyes off Dad.

They drove home, crammed in the back seat of a Russian Humvee-looking vehicle. Theirs was sandwiched between two other Humvees, one leading the way and one bringing up the rear. Emma sat in the middle of Mom and Matt, fighting the lump in her throat.

So much of the city was gone. All the familiarity gone. They might as well be on a different planet. Emma's skin crawled.

At least Aaron and Claire are okay. And Jack. Jack must be okay.

Matt took her hand again. He hadn't said a word all day.

Things remained unfamiliar as they made their way toward the outer suburbs. She could barely tell which streets they were on as they followed the directions of the GPS. Matt gaped out the window as they spotted people loading dead bodies into trucks. Emma turned away.

There were Russians with guns everywhere. Three guarded a power pole where American linemen were working. Others watched over men working on a piping with water bursting from the sidewalk. Matt turned and looked at Emma with wide eyes. He shook his head.

The driver turned on the radio. A tense voice, with a Texan accent, came through the airwaves. "We've seen higher rates of unemployment and homelessness in recent years, and our own government has done almost nothing to change that. The new regime aims for a better America. We will soon see cleaner streets, lower crime rates, and more job opportunities—"

"Turn it off." Matt startled everyone.

The driver glared back at him, then barked a sadistic laugh before facing the road again.

Emma shivered but had stopped crying. The cereal sat in an uncomfortable ball in her stomach.

When they entered their cul-de-sac, the cereal threatened to make another appearance.

The house was gone.

Mom let out a cry that chilled Emma to the core. Matt threw his arms around Emma and Mom. Tears fell, silent, down his cheeks.

Emma caught the guard's eye in the mirror and thought she detected sympathy. Her heart pounded, and angry adrenaline surged through her whole body.

"Take us back." The words came from Matt with force.

As the guard turned the Humvee around, Emma's stomach lurched. One thought seared through her mind. She turned in her seat and reached back to the rubble that used to be their home.

"My dress. My wedding dress. Mom!"

Saturday 7:23AM //

"Mr. Smith, I am Lev Popov. We understand you have been running the operations here for some time, yes?" The man at the head of the table touched his fingertips together and peered at Joe.

Joe ducked his head in confirmation. He met the man's gaze without wavering, fighting the urge to look in Bobby's direction again.

I won't tell him I was only promoted a few days ago. The value of my life might go down. What happened to Hooper? What's going to happen to my family? Joe clutched at the knees of his slacks under the table.

"Excellent. I think you will find us to be very accommodating to you and your family if you will agree to our terms." Popov's grin made Joe's stomach churn.

"Which are?"

"Simply that you continue your work and communicate everything you do to my assistant, Dimitri." Popov nodded his head toward the man on his right.

He was a thin, greasy-looking man with black eyes whose look caused Joe to shudder.

"As you can see, we have a few of your employees here to make sure things run smoothly, and we will also employ many of our own in the operations." Popov encompassed all in the room with his hands.

"And my family?" Joe's jaw clenched as he spoke.

"They will be very useful to us as well. Have no fear, Mr. Smith. Now, let's carry on as normal, shall we?" Popov looked down at the tablet in front of him and everyone stood.

The meeting was over. Bobby followed Joe out of the room but didn't make eye contact.

"We're getting out of here as soon as we can. They're likely going to close the borders soon." Bobby moved his lips as little as possible and continued to stare straight ahead. "I know some coyotes who can get you through too."

Joe stopped outside his office and watched Bobby continue down the hall without acknowledging him. His office was unchanged, except for the cell phone next to his laptop and the note beside it with bold, black letters, saying, "To communicate with Dimitri."

Joe sat in his desk chair and ran his hands through his hair. He heard footsteps in the hall and looked out the glass door to see a guard with a gun watching him. Joe understood. If he didn't work, he would be reported, or maybe shot.

Staring up his laptop, Joe closed his eyes and thought of Carol. *I hope they're safe. I hadn't even thought of fleeing, but we have to get out of here. Even if I can only get Carol and the kids to go with Bobby.*

Joe started his day's work as usual, save for the sick knot in his stomach and the sweat beading on his brow. *Everything I do will benefit Russia and help them gain power. I can't do anything to jeopardize Carol and the kids though. How did this happen so fast? Emma was right, what happened to our defenses?*

With the man and his gun looking over Joe's shoulder, he worked on through the morning. They delivered a gummy cheese sandwich to him at noon.

"Where's my family?" Joe stood and glared at the man who set the sandwich on his desk.

"They are safe. They are eating lunch too. They had a pleasant morning out in the city." The man's grin was cold.

Joe clenched his fists at his sides to keep himself from punching the man's face. "What do you mean?"

"I'm sure they will tell you all about it tonight after work." The man walked to the door, laughing.

"I want to see them now. Take me to them." Joe followed on the man's heels.

"I'm afraid that is not possible." Dimitri entered as the other man disappeared around the corner. "How are things running?"

"Just great. Except it's hard to run like normal when half the power lines are down, and communication is spotty." Joe met Dimitri's stare, glowering.

"Well, do your best. Bobby seems to know what he is doing on the field. Mr. Popov will be pleased. Now, I have done this work for many years back home. Give me the specifics, Mr. Smith." Dimitri's gaze was steel and threatening.

Joe filled him in on the morning's work, using all the technical jargon he could. Dimitri appeared to keep up. When he had left, Joe chomped into his sandwich.

As he threw the plastic cellophane into the trash by his desk, a new message from the field popped up on his monitor. It was from Bobby, as indicated by the "BS124" user name.

The message appeared to be a normal report on the activities in the field, but Joe looked deeper. Typing the series of letters onto the notepad on his laptop, Joe worked through a few encryptions he thought Bobby might use.

When he found the pattern and discovered the message, Joe sat back in his chair, heart pounding.

Saturday 1:34PM //

Matt's stomach growled, and he stood straight to wipe his sweaty forehead with the bottom of his t-shirt. Tears were so close to the surface, he was afraid he wouldn't be able to hold them back much longer. Looking over at Emma and Mom, bent over as they shoveled debris, Matt cleared his throat and gripped his own shovel tighter.

Breakfast and lunch had done almost nothing to satisfy the hunger raging in his belly. They had been working out here all morning, shoveling brick, glass, and splinters of wood, and moving the larger pieces of the bombed buildings off the streets. This was the Russians' idea of putting them to work to "help the common good."

Matt was just thankful all the bodies had disappeared before they were forced to work in the streets. Other city workers were out repairing damages, always with the presence of a Russian and a gun.

Emma hadn't stopped crying and she leaned against her shovel often. She checked her phone, though there was still no cell service. She hadn't been able to keep her lunch down. Most of Matt's threatening tears came from watching his sister's grief.

He was amazed to see Mom work without pause and with more strength than he would've given her credit for. He couldn't trust himself to say anything since demanding the guard to leave their cul-de-sac.

As Matt bent to shovel another load, he noticed a man crouched and shaking in a free-standing doorway. The rest of the building had been blown away. *I wonder if Aaron knows that guy.*

Matt looked at the guard standing nearby with his gun on his shoulder. He caught Mom's eye and tilted his head toward the man. Mom watched the man for a moment, then met Matt's eyes again. She pressed her lips together and glanced at the guard too before moving closer to Matt.

"Aaron's apartment is a mile away. There's no way we could suggest going over there without sounding suspicious." Mom spoke so low, Matt almost didn't hear her.

"Maybe we could just ask to go see him." Matt shrugged.

Mom looked at Matt with sad eyes, crinkled in the corners. His stomach clenched as he watched her familiar face. His eyes burned, and he closed them. The guard grunted. Matt took a deep breath and dug his shovel under the rubble at his feet.

He looked up at the end of the street, willing Aaron and Claire to come around the corner. Aaron's quick grin and Claire's kind brown eyes were so clear in his mind. Mom whimpered as she worked. Emma glared at the bricks and glass and shoveled, tears flowing, as if she were burying the Russians.

Monday, June 11th
4:54PM //

Aaron looked down at Claire lying on the bed. She was pale and dark bags hung under her eyes. She smiled up at him and reached out to take his hand.

"Are you sure you'll be okay?" Aaron sat down next to her and smoothed a few locks of hair out of her eyes.

"I'll be fine. My stomach is just a little upset. Go. Your family needs to see you." Claire squeezed his hand.

"Do you want me to bring you anything?"

Claire thought for a moment. "Maybe some saltines and ginger ale. If you can find anything that's still open."

"Okay. I won't be gone long." Aaron sat for another moment at Claire's side. *Life is so fragile these days.*

"I love you." Claire kissed his hand before letting him go.

"I love you too." The tightness in his chest surprised him as he stepped away from her.

She'll be fine, and I'll be right back. You're being irrational.

On his way to the refinery, Aaron pulled over when a police car turned its lights on behind him. A man in a police uniform and dark sunglasses sauntered up to Aaron's window.

I don't even know what to expect anymore. I just hope I don't get arrested.

"Hello Officer, how's your day going?" Aaron leaned out the window as if he had all the time in the world.

The officer scuffed his feet on the ground and looked down before meeting Aaron's steady gaze. "Can I see your license and registration?"

Aaron handed over the documents and the cop returned to his car.

This seems par for the course. Maybe I have a tail light out or something. Aaron peered in his rearview mirror.

There was someone else in the police car. In the passenger's seat sat a man with a large gun.

Is that the only tactic they know how to implement?

The cop came back, and Aaron met him with his friendliest smile. "Any trouble?" He took his ID and registration when the cop held them out.

"If you can answer a few questions, hopefully I can get you on your way. You're twenty-eight years old?" The man crossed his arms over his chest.

"Yes, sir."

"What's your occupation?"

"I'm in social services. I serve the homeless and low-income people in our city." Aaron kept his tone light, only guessing what this guy had on the line.

"Are you affiliated with any military group, local or national?"

"No, sir."

"Have you ever been charged with a crime, or served a sentence of any kind?"

"No, sir."

"You live in an apartment downtown with your wife, correct?"

"Yes, sir."

"Is there anyone else living with you?"

"Nope."

"And where are you headed right now?" The police officer had kept a straight face through the whole interview.

"My family is being held at the oil refinery. My dad works there and so I guess they decided to keep the whole family around. I'm going to visit them, hopefully."

The officer pulled a pad of paper out of his breast pocket. He scribbled on the top sheet, tore it off, and handed it to Aaron. "This is your pass. You must not go anywhere without this pass. Your wife may be questioned and given a pass, or not, if she is caught out of the apartment. The government reserves the right to retract your pass at any time for any reason."

"Great." Aaron glanced at the pass but wasn't ready to let the officer go. "Are you going to be alright, sir?"

The man didn't change his expression or the inflection of his voice. "He's been with the force for the last twenty-five years. No one knew he was a Russian spy until Friday. Said he's been waiting for this day for a hell of a long time. Red bastard."

Aaron's eyebrows rose. "No way."

"Yeah, well. I'll be fine. If it weren't for the wife and kids, I'd go after every last one of them. But, got to keep it under my hat. You have a good night, son." The officer made his way back to the patrol car without another look at Aaron.

As the police car sped around him, Aaron sat and let the man's words sink in. *A Russian spy has been a part of the Houston police force for twenty-five years. . . Waiting for this to happen.* His eyes fell to the piece of paper on his lap.

It was a pass stating he had the government's permission to move about the city of Houston freely.

He shook his head and pulled back onto the road. He thought of Claire stuck in the apartment, and Marie and the kids, gone. *Nothing will ever be the same. But we have to push through and fight back in our own way.*

It was dinner time when he reached the refinery, and he found his family huddled close at one end of a long table in the cafeteria. After waving his pass at all the guards he'd come across, he got in without a problem.

Matt stood when he spotted Aaron and met him with a hug. Ruffling Matt's hair, Aaron sat down next to his mom and put an arm around her shoulders.

"Hey. It's good to see you, Son." Dad squeezed his shoulder.

"You too." Aaron met each of their gazes.

Then his eyes went to the large flat screen on the wall where a news reporter blared out bogus reports in a Russian accent. *They've wasted no time on propaganda.*

Images of happy Americans under the new control of the Russians filled the screen. Next, a story of Russian soldiers rescuing people from the ruined city came up.

It was like a nineteen-fifties TV show with Americans seated at tables full of food, smiling and laughing. And the hero, the Russian soldier, always in the right place at the right time.

Aaron turned away as a sourness grew in the pit of his stomach. He told his family about being pulled over and questioned on the way. "Apparently, the man in the car has been here for over twenty years as a spy, just waiting."

Dad shook his head and rubbed the back of his neck. "I can't believe this is happening."

"How are you and Claire doing?" Mom's face was a mask of concern and anxiety, as usual.

"Claire's not feeling great, unfortunately. But we're doing all right. Kids stopped showing up for school, so Claire doesn't go to work anymore. Parents don't trust their kids out of their sight and I don't blame them. I'm always afraid to leave Claire for too long." Aaron's voice faded, and he looked down at the table.

"We've been cleaning up the streets for days." Matt leaned his forehead on his hand. "We keep hoping to get near your place, but we haven't yet."

No wonder they all look exhausted.

"Are you still out working?" Emma's eyes were bloodshot, and Aaron wondered for a moment what had happened to Jack.

"I'm still going to try to visit the people. A lot of the poorest neighborhoods were hit, a lot of our previous clients. . . Also, our funders are gone. We have some money saved up, and we'll dip into our own savings. I'll keep doing what I can. I don't think Claire will get out much. I think she's really shaken up."

"You know our bank information if you need access to more money." Dad's tone was hopeless for their future. Then his eyes brightened. "Actually, can you do us a favor? Could you go to our bank and withdraw as much money as you can? Keep plenty for yourself. Bring it with you in the next few days."

"Can you empty out my accounts too?" Emma leaned across the table toward Aaron.

"Yeah, write down your information." Aaron pulled a scrap of paper and a pen out of his pocket. Being prepared with these implements was an old habit from writing down the needs of people he met on the streets.

"I've been taking our money out of the bank slowly. You can only take so much out in a day. The banks don't have that much cash on hand, and it's probably a matter of time before the Russians gain control of the banks too. I'll do what I can though." Aaron whispered under his hands. "You know they mobilized US, English, and French troops from overseas right after we were attacked, but all the planes are being shot down over the ocean."

Dad's eyes widened. "Hopefully someone can get through soon. What about the National Guard?"

"They were obviously targeted. I've heard of some companies trying to get here, but Houston is so entrenched that what forces we do have are stretched thin to other, less controlled areas."

Dad shook his head and Emma dropped her forehead into her hands.

Aaron talked with his family a while longer. When he stood to go, Dad walked to the entrance of the cafeteria with him.

They stopped, and Aaron crossed his arms over his chest.

Dad glanced around and spoke in a low voice. "Bobby's talked to me about getting us all across the border, but we'll need some money, so be sure to get to the bank as much as you can."

"I can do that. Bobby. Has he heard from his family?" Aaron's heart pounded with wild hope.

"I think so. I think he's talked to them through the fence outside. Marie and the kids were at Bobby's parents' house when the bombs hit. They've arranged a place to meet and everything. Bobby's a smart guy. He's come up with a way to communicate—"

"Alright. Break it up. Move along." A guard butted in, shoving Aaron aside with the end of his gun.

"I'm going." Aaron held has hands up and shot an apologetic look to his dad.

"Hope Claire feels better. Send her our love." Dad pulled Aaron into an embrace. Something he wouldn't have done before the Russians came.

Aaron breathed in his familiar smell as memories of his childhood flashed through his mind. He couldn't wait to tell Claire the good news about Marie and the kids. As he walked out of the cafeteria the guard followed him with an intent gaze.

Tuesday, June 12th
12:04PM //

"Let me in!" Jack shook the chain link fence surrounding the oil refinery. "I know my fiancée's in there. I don't care if you take me hostage, or whatever, just let me in. I have a pass."

Neither of the guards by the door acknowledged him. There were no heartstrings to tug.

"Could you at least go find Emma Smith and tell her Jack is out here? Come on!" Jack gave the fence one final, violent shake, then stepped away.

He had been around the whole compound. There were guards everywhere and no feasible way to get in.

He wondered if she knew about their house, and the coffee shop. He couldn't imagine how Emma was taking it.

Jack sat on the trunk of his car and stared at the guards. His mind turned around a faint idea. His apartment was still standing but the accounting firm where he'd worked had been destroyed. Nothing would be as it had been just days before.

For the first time, anger flared through Jack's veins. *How did this happen in America? How could we let this happen?*

An image formed in his mind as the idea solidified. He smirked and narrowed his eyes at the guards. One shifted his weight to his other foot. Jack just had to figure out how to get to Emma, or to let her know he was here.

He sat on his car all afternoon, except when he drove a few miles into town to get a late lunch, which he took right back to the entrance of the refinery to eat.

Jack raised a taco at the guards before taking a bite. When he finished eating, he lay back on the hood of his car and closed his eyes. His thoughts kept wandering to Emma. The Texas sun boiled the metal hood of his car and sweat was soon dripping from his forehead and back.

"Jack?" The familiar voice startled Jack out of a hazy sleep.

He sat up to find Aaron standing in front of him. Jack hopped from the car. "Aaron! Do they let you in? You have to tell Emma I'm out here. I've been trying to get in for days."

"Whoa, slow down. I'll let her know you're here. How're you holding up?"

"Fine." Jack shrugged and scanned Aaron's face. It was so good to see someone he knew.

"Where are you staying? Did your apartment get hit?" Aaron spoke in low tones.

Jack clenched his hands into fists. *These are the conversations we're having now?* "My apartment's fine. I've been staying there. Please go tell Emma I'm here."

"I'm gone." Aaron gave Jack's shoulder a squeeze before heading to the chain link gate.

The guards let him through without a question. Jack's heart skipped at the thought of Emma coming out those doors in minutes.

And then she was there, yelling his name. She was in his arms and he could barely stay on his feet for the realness of her. The coconutty Emma-smell, her soft hair against his cheek. Her slim figure, now even slimmer, in his arms. Her skin under his fingers.

Jack let the tears come.

"You're here. You're alive. I thought you were dead." Emma sobbed into his shoulder.

He pulled away from her. "You thought I was dead?"

"Well, yeah. The way our last call got cut off." Emma took a deep, shaky breath.

Jack pulled her close again. "I'm so sorry. How've you been handling everything?"

"I haven't been handling anything. I couldn't imagine my life going on without you." Emma held him so tight he almost couldn't breathe. "I was devastated when I saw our house was gone, and my wedding dress is gone, Jack. But when I thought I'd lost you, none of that mattered." Emma dissolved into more sobs.

"Shhh, it's okay. I'm here now. Everything's fine."

"Yeah. But, when will this nightmare end?" Emma put her forehead against Jack's.

Jack kissed her lips. He didn't know what to say. "What have you been doing? Just sitting in there like a prisoner?"

"No, we've been cleaning the rubble off the streets. And they don't feed us enough. It's been awful."

"You don't look good. I mean, you're still the best thing I've ever seen, but you're not healthy." Jack's gaze roamed over her body. "Let's go get some real food in you."

He avoided the street where Common Grounds once stood on his way to the Panaderia, which was still open for business.

"So what happened to you when our call was dropped?" Emma slumped into the booth right next to Jack after ordering food.

"I ran into a blockade of military vehicles. They stopped me and questioned me for a long time, then gave me a pass. I don't trust it though. It feels too easy."

Emma laid her head on his shoulder. As they sat in a bliss of cool silence and ate, Jack's mind wandered to an old, sweet memory.

Ten Years Earlier //

"Can we get some food? I'm starving." Jack leaned against Emma's Jeep, hands in the pockets of his jeans.

"You're pathetic." Emma rolled her eyes.

"Come on, let's go get tacos." Jack grabbed the keys from her hand.

"Hey! You are not driving my car. Give those back." Emma took the keys back.

Jack sauntered to the passenger's side. "Fine with me. I can't be seen carrying a keyring with a huge pink E on it anyway."

Emma started the Jeep without looking at him.

It's only been a week of working on this stupid project and I've never wanted anyone more. How can she have such an effect on me?

"Why is everyone so obsessed with tacos anyway?" Emma pulled out of the school's parking lot.

"Obviously, you've never had the right tacos. Turn left here."

Emma raised an eyebrow at him.

"Do you trust me?"

"Yes, Aladdin." Emma took the turn.

"What? Who's Aladdin?"

"Never mind, I forgot you had a deprived childhood."

"My childhood was deprived? You haven't even had a decent taco." Jack couldn't help but slug her on the arm just to touch her.

He was rewarded with a brilliant grin that stopped his breath. "You don't know that. Maybe I just don't like tacos. Is it really the end of the world?"

Jack recovered in time to respond without skipping a beat. "Yes. It is. You'll like these ones, I promise."

"Wow, a promise. That's serious stuff in my world, Davidson. Where am I going, anyway?"

"Turn right at the next light." Jack pointed. "Why are promises such a big deal? I said turn right, Em, not left."

Emma changed lanes, her cheeks softened into pink. "Promises are to be kept, never broken." She was quiet for a moment. She met his eyes as she stopped at the red light. "I guess your mom must have broken a lot of promises."

Jack looked out the windshield. "You can turn if there's no traffic, you know."

Emma looked to her left before swinging to the right. Jack directed her to park in front of Anna's Panaderia. He braced himself in horror as she nosed into the parallel parking spot.

"You're never going to fit in this way with your Jeep." He raised his eyebrows at her.

Her cheeks flushed again. She dropped her hands from the steering wheel. "Would you like to park then?"

Stop being so adorable. "Back out and pull up alongside this car. I'll steer."

A honk sounded from behind them and Jack waved the guy around.

"I hate this." Emma eased up next to the parked car.

Jack put one hand on her headrest and one on the steering wheel. "I'll show you how, it's no big deal."

Her eyes locked onto his. Was there something inviting in her gaze? Her lips were definitely calling to him. Heat rose up Jack's neck. He swallowed.

"You just start up here, now put it in reverse and give it just a little gas. Good." Jack steered, looking over his shoulder. "Now stop. Put it back in drive, and we're in. Nothing to it."

Emma killed the engine and lifted her eyes from the steering wheel again. "Thanks."

Jack got out and jogged around to her side, opening her door. Her eyes narrowed when he also opened the door to the Panaderia for her and stayed suspicious as he placed her order.

"Have you always been such a gentleman?" Emma crossed her arms as after sliding into an empty booth.

Jack gave what he hoped was a look of incredulity. "Of course. You and I have never even been in the same plane of reality until now. How would you know what I'm really like?" It was all a lie. He'd never cared to treat anyone like this until about a week ago when Emma came into his life.

"Okay, point taken." Emma held up her hands. "Hola, Rosa."

A girl from their school walked up with a plate in each hand. "Bonjour, Emma."

A conversation flowed around him, but Jack knew they weren't speaking Spanish.

"What was that?" Jack leaned forward after Rosa left. "How do you even know her?"

"She's in my French class, what?"

"French?"

"She already knows English and Spanish. What do you expect?"

"So, you guys were speaking French?" Jack poured a little made-from-scratch salsa onto his taco.

"Oui, mon petit garçon."

Jack glared across the table at her. He reached out to grab her wrist as she went for the salsa. "No, wait. Try it without anything on it first."

Emma looked down at his hand and pulled her arm back. "Alright. Here goes nothing." She winked as she raised the taco to her mouth. She set the taco down and chewed but wouldn't meet his eyes again. "Shoot, that is good."

Jack's face broke over a grin he couldn't suppress. "Told ya."

"Well, I'm glad to see you can keep your promises. I had my doubts." Emma bit into the taco again and closed her eyes.

Jack's stomach flopped. He turned his attention back to his own plate.

"So, we never did come up with an idea of how to present the book." Emma poured a little salsa on the taco for her next bite.

"Yeah, you wouldn't stop asking my opinion of different parts of it."

"That's cause it's so good. Gosh, just like this taco."

"Jeez, get a room." Emma's eyes pierced him with their disdain and he wished he could take back the crude comment.

Everything about her is sweet and innocent. I really have to watch what I say around her. The day she learns the whole truth about my past is going to suck.

Saturday, June 16th
6:13PM //

Every muscle in her body screamed as Carol and the kids made their way down the hall to their room. They'd left at eight o'clock and worked out in the streets all day. The room was empty.

"Let's go to the cafeteria. Dad will probably be there." Carol put her arm around Matt's shoulders.

She didn't know what to do with the magnitudes of heartache compounding one on top of the other. There was a perpetual tightness in her chest as she watched her kids and her husband suffer.

And there's just nothing I can do to make things better for any of them.

They went through the line and filled their plates with chewy sandwiches, similar to the ones they'd eaten for lunch. *This isn't how I imagined losing weight.*

Matt took three sandwiches, though he received a glare from the guard overseeing the food line. Emma was green just looking at her food. Carol's heartache went deeper.

Tears flooded her eyes as they had so many times in the past week. *It's only been a week, but it feels like a lifetime ago that things were normal.*

As they sat at the nearest table, Joe walked in and the knot in Carol's chest loosened. He grabbed some sandwiches and joined them. Joe sat close to Carol and kissed her before lifting a sandwich to his mouth. He made a disgusted face as he bit into it.

"What have you been doing all day?" Joe looked from Carol to the kids.

"The usual." Carol put a hand on Joe's thigh and sighed. "I'm exhausted."

Joe rubbed her back, his eyes bloodshot. "I'm sure you are. We all are. Sorry guys. Listen, Emma, Matt."

The kids looked up from their plates.

"Please stay calm, we're being watched. Bobby has a plan to get us out of here in the next few days." Joe's voice was a tremulous whisper.

Carol suppressed a sob. Hope and fear fought for dominance in her heart.

"We're not sure how long the border will be open, so we have to act fast. I'll fill you in on the plan later." Joe turned to Emma. "Jack's been outside all day. Maybe you'll see him in the morning when you go out again."

Emma closed her eyes for a moment, then stared hard at Carol and Joe. "I'm going to see him right now. I can't leave him waiting out there all night." Emma stood and walked away before any of them could stop her.

Carol rose as Emma hurried to the door.

"I'm going to be sick!" Emma rushed past a guard, who backed away to let her through.

"Joe, do you think she'll come back?" Carol sat down again.

"I don't know." Joe's voice broke. "She came back last time."

Matt reached for Carol's hand, his eyes fixed on the spot his sister had been a moment before.

"Is Bobby really going to get us out of here?" Carol met her husband's eyes.

"He says he can." Joe shrugged, deep lines etched above his brow.

A loud bang sounded from the flat screen TV. Carol watched as an American fell to his death in front of an armed soldier. The reporter called him a criminal, someone who threatened to disturb the established peace.

"That's different." Matt startled Carol.

She became aware of her body shaking.

Joe nodded slowly. "Is that the first negative news story they've aired?"

"That I've seen." Matt's eyes were still glued to the screen.

"Come on, you two. You know it's all fake. You don't believe what they're telling you now, do you?" Carol dropped her cheek into one hand with her elbow propped on the table.

Joe shook his head. "It's not what they're telling us. It's what they're doing. They're trying to show us that 'criminals' get killed."

Saturday 7:01PM //

"I'm here. I'm here." Jack's murmured words were like a balm on Emma's raw heart. "Come on, come with me."

"Where are we going?" Emma pulled back.

"There's something I want to do with you." Something in Jack's dark, blue eyes compelled Emma.

She glanced back, then slid into the passenger's seat of Jack's car. The guards, just like last time, hadn't followed her.

Jack drove into the city. Though the streets were now clean, too clean, the sidewalks were littered with displaced people, children standing alone, crying, and every block displayed multiple Russian soldiers with their guns. Emma closed her eyes to it all. She was with Jack now.

She clung to his hand and studied his profile. Her heart somersaulted as Jack glanced at her with his dimpled smile, which always quickened her pulse.

"I don't know what's going to happen to us, but—"

"One of Dad's coworkers is going to get us across the border. He can get you across too. You have to come with us." Hope surged like a sudden spring from Emma's heart.

"Really? When?" Jack swerved around a street sweeper.

"I don't know. I think in the next couple of days. Dad just told us at dinner. Aaron has been emptying our bank accounts and brought all the money to us in paper bags hidden in his pants."

Jack parked on the side of the road in front of Anna's. He didn't say anything as he opened her door. Emma ate a burrito and as many chips and salsa as Rosa would bring out.

They spoke little while she ate, the silence punctuated by Emma's satisfied murmurs. Jack sat across from her, eating an occasional chip as he watched her. Emma might have felt more self-conscious if she hadn't been so hungry.

The mariachi music playing over the speakers, and Rosa's usual routine of wiping down the tables were soothing to Emma's raw nerves. She wished she could curl up in the booth and fall asleep forever.

When they went to the counter to pay, Rosa held up a hand. "No, it's on me."

"We can pay. Let us pay you. We all have to survive this somehow. Are you staying here, or are you going to go south?" Jack thrust a twenty across the counter, which more than paid for the food.

"Gracias. I'm leaving in a few days. Hopefully they won't close the border. I wanted to serve customers as long as I could." Rosa eyed Emma with obvious concern.

"I'm really glad you've been here. We'll miss you." Emma reached out to squeeze the girl's hand. "You've always served everyone with quiet grace. Ever since high school days."

Tears welled in Rosa's eyes. "That's the nicest thing anyone's said to me."

Jack put an arm around Emma's shoulders and steered her out of the restaurant. Emma looked back to see Rosa sobbing behind the counter.

Emma ached to go back inside. She yearned to stay among the familiarity of the décor and lighting of their favorite place to eat since she and Jack had met.

"Wait, Common Grounds is just around the corner. Is it—" Emma read the sympathy in Jack's eyes. "It's gone?"

Jack drove around the block and stopped along the curb where Common Grounds once stood.

Emma stared out the window at the ruins. "It's gone?" She looked at Jack as though he could tell her it wasn't true. It was all a dream.

He took her hand and kissed it. "I'm sorry, Em."

Emma looked out the window again. Someone was in among the ruins working on some pipes. He wasn't accompanied by the usual entourage of Russian guards, but they were never far off.

Emma rolled down her window. "Maybe we can rebuild and get it going again. It would take time, but we could do it."

When she turned back to Jack, his face was buried in his hand. He lifted his head to reveal bloodshot eyes. "I'm so sorry but think about what you're saying. What money would we use to rebuild? Who would we serve? Do you really want to stay here, where the Russians are using their control in more heinous ways every day? Things are only going to get worse."

"You don't know that. Things could blow over." Emma's mind reached for scenarios in which things would be better. "I just—I just want everything to go back to the way it was."

"I know, Em." Jack stroked her hair. "I don't know if things will ever be the same. Even if we were able to drive the Russians out, our country will never be the same. Our lives may never be the same. The sooner we get that through our heads, the better."

Emma pulled her knees up to her chest. She glanced out the window one more time before dropping her forehead onto her knees. "This is all so wrong. It's so unfair. How could this happen to us?" She couldn't stop her tears. A vice gripped her heart and squeezed. "Let's go. Please. Let's go."

Jack started the car again and eased away from the curb.

"We have to get out of here. We can't stay here, Jack. There's nothing left for us here."

Jack drove around a couple of blocks before turning onto a side street. He stopped in front of what appeared to be an abandoned building and killed the engine again. They sat in silence while Emma's tears dried.

"Where are we now?" Emma didn't take her eyes off her fiancé.

He pulled a piece of paper out of his jeans' pocket. "Look, whatever happens to us, I want you to know how much I love you. Even though the Russians have taken over our country, and have destroyed everything we've known, they can't destroy our hope. They can't tell us who we are. We still have a future."

"Jack, you're scaring me." Emma's eyes widened.

"Remember when you said you wanted to get a tattoo? I think now is as good a time as any to get one. I drew this, and I think we should get tattoos to remember that even if we run to Mexico, this is our way of fighting against Russian domination or anyone who tries to hold us down." Jack held out the picture.

It was a sketch of two feathers bursting into birds in flight.

"It's beautiful. Wait, this is Jennie's tattoo shop?" Emma looked out the window.

"Yep. She's still in business, despite being almost bombed out. I told her my idea and she loved it. She even wants to suggest it to other potential customers." Jack shrugged, then put a hand on Emma's shoulder, stroking her long hair.

He looked down at his lap. "I also thought that getting the same tattoo together could symbolize our unity since our wedding has been put on the backburner. I still want to marry you more than anything. And you know I have enough cash saved to make it happen. But I don't want it to happen here, like this. I thought this tattoo could remind us of our promise to each other. What do you think?"

Emma's eyes burned with tears. "Let's do it, Jack. I love it."

He pulled her closer to rest his forehead on hers. "I don't think you'll ever know how much I love you." His eyes were closed, his voice broken.

"I love you too."

Jennie's greeting was curt, and she pointed to a sagging leather bench in the middle of the tiny room, but she seemed pleased to see them. Jack jumped onto the bench. The room and the equipment were as clean as they could be given the circumstances.

"I want this done. This size. Where should I do it, Em?" Jack handed Jennie his drawing and looked at Emma.

"I always wanted to get one just below my elbow, on the inside of my arm." Emma pointed to the spot on her right arm.

"Cool. I'll do the same." Jack slapped the skin and gave Emma a comforting grin.

"This is a cool design." Jennie studied the drawing before putting it through the copier. It came out on translucent paper, which Jennie placed on Jack's arm.

She traced over the design, leaving an imprint of it on his tan skin. "Does that look good?"

Emma and Jack leaned over his arm. Their eyes met. Emma took Jack's other hand, fresh tears welling in her eyes. She nodded.

"Let's do this." Jack took a deep breath.

He gritted his teeth while the needle dragged through his skin, but he didn't make a sound.

When it was Emma's turn, Jennie made the drawing smaller on her computer before tracing it on her skin. Emma clasped Jack's hand and held his gaze as Jennie went to work. The needle tore into Emma's flesh, her whole body tensed, and she bit her lips together. Her eyes didn't waver from Jack's.

"You're a rock star, Em." Jack squeezed her hand, his dimples peeking out on both cheeks.

Emma's arm went numb, aside from the searing pain concentrated just below her elbow.

"Don't forget to breathe." Jennie didn't take her focus off her task.

Emma exhaled, then took a deep breath in. It seemed to ease the pain. She hadn't realized she'd been holding her breath.

Then it was over. Jennie covered the area with a clean bandage and stood, stretching. Jack pulled a wad of bills out of his back pocket and held them out to Jennie.

Jennie rifled through the stack. "This is too much. I can't take all this. You need it."

"No, take it." Jack put his untattooed arm around Emma's shoulders.

"Here, compromise." Jennie held out a small chunk of the wad.

Jack sighed and took the money. "Thanks. Thanks for doing this for us."

"Thank you. Good luck, both of you." Jennie wrapped an arm around Jack and Emma, pulling them into a hug.

"You're staying here?" Emma glanced around the tiny shop.

"Yep. I'm not going anywhere." A gleam of defiance lit Jennie's dark eyes.

Jack and Emma left the shop.

"Can we go to Aaron and Claire's, and tell them Dad's plan?" Emma looked up at her fiancé before he could shut the passenger's side door.

"Sure." He leaned over and placed a light kiss on her lips.

On their way to Aaron and Claire's, they passed by Houston's downtown plaza. A mob of Americans were running at the Russian guards scattered throughout the square. Jack slowed down as they watched the Americans' rage, and the Russians greet them with the ends of their guns to the head or bullets to the heart.

"Go!" Emma ducked down, unsure where the bullets were flying.

Jack hunched in his seat and accelerated, speeding through the streets until they were several blocks away. He didn't stop until they reached the apartment building where Aaron and Claire lived.

Jack killed the engine and leaned over to wrap his arms around Emma. He was shaking. "Are you okay?"

He planted kisses everywhere he could reach.

Emma clutched Jack as he held her. "We have to get out of here." She pulled away and he ran his fingers through her hair.

"You still want to see your brother?"

Emma nodded.

"Okay, let's get in there quickly. Wait here." Jack got out and ran to Emma's door. He grabbed her hand and pulled her up the steps to the apartment building.

When they knocked on Aaron and Claire's door, Aaron opened it a crack.

"Emma? Jack?" Opening the door wider, he stepped aside to let them in

Aaron pulled Emma into a hug. He had always given great hugs, and Emma savored this one.

"What's going on? I thought you were stuck at the oil plant." Aaron held Emma's gaze while she hugged Claire.

"They don't seem to care if I leave. It's pretty strange. I don't even have a pass like Jack or you." Emma shrugged and returned to Jack's side.

Aaron exchanged a glance with Claire. "That's so—none of this makes sense. You got a pass too?" He rubbed the back of his neck and looked at Jack.

Jack nodded. "But I think they're biding their time. Why would they let capable young men, or women, go free without forcing us to join the military or some other group 'for the good of society'? I think they're establishing their new order before they start rounding people up."

Aaron's eyes widened. "Jack, man, I hope you're wrong."

"Gas prices have dropped so low. I think they're doing what they can to win everyone over. All this talk about a better government, they're trying to get us all to side with them."

Claire tightened her grip on Aaron's arm.

"Bobby's going to get us across the border in the next couple of days. Please come with us. Do you know what it's like out there? It's crazy. We just saw a mob of people get mauled down by Russians, who of course had their guns ready. You have to come with us." Emma looked from Aaron to Claire.

"I'm so sorry." Aaron's eyes flooded. He cleared his throat. "I know how bad it is. That's really tempting, but we're going to stay put. The people here need help more than ever, and there's no one to help them. We have to stay."

Emma's eyes welled with tears. "It's dangerous. Dad said they might close the borders off soon. This might be our only chance."

Aaron blinked and turned his back on them.

"We're not going, Emma." Claire laid a hand on Emma's arm. Her expression was gentle, apologetic, but firm.

Aaron turned around again. "What happened to your arms?" All trace of his tears vanished as he pointed to Emma's bandaged arm.

Emma looked at Jack. "We just got tattoos."

Jack pulled the original design out of his pocket. "This is what they look like. We wanted to have a reminder that even though the Russians have taken everything from us, they can't take our hope. America will come together again."

Aaron took the small piece of paper from Jack and studied it. "This is really cool."

"You should get it too, man. Add it to your collection. Jennie's still in business and she's going to spread the word." Jack winked at Aaron.

"Cool. Maybe I will get one." Aaron pocketed the paper.

"Maybe I'll get one too." Everyone stared at Claire for a surprised moment.
Aaron put his arm around her.

"I'll miss you guys, so much." Emma took a step forward.

They all gravitated together in an embrace.

"You two will have a good life down there." Aaron grin, though tears stood again in the smile lines around his eyes.

"Love you guys." Emma looked from Aaron to Claire and back.

"Here, take some jackets." Claire hurried to the coat closet and pulled out three or four zip-up hoodie sweatshirts. She handed them to Emma.

Ten minutes later, she and Jack were weaving through the streets again, back to the oil refinery.

"I can't believe I may never see him again." Emma gazed at the sweatshirts on her lap, unwilling to watch the crumbling world speed by.

Jack took her hand. "You will see him again. You think the rest of the world is going to sit by and watch the Russians take over America? This will all be over in a few months and we'll be able to come back and start fresh."

Emma lifted an eyebrow and squeezed his hand. "I hope you're right.

Jack pulled up to the curb, a block away from the front entrance and jogged around to Emma's door. When she stepped out and reached for his hand, he pulled her into an embrace instead.

"I love you, Em." His voice was thick.

"What's wrong?" Emma pulled back to look into his face.

His eyes were full of an anguish she'd never seen there before.

What now?

He held her by the shoulders. "Em, I—I need to go make sure my mom is okay, then I'll come find you."

The spinning world stopped.

If Jack hadn't been holding her up, Emma would've collapsed. She couldn't catch her breath. "No, don't leave me again. Let me go with you. Please!" Sobs tore from Emma's throat.

Jack swallowed hard and blinked several times. "You'll be safer here than with me. I'll meet you at the border. I promise." His voice broke.

Promise was a complicated word between them.

"Jack, please. You don't know where we'll be or when we'll get there."

"Call me when you get there. Where I'm going isn't far from the border. Call me." He pried Emma's fingers off his arm.

Tears fell down Jack's cheeks as he walked around the car and slid into the driver's side.

Then he was gone.

Emma's legs buckled, and she slumped to the ground. A gnawing ache spread from her chest, filling her all the way to her fingertips.

How could he leave me? What if I never see him again? I could roll into the street. Nothing is fair. Nothing. Why is every last thing being ripped from me?

After a long time, or maybe just a moment, a Humvee drove by and brought Emma back from the blackness. She stood on unsteady legs and held onto the chain link fence, with the barbed wire around the top, all the way back to the front door. She didn't know if the guards paid her any attention or not.

When she was inside again, Emma fell to the cold linoleum floor and lay motionless, staring at the wall. She pulled herself up and wound through the maze of hallways back to her family's room. They were all there.

"Honey, is Jack okay? Where have you been? Oh my God. What happened to your arm?" Mom stood as her hand flew to her mouth.

"He left. He left me. He had to go find his mom." Emma lowered herself onto her makeshift bed and curled into a ball.

"What happened, Sweetie?" Dad crouched over her and smoothed her hair away from her face.

Emma closed her eyes as the gnawing ache ebbed a little. Dad lifted her bandaged arm.

"It's a tattoo." Emma didn't open her eyes.

"A what?" Shock and confusion reverberated through Mom's voice.

Emma sighed, opened her eyes and removed the bandage. "Jack drew it. He wanted me to remember that even though the Russians have taken away our home and taken over our lives, they can't take away our hope and we will be free again."

They all hovered over Emma now.

Matt caught her gaze. "Sick."

The   corners   of   Emma's   lips   twitched.

Sunday, June 17th
8:16AM //

Slumped over his desk, peering at his laptop, Joe typed the most recent encrypted message sent by Bobby onto his computer's notepad. Perspiration trickled between his shoulder blades despite the air-conditioning. The guard watching him just outside the door would be stupid not to suspect something.

The decoded message read, "Tonight or never. It's only getting harder to cross. Come talk."

Joe stood and was followed out to the field by his guard. He found Bobby, yellow vest and hard hat on, checking in with one of the Russian employees. He turned to Joe and dove into business without a glance at the guard. Joe was surprised when he didn't attempt to say anything under his breath, but the guard was standing very close by.

When matters were settled with Bobby, Joe spent the rest of the morning making rounds through the warehouse. When he went to the cafeteria for lunch, the guard left him to get his lunch elsewhere. Joe got in line for food and spotted his family at a table across the room.

With as much food as he could stomach piled on his tray, Joe sat down next to Carol. Something crinkled in the back pocket of his jeans. Joe fished a piece of paper out. It was a note scribbled in apparent haste by Bobby. *Meet me by the south gate with your family at 10:00 tonight.*

Joe crumpled the paper and eyed the guard at the door who seemed preoccupied with watching a man in the line who was crying loud and without shame.

"Poor man." Carol shook her head.

Many of his coworkers' families had already been killed in the bombings, or had just disappeared, but they were still forced to work. Joe put an arm around Carol's shoulders, pulling her closer.

"Aaron!" Matt was on his feet a second later, running across the cafeteria to meet his older brother.

Joe and Carol turned to see Aaron sauntering through the door, past the guard, as though he owned the place.

Aaron and Matt embraced in the middle of the room. Carol and Emma rose to join them. Joe followed.

"Back so soon?" Joe put a hand on Aaron's shoulder and steered him to their table.

"Emma and Jack came by our place yesterday and said you guys were leaving soon, so I wanted to come see you one more time. Do you have everything you need?"

"I think so. Thanks." Joe put a hand on his son's shoulder.

Carol held his hand, as they talked as though everything were normal.

"All right! That's enough. Time to get back to work." A guard stalked up behind them.

Aaron hugged them each one last time. Joe's gut dropped as he watched Aaron walk out.

Back in his office, Joe worked in a state of distraction. Nine o'clock was lights out time. They would have to be careful. He planned their escape route over and over throughout the afternoon. *How can we possibly get by all the guards?*

Thirty-two Years Earlier //

"I can't believe you talked me into coming to a Christian singles group, Fay. I should be home researching for my lit paper." Carol unbuckled her seatbelt and climbed out of the car.

Fay joined her on the sidewalk. "You're a good friend, Carol. You're going to give me moral support when I talk to David. You know how I hate parties—"

"But you knew David would be here. Yes, I know."

"Not everyone can score a date as easily as you and Ruby. Plus, it's a great excuse to wear your new dress and jacket. The blue really makes your eyes pop."

"Oh, well in that case, let's go." Carol chuckled and turned up the short walk to a large house. "Where is Ruby anyway?"

"On a date."

Carol laughed and knocked on the door.

"Come in!" A voice sailed through the open window to their right.

Carol and Fay stepped into the formal entryway and took off their jackets.

"Whose house is this? It's really nice." Carol stopped to study a family portrait with a young couple and five little kids. *That's a lot of kids. No thanks.*

"This is the young adult pastor's house." Fay peeked into the living room.

"Your church has a young adult pastor? Gag me." Carol muttered this last part under her breath. *What's Fay getting herself into going to church?*

Carol stepped up beside Fay and scanned the living room. "There are a lot of women here. Where are all the men?"

"Over there." Fay pointed to a cluster of guys in the far corner.

Carol grabbed Fay's elbow. "Let's go mingle."

Fay pulled back. "Wait, no one's mingling yet."

"I know. What's their damage? Are they all waiting for an air horn or something? If you're the first one over there, you'll have much better odds." Carol hooked her arm under Fay's and led her across the room.

When they reached the group of guys, a silence fell, and six pairs of eyes landed on Carol and Fay.

"Hi, I'm Carol. Have you met Fay?" Carol nudged Fay into the circle.

She let out a breath of relief when a few of them started a conversation with her. *Fay would've stood there for who knows how long without saying a word.*

Carol looked around and decided to make a beeline for the refreshment table when a pair of amused, frost-blue eyes stopped her. He was tall and broad-shouldered, and he worked his way out of the tight circle.

"Hi, Carol. I'm Joe, Joe Smith." Joe leaned against the wall and put his hands in his pockets.

Carol placed a hand on the curve of her hip. "Hi."

"You go to UH?"

"Yeah. You?" Carol brought her hand up to her hair and curled it around her fingers.

Something in Joe's open, kind face stopped her from continuing her usual games.

"No. I go to Rice. What's your major?" Joe's eyes hadn't left her face. He seemed interested in her for her own sake.

This is different. "English. Rice, huh?"

"Yeah, I'm an engineering student. So, Fay must have convinced you to come?"

"Yeah, she did. She doesn't really like these things, but she likes someone here, I think." Carol's voice grew tender as she looked at her friend.

When she glanced back at Joe, a wide smile had engulfed his features.

"What?"

Joe turned to look at the guys still talking with Fay. "Who does she like?"

"Oh, I don't know, she's said his name a thousand times." Carol scrutinized the guys in the group. "I think his name is David. Does that ring a bell?"

"Oh yeah, David's the one in the blazer of many colors. People keep calling him Joseph tonight." Joe chuckled and met Carol's bewildered look. "You know, like Joseph from the Bible and his coat of many colors?"

Carol raised an eyebrow and shook her head.

"Oh, sorry. I guess I assumed. . ."

"Well, guess you assumed wrong, huh." Carol turned on her heel. *Perfect. Just what I need. A judgmental Christian making eyes at me.*

"Hey, wait. Where are you going?" Joe caught up with her.

"I was thinking about spiking the punch." Carol rolled her eyes and stopped walking. Her words died in her throat at the amusement in Joe's blue eyes. "What?"

"What do you have on you to spike the punch? There's no hiding room in that dress, or that tiny purse."

Instead of anger boiling inside her, laughter bubbled up to Carol's lips. "You're right about that. I wasn't going to spike the punch. I've never done anything like that in my life."

"It must be weird being in a room full of people with a very different background from your own. Want to get out of here?" Joe pulled his keys out of his pocket.

"Yeah. Let me tell Fay." *He can't possibly know how different my life's been from these people. Can he?*

After a quick good-bye to Fay, who was too entranced in a conversation with David to care, Carol grabbed her jacket from the coat rack and followed Joe out to his car.

"This is your car?" Carol looked at Joe over the brand-new red Corvette convertible.

Joe rubbed the back of his neck and shrugged as though he was embarrassed. "Yeah, my grandparents got it for me."

"This is so rad. I've never ridden in a convertible before." Carol climbed in, careful not to damage the upholstery.

Joe slid into the driver's seat with less care. He started the engine, and something ignited within Carol.

She studied him out of the corner of her eye. *Who is this guy? He rescues me from a drag of a party and whisks me off in a Corvette. He seems interested in me, not just my dress, and he's really cute.*

"What?" Joe caught her staring at him.

Carol turned her gaze forward. "Do you play sports at Rice?"

"Nah. No time in the engineering program. But I like to run. I'd try out for cross country if I had time to compete. You?"

"No way. Do I look like an athlete to you?" Carol raised an eyebrow at Joe.

Still he only glanced at her face and shrugged.

Carol crossed her arms over her middle and slumped in her seat. "Where are we going?"

"Just a little place I like to hang out." They drove through the suburbs of Houston, and passed the turnoff to the Lookout, the spot where couples "parked."

Joe handled the Corvette well and maneuvered into the city. It was like riding an eager, well-trained horse.

Joe pulled up to the curb outside an arcade.

Carol's scornful glare was met with a boyish grin and a twinkle from the depths of Joe's eyes.

"You really love the arcade?" Carol raised an eyebrow.

Joe shrugged. "Sure. It's not the arcade we're here for though. My buddy works here, and I owe him for pranking me last week. Wanna help me pull one over on him?"

Carol stared, bemused, before she burst out laughing. "You're one of a kind, aren't you Joe?"

"Does that mean you're in?"

"I guess I should make sure we're not about to do something illegal." Carol narrowed her eyes at Joe, keeping her smile in check. "Okay, what's your plan?"

Joe outlined the prank to her with a lot of animation and arm-waving. He had Carol muffling her laughter by the end. "Okay, are you ready? You know what you're going to do?"

Carol nodded.

"Come on, this way." Joe led the way down the alley to the back door of the arcade.

He looked through the narrow window before opening the door, being careful not to make any noise. Carol slipped through the open door and waited in the dark hallway as Joe eased the door shut behind him.

In the dim light from a streetlamp outside, Carol could see Joe biting his lower lip to keep from laughing.

He took Carol's hand and a warm shock went through her. A steady protection and safety seemed to surround her. She stopped to stare at their joined hands until Joe drew her forward. Her heart pounding over more than just the prank they were about to pull, Carol followed close behind Joe.

Sunday, June 17th
9:47PM //

Shaking, heart pounding, Carol followed close behind Joe as they walked the halls of the oil refinery. Emma and Matt were on her heels. They carried their shoes in an attempt to be as quiet as possible, and they wore the jackets Claire had given to Emma.

Joe peered around every corner, checking for guards before they continued. The silence in the building seemed alive, as though the walls were listening and watching their every move. The hair on Carol's neck stood up.

The maze of halls was never-ending. Carol got so turned around, she couldn't say with any confidence where they were. But she trusted Joe. When Joe peered around the umpteenth corner, he flattened against the wall and put a finger to his lips. Carol heard heavy footsteps pacing the hall.

Joe took her hand. He clenched his eyes shut, trembling. Sweat beaded on his forehead.

Carol squeezed his hand. He looked around the corner again and pushed Carol forward. Alarmed, she hurried for cover behind the wall across from Joe and the kids. She flattened against it, her heart pounding, trying to catch her breath without making a sound. She stared across the hall at Joe with wide eyes. He was pale as a sheet, and stiff as a board.

Joe waited a few moments, then checked for clearance again and sent Emma after Carol. Next, Matt scurried over. When Joe made it across, the boots stopped.

They all froze, not daring to breathe. Matt shook against her. The guard grunted, causing Carol's heart to leap to her throat. Then the pacing began again.

Joe hurried them on. When they made it to an outside door, Joe opened it and they all slipped on their shoes.

"Don't relax yet. There are probably more guards out here." Joe looked around before leading the way to the south gate.

There was no one in sight the whole way. They ducked around hiding places, staying in the shadows as much as they could, but it didn't seem necessary.

Carol couldn't help but smile as they neared the gate. Bobby was there waiting. Her pulse quickened. Bobby ushered them through the gate behind some bushes on the other side where his family was waiting.

"Hey!" The voice came out of the dim. A beam from a flashlight bobbed up and down. "Who's there?"

Carol pulled the kids down. She clasped a hand to her mouth when she saw Joe caught in the flashlight's beam.

"I—I thought I heard something, so I came over here to check it out. Then I saw that the gate was open. I was just about to shut it." Joe crossed his arms, his legs spread in a firm stance.

"It's past lights out. Why are you out here anyway?" The guard came to the gate and swung his light around.

Carol and the kids didn't move.

"I had to get some fresh air." Joe cleared his throat.

"Come on. I'll walk you back in." The guard shoved Joe from behind.

Carol bit her lips together. Tears stung her eyes. Joe's hand pressed against his back, making the sign they had used long ago to say, "I love you." Carol stood and made for the gate but was caught by Bobby.

"We must go now. He would want you to take the kids and go." Bobby spoke in a firm, but gentle whisper.

Carol bent over with her hands on her knees, dragging in unsteady breaths.

Emma took her arm and pulled her along. Carol walked on, but her heart had been left behind. A hollow ache in her chest threatened to consume her.

Monday, June 18th
4:16AM //

Matt extricated himself from the sticky mass of bodies. They'd been crammed into the car for over seven hours.

Nausea and hunger wrestled in his stomach, and he couldn't bring himself to look at his mom. Tears had been falling steadily down her cheeks the whole drive.

A cascade of emotions washed over Matt as the hours passed. Anger at Dad for getting caught. Fear. An aching for Dad to be there. More fear.

Bobby and Marie's kids had slept and cried and slept some more. Matt kept his gaze out the window.

They were almost to the border. He didn't know the plan. Helplessness squashed the urge to take care of his mom and Emma. Matt looked at Bobby. He signaled for everyone to follow him. They abandoned the car and continued on foot.

Bobby approached an old phone booth next to a dark alleyway where a man in a black hoodie stood. Emma took Matt's hand, and Matt took his mom's hand. Bobby spoke to the man in Spanish.

Matt picked up a few of their muttered words. *Money. Five thousand dollars. Safe.* Bobby handed the man a fat, white envelope. The man flicked it open and rifled through the bills.

"Bueno." The man looked the group over, contempt written over his dark features. He beckoned them to follow him.

"Is he a coyote?" Emma pulled on Bobby's arm, whispering. "We're going to trust a coyote?"

"It's the only way. They aren't letting many people across the border anymore. He will make sure we get across safely."

Emma stared at Bobby, eyes wide.

Matt had heard about coyotes on the news. "I thought coyotes helped Mexicans get into America."

Emma frowned at him.

Matt looked from Bobby to the man leading them. *What are we doing? Why didn't we just stay back with Dad?*

Matt took a few deep breaths. Mom still appeared catatonic. He reached up and rubbed her back. For the first time since they'd left Houston, she looked at him.

His fear and uncertainty were mirrored in her eyes. The ground had been pulled out from under them, and they were all left hanging onto a limb that might snap at any second.

They walked on and on. Matt fought against his tears the whole way. A few escaped, leaking down his cheeks. Emma put an arm around him, making it harder not to cry.

"You should be looking forward to summer break, to all those free days." Emma's voice was a broken whisper in the darkness. "You're just a kid. Who knows what we're heading into now."

Matt bit back his sobs as the tears flowed, silent and hot. He put an arm around Emma's waist.

After walking for what seemed like an hour, they came to the border. The air was thick and musty with the smell of sweat, sun-drenched earth, and something like tar. Bobby's eyes were wide. He looked all around. One of his babies was asleep on his shoulder.

The night was dark, pierced by the bright lights of the border checkpoints. Matt peered, wary, into the deep shadows.

Some of the checkpoints had been bombed, but police and guards stood everywhere. Whether they were Mexican or Russian wasn't clear in the darkness.

The coyote led all of them to a police officer at the border and spoke in rapid Spanish. He shoved a large wad of bills into the policeman's hand.

"What about Jack? I have to call him. He said he'd meet me here." Emma pulled out her cell phone and tried putting a call through. "It's not working. I have to get a hold of him." Her tone was hysterical.

Matt swallowed. Mom stared straight ahead, unseeing. *So I'm the only one thinking clearly.*

"This is our only chance. We have to go now." Matt tugged on Emma's hand as they moved forward.

She looked around as if Jack would materialize out of nowhere. She tried to pull her hand free, but Matt held on tight. He placed his other hand on the small of Mom's back and guided both of them after Bobby and his family.

As they passed over the border, the police officer stared ahead, still as stone.

They entered Matamoros.

Everything was quiet and dark. It was five forty-six in the morning by Matt's watch. Mom and Emma walked alongside Matt like zombies.

They followed Bobby through the streets as a seam of gold appeared in the east.

On the outskirts of town, Bobby and his family stopped at a cluster of houses.

"This is where we part ways." Bobby shifted his sleeping baby to his other arm. "The coyote told me you guys will have to go to a camp outside the city. That way." Bobby pointed to the east. Just keep on this road, I'm sure you'll find it."

Matt looked down the dark street.

"Adios." Bobby waved as his wife herded their other children toward one of the houses.

"Thanks Bobby." Matt found his voice as Bobby disappeared into the darkness.

Gunshots rang loud in Matt's ears. Rough, urgent voices came from an alley nearby. Matt pulled on Emma's and Mom's hands. They trotted away.

"I wonder what kind of camp he's talking about." Emma trembled beside him, fifteen minutes later.

They walked on, past small stucco houses, into an industrial area as the sun rose. Golden light covered everything like honey.

Soon, a mass of tents loomed before them. One large tent stood to the right. A line of American refugees snaked out of the tent's opening.

Refugees.

Emma's hand tightened around Matt's. Mom stopped in her tracks. Matt's stomach grumbled.

"You hear about refugees on the news. I never thought we would become them." Matt muttered his thoughts out loud.

Emma whipped around as though he startled her. "What did you say?"

"Nothing."

"What is this place?" Mom's voice sounded far off.

"It's a camp, I guess. Bobby sent us this way." Matt took Mom's hand with his free one. "Are you okay?"

"I can't believe we've made it this far. What are we supposed to do?" Tears trickled down Mom's cheeks.

"Get in line and wait, I guess. Matt's starving." Emma tugged them forward. Her voice was thin and quivered.

Mom stared into the sea of tents. Matt couldn't tell if she was really seeing them.

Everyone in line ahead of them seemed too tired or shocked to do anything but wait. They stood in line for an hour before they reached the entrance to the tent. Matt's stomach grumbled again and tightened. Emma cried off and on. Mom didn't make a sound.

The check-in tent was lined with tables, and volunteers bustled around, organizing groups of families who looked as lost as Matt felt.

Emma approached a man behind a nearby table. "Hi, hola. Do we need to check in or something?" She seemed beyond caring about anything.

"Yes, please fill out these forms." He shoved a couple of forms and a pen under her nose.

Emma picked up the forms and began filling them out.

Matt scanned the tent. The volunteers looked like they hadn't slept in several nights, though they still wore tired smiles.

American refugees crowded the tent. Loud voices were absorbed by the tent walls. A rank smell of body odor filled the close space.

For the first time in weeks, Matt thought of home and every fiber of his being wanted to be back in his own room, with the smells of his mom cooking dinner wafting up from downstairs.

Several families with small kids huddled together, dazed. Nothing could appease all the tears.

Nothing will ever be the same. There's no going back to the way things used to be. A heaviness settled over Matt's shoulders as he took in the chaos and confusion around him.

The refugees outnumbered the workers by a large number. *Aaron should have come with us. He would've known what to do.*

Emma filled out several forms as well as she could without their IDs. After getting their pictures taken, Matt, Emma, and Mom stood in another line for twenty minutes. When they reached the front, a weary Mexican handed over three sleeping bags, two buckets, a cooking pot, and a few eating utensils.

"This is what we get?" Emma stared at the sleeping bag in her arms. "This is all we have."

"Hello, can I help you guys get settled?" A girl approached them.

Emma fell on her shoulder, crying.

Monday 10:12AM //

She wasn't there. No one knew where she was. She hadn't been seen in weeks.

Well, I tried. Jack sighed, grappling with a tinge a guilt. *It's not like I've talked to her in the last seven years. She probably wouldn't know me if she saw me.*

Jack drove around downtown. Just like in Houston, the people of Corpus Christi were trying to survive. The streets were a mess and littered with Russians, though not as many as in Houston. And he hadn't seen as much public violence. Jack found he could look around instead of keeping his eyes focused straight ahead.

He fished some cash out of his pocket as he stepped up to the counter at the coffee shop he'd found. The girl behind the counter reminded him of Emma. He saw Emma everywhere.

I hope she's okay. I have to get to her. Why did I leave her to look for my stupid mom? How could I leave her right after she found out about the coffee shop? Right when she was going to leave the country? I'm such an idiot! Jack wanted to hit something, but also didn't want to attract attention.

He bought a latte and a sandwich and returned to his car. He ate as he drove. Emma flooded his thoughts the whole way to the border.

Jack arrived at the border around two o'clock and abandoned his car. He took a deep breath as he approached the guards. Emma was so close.

The guard held up a hand. Jack stared at it. No words came.

"Border's closed."

"Wha— How? It's only been a couple of weeks since—"

"We can't let you through."

Jack backed away and noticed all the people loitering around the border. A few leaned against the border fence, eyes closed, or peering around with desperation.

Some families sat on benches nearby. The area was littered with people. Many of them had probably abandoned everything they knew and were now homeless, waiting for a miracle.

Anger boiled to the surface, and Jack marched forward. The guard barred him with his gun and pushed back hard. Jack stared at the man's dark sunglasses.

Like an overloaded rope breaking under its burden, whatever it was that held everything together inside Jack snapped. He pushed the guard, felt the butt of a gun against his head, heard a crack, and everything went black.

Ten Years Earlier //

The room spun around him and blackness crowded his vision. Jack closed his eyes and fought the tears that sprang to the surface. He took two deep breaths before opening his eyes again.

Emma stood before him, her hand over her mouth. The horror and anger in her eyes were more than he could handle. He closed his eyes again.

"How dare you? I trusted you. I thought I knew you." Emma's voice wobbled, and Jack could picture the tears streaming down her perfect face.

His cheek was on fire from her slap. An instinctive move he deserved. *I deserve even worse. I can't believe I just blew it.*

"Emma. I'm sorry. I thought that's what you wanted." Jack's ragged voice begged for forgiveness. He opened his eyes.

Emma's hand was still over her lips, and tears were streaming from her clear, blue eyes. She shook her head. "How could you—"

"I know. I don't know what I was thinking. Please let me tell you the truth. Sit down." Jack patted the top of the Smith's kitchen table next to him.

Emma shook her head again and stood her ground.

Jack buried his raw face in his hands before meeting her gaze. "Until I met you, I lived differently. This is the only way I know how to be in a relationship. Maybe it has to do with my absentee mom, I don't know."

Emma rolled her eyes.

"I know that's no excuse. I've never hurt anyone. I swear. The last thing I want to do is lose you. I'm so sorry." Jack's voice broke and he cleared his throat.

Embarrassment grew like a monster inside him, but he didn't back off. "I'm acting like a sleaze-ball. I never deserved you Emma, and I definitely don't now."

He jumped off the table and headed toward the front door.

"Where are you going?"

Jack turned back to see Emma with hands on her hips. "We never should have mixed in the first place, you're way out of my league. Look at this house. I sleep on the floor every night. It doesn't make sense. I'm leaving. Isn't that what you want?"

"Maybe in your family you just leave, but that's not how our family handles things. Sit down." Emma pulled a chair out from the table.

Her eyes were cold as ice, but Jack's heart pounded with hope. An urge to smile came over him, but he fought it as he dropped into the chair.

Emma waited until their eyes locked. A sorrow and tenderness filled hers. "Jack Davidson, I forgive you." She stood up straighter. "But if you ever treat me or anyone like that again, that will be it. No more chances. You're better than that."

Jack let out his breath. "I won't ever do anything like that again. I'll follow your lead when it comes to that stuff. Do you trust me?"

Emma raised an eyebrow. "The question is, do you trust me, Jack?"

"Of course I do."

"It's considered old-fashioned now, but I plan to save myself for marriage. It feels right to me. Can you still follow my lead knowing that?" Emma was a mixture of timidity and defiance.

Jack's mind raced. *Until marriage? This girl is something else.*

"Yes, I will wait, if that's what you want." As the words came through Jack's lips, they took root and he knew he wasn't lying as he had to other girls in the past.

"Then I can trust you." Emma held out a hand.

When Jack took it, she pulled him up and wrapped her arms around his waist. He inhaled the sweet scent of her hair. "Thank you."

Monday, June 18th
11:16AM //

As they finally left the processing tent, the stench of sweat and feces crashed over them like a wave. Rows of patched-up tents faced each other, creating an avenue they walked down.

A deep well of despair filled Emma. And anger at Jack, for leaving her.

He should be here with us. We shouldn't even be here. We should be going about our lives in Houston.

People stood or sat everywhere. Listless, hopeless, bloodshot expressions met her at every turn. Many had tears in their eyes. As they passed one tent, a man sat, almost naked, crying and stamping his fists on the ground. Emma looked the other way.

The silence, pierced by jarring cries, clung to Emma, heavy as the humidity. The girl who'd helped them through the check in process, Margot, now led them down the avenue and took a few turns. Emma's sneakers were covered in dust as she shuffled through the garbage littered along the ground.

Some invisible claw tore at her heart. *This can't be happening. Where's Jack? I just want Jack.*

Margot stopped outside a tent, numbered fifty-nine. It looked like every other tent, patched in places, half falling down.

"The supply tent is that way." Margot pointed behind her. "That's where you can get wood to build fires to cook over, as well as clothes and toiletries. You have to get meal vouchers for each week, because of the limited food supply. At the food tent you can pick up your weekly rations of rice and beans. Porta potties and showers are that way." Margot turned to the right. "You'll need to come back to the processing tent we just left in two days to pick up your temporary refugee ID cards."

A strange mix of empathy and apathy fought over Margot's features. Her lips turned up at the corners. "If you need anything just go to the supply tent. Okay, I'd better get back."

Margot left. Emma led the way into the tent. It was spacious for the three of them. They unrolled their sleeping bags on the ground. Mom dropped onto one and gave in to tears. Matt gazed around the tent until his eyes locked with Emma's. He blinked quickly.

Emma was overcome by a nasty, sick gnawing in her gut. Her skin bristled with discomfort. The air was close and musty. Dust kicked up from the ground seemed to coat her tongue. It covered everything.

She sat down and wrapped her arms around Mom's shoulders. Matt lowered himself onto the closest sleeping bag.

The silence was rent with sobs for an unknown amount of time. Mom muttered Dad's name. Emma's heart was heavy with grief and the absence of Jack. "I'm hungry." Matt's voice was hoarse, and he wiped at his cheeks.

Emma exhaled a fresh cry. "Do you want me to look for the food tent with you?"

Matt nodded.

"Mom, just stay here. We'll bring you something." Emma waited until Mom had laid down, then left with Matt.

"How are we going to find the food tent in this maze?" Matt stopped once they'd stepped outside.

"I guess we just walk that way. Hopefully it's obvious." Emma pointed in the direction Margot had indicated earlier.

Matt grabbed her hand as they started down the rows of tents. "It's weird how quiet it is, with all these people."

"Yeah, it is." Emma cleared her throat to suppress another sob. Her body ached with trying to hold herself together.

"Is Mom going to be okay?" Matt kept his eyes forward as they walked on.

"As okay as any of us, I guess."

They didn't walk far before a large white, open canopy rose up ahead. Long lines stretched out in every direction as people waited for their rations. Mexicans served uncooked rice and beans into small buckets for the American refugees.

A sign reading "Vouchers" hung to the right. Emma pulled Matt in that direction. They reached the end of another long line and waited.

A large, red-faced man, who was at the front of a food line being served rice and beans, threw the rice into a server's face. "You expect me to eat this garbage morning, noon, and night, after cooking it myself over a fire in this sweltering heat? You'd better get some good food here! I'm a lawyer, and I can — "

"You can what?" A muscly American man appeared behind the server. A sadistic smile matched the malicious look in his eyes.

"I'll get you back for this! As soon as this is over, I'll come after you! I'll come after the whole Mexican government!"

Emma squeezed Matt's hand. The look in the man's eyes darkened. He walked around to the irate lawyer and took him by the shoulders, pushing him away from the line.

"Okay, okay. It's fine. I'll eat it. Just let me go." The red-faced man tried to shrug the other American off. But he only pushed harder.

Everyone stared after them before going about their own business in hushed tones.

"What are the chances anyone sees him again?" The woman behind Emma shifted the baby on her hip and raised an eyebrow.

"What do you mean?" Emma took in the woman's short shorts, crop top, and heavy eyeliner, and made some nasty assumptions. Somehow, she didn't want Matt near this woman. Not to mention that emaciated baby on her hip.

"Usually when people raise a fuss like that, they disappear. Gangs, honey. This camp's full of them." The women's southern accent was thick. She barked a harsh laugh.

Emma put an arm around Matt's shoulders and steered him forward. It was almost their turn. The men behind the voucher table seemed kind, but did their eyes had a hunted look.

Emma and Matt approached the table a moment later.

"How do we get vouchers?" Matt's arms were crossed over his chest.

Emma closed her eyes. *Where's Jack? Where's Dad? Where the hell are we?*

"Fill out this form first. Then get back in line." One of the men pushed a paper across the table.

"We stood in line this whole time just to get a piece of paper and get back—"

Emma pulled hard on Matt's arm and took the paper and a pen from the table. She stalked away with Matt.

"Remember what just happened to that man? People apparently disappear for making a fuss. I think it's best to just go with it if we ever want to get food or see the rest of our family again."

Matt paced back and forth as Emma looked at the form. It was very similar to the one they'd filled out when they'd arrived. How many were in the family unit? Ages? Genders? Height? Weight?

Emma put a hand over her eyes, shielding them from the bright sun, and took a deep breath. "Stop pacing and come here. I need to use your back."

Matt stood in front of Emma, acting as a desk while she filled in the answers. "How much do you think Mom weighs?"

"They want to know our weight? What is this?" Matt let out an exasperated breath.

"I know, I know. Come on. What do you think?"

"She'd say, 'Too much. I'm not giving you a number.'" Matt put a hand on his hip just like their mom would do.

"You're right." Emma suppressed a laugh. "I'll just guess. And you're how tall?"

"Five, four. One hundred and twelve pounds."

"Gosh, you're scrawny."

"Well, I don't think this place will help much." Matt turned around when Emma took the paper off his back.

The heat, the noise of hundreds of people, the smells of body odor mixed with nearby cooking fires, turned Emma's stomach.

"Let's get our food and get out of here." She walked to the back of the line again.

"Hey you!" A man standing beside the tent pointed at Emma.

Emma gave Matt a quizzical look before turning back to the man. "Me?"

The man lifted his chin, beckoning her to him.

"Stay here." Emma handed Matt the form and left the line.

With baggy shorts and a demanding gaze, the man acted as though he was in charge. *How could that be? What's he in charge of?*

"Hey, pretty girl. You gettin' food tickets, huh?" The man drank every inch of her in with wandering eyes.

Emma crossed her arms, trying to steady their shaking. "Yeah. Obviously." She held the man's gaze, though nausea swooped through her stomach.

"Yeah, obviously everyone else is too. You get maybe enough tickets to eat one or two times a day. I know how they work it here. You need more, you just come find me, JD. We work something out." JD ended his proposition with another lingering look over Emma's figure.

Emma turned and walked away, shaking all over.

Monday 6:47PM //

Pushing food around his plate with his fork, Joe glanced around the cafeteria. Fewer people than ever sat at the long tables.

Not that many people could have escaped. Joe cleared his throat in lieu of another long sigh.

"Hey Dad."

Joe lifted his head. There was Aaron, standing on the other side of the table. Joe stood and embraced him.

He pulled back and put a hand on each of Aaron's shoulders. "It's good to see you. What are you doing here?"

"I wanted to come and make sure you guys got out last night. God, what happened to you?" He reached up to touch Joe's black and blue face. "Where is everyone?" Aaron looked around for the rest of the family.

Joe pulled his head away. "They caught me last night. The others got out. They've been keeping me in my room all day. I'm fine. How's Claire?"

"She's still under the weather. I think she's pregnant." Though he didn't smile, pride filled Aaron's eyes.

Joe looked down at the table as tears rushed to the surface. He swallowed a few times before meeting Aaron's gaze. "I know you two have wanted kids for a while now, but do you really want to bring a child into this environment?"

"No, of course not. But if it's happened, there's nothing we can do, or would do about it. We'll be happy to have a baby. And we'll figure things out. If she's not pregnant, we'll be more careful to not get pregnant until things have calmed down. You're here every day with the Russians. What do you think's going to happen? How have we still not heard anything from the National Guard at least?"

Joe exhaled and spoke as soft as he could. "I don't know. It's strange. The Russians are keeping everything really quiet. Other countries don't seem eager to come up against them to our defense. You know how it's been the last few years. Russia's been slowly taking over. It could be World War III, except that if other countries enter into the nuclear war, they could end up taking out the whole planet."

Aaron ran his hands through his hair. "It's that bad, huh? How do you know all this outside information? All I see on the news is propaganda."

"There's a radio station that somehow gets the real news out. I found an old radio in one of the offices one day." Joe rattled off the frequency. "Do you think I'd send your mother and Emma and Mattie into a completely unknown situation in Mexico if it wasn't that bad? The only reason I'm not dead is because I'm useful to them here. The rest of the family were expendable. I didn't want them to be disposed of." Joe's voice trailed off.

The cafeteria rang with silence. A prickling on the back of Joe's neck told him the guards were watching close by.

"I wish you'd come more often. It's awful here."

"I'll come back tomorrow. Can I bring you anything?"

"Just seeing you is more than enough for me. Give your beautiful wife a hug for me and tell her I hope she feels better."

Aaron raised an eyebrow.

"Even if she's pregnant. I wouldn't wish morning sickness on anyone." Joe held his hands up in defense.

"I'd better get back to her. She's been eating a lot of frozen yogurt lately."

Joe chuckled.

Later, lying alone in the spacious office turned sleeping chamber, the faces of Carol, Emma, and Matt filled Joe's mind. Their faces had kept him going through the beatings that day, and now at night he couldn't sleep for the pain, and for wondering what they were doing, and how they were.

Thirty-two Years Earlier //

"How are you?" Joe held the phone close to his ear and turned away from his roommate who sat doing homework on his bed.

"I'm okay, I'll be fine. It's—it's happened before." Carol's voice quivered.

"I know. I ran into Fay today. She said you weren't home, but I should call you later. Then she told me you had gone to your dad's house. She told me everything. Why did you go? Why didn't you tell me?" Joe's heart melted like hot wax at the sound of Carol's tears.

"I'm sorry I didn't tell you. It's embarrassing, you know. My dad is a drunk. I've been able to stay away from him during college, but I decided to go back there yesterday to—so I could tell him about you." Carol chuckled through her tears.

Joe pressed the earpiece to his forehead for a moment before bringing it back to his ear. "Can I come over?"

"I don't know, Joe. I don't want you to—"

"I'm on my way." Joe dropped the phone onto the receiver and grabbed his university sweater.

He tested the speed limits through town and reached Carol's apartment in ten minutes.

When she opened the door at his knock, Joe's stomach dropped. Her beautiful face was marred with a black and blue bruise surrounding her right eye. A bloody gash covered her right cheek. Without a word, Joe walked through the door and pulled her into his arms. As his arms tightened around her, Carol drew a sharp breath and pulled back.

Joe stepped away from her and tilted her chin up. "What's wrong?"

Tears pooled in Carol's eyes, magnifying their cornflower blue color, but she smiled. "It's nothing. I'm fine. I'm glad you're here."

"Me too." Joe put his arms around her again and felt her body go rigid. "What is it?"

"It's just my ribs. I think he cracked a few." Carol kept her gaze on the floor.

Joe's hands went to the bottom of Carol's blouse. "Can I see?"

Her eyes shot up to his again. She nodded and slowly lifted her shirt, stopping at her bra line. The silky skin around her rib cage was in worse shape than her eye. Joe's fingers drifted up her sides and caressed her bruised skin.

He swallowed and met Carol's gaze again. "I can't believe he did this to you. You shouldn't have gone over there. If I ever meet him—"

Carol dropped her shirt and covered her face. Joe suppressed his anger. With the greatest care, he embraced her.

After a few moments, she looked up at Joe, her eyes clearer. "I wanted to tell him about you. Dating you has made me brave and has healed me in some ways. I'm proud of you, and I guess I wanted to show my dad how strong I am. But it was bad timing. He was in one of his drunk rages. My mom was passed out on the floor."

Joe drew a deep breath and cleared his throat. "Carol don't ever go back there again. Please. I love you. And I can't imagine what I'd do if anything happened to you."

A wide, tremulous smile spread up Carol's rosy cheeks. "That's the first time you've said that to me."

"It's the first time I've said that to anyone. And I mean it. I love you."

"I love you too." A sob escaped Carol's lips as Joe pressed his mouth against hers. This time, when he held her close, she didn't pull away.

Monday, June 18th
7:31PM //

The first thing he knew was a pounding in his head. Jack was afraid to move. He opened his eyes just a fraction. Everything was blurry, the lowering sun seemed too bright.

Taking inventory of his limbs, Jack became aware of the heaviness of his body. Nothing else hurt though, just his head. He opened his eyes wider as things came into focus.

He was lying in an alley next to a dumpster. He seemed to be alone. He took his time standing.

How am I not in jail? I attacked an officer. They probably thought they were leaving me for dead.

Jack peered around the buildings on either side of the alley. He wasn't far from the border where he'd tried to get through. He turned and headed in the opposite direction.

After finding his way back to the car, Jack climbed in, and lay his head against the steering wheel. He took a few deep breaths.

Throbbing pain surged through his head. Pulling his cell phone out of his jeans, Jack plugged it into the cigarette lighter.

Just in case. He started the engine and drove east on Boca Chica boulevard.

The land was desolate on either side, the road stretching on as far as Jack could see. He didn't pass any other cars the whole way. The waning sunlight winked on the Rio Grande as the road curved closer to the river. He could see Mexico.

Where is everyone? Maybe they fled as soon as the Russians hit US soil. It would've been so easy. I wonder where Emma crossed over. And when? I can't believe I'm trying to get out of America.

Flashes of Independence Day celebrations filled Jack's mind. The Smiths annual baseball game, tables laden with good food, and fireworks at the end of the day with Emma in his arms.

Something caught Jack's eye along the river. He pulled over and peered into the bushes.

His tongue stuck to the roof of his mouth. He looked in the seats behind him, on the floor, and found a water bottle behind the passenger's seat. The water was warm, but wet. He took a few sips, then twisted the cap back on.

Opening the glove box, he found three granola bars. He peeled back the wrapper on one and took a few small bites, then curled the wrapper back over the rest of the bar and stashed all three in the pocket of his jeans. He unearthed a wad of cash under the granola bars.

After leaning forward to pull the bills out, Jack reached into his back pocket for his wallet. It was gone. *Of course they took everything.*

He unplugged his phone and jammed it into his back pocket with the loose bills.

Jack climbed out of the car and walked to the water's edge. A small, wooden boat poked above the bushes. He yanked on the boat and pulled it to the river bank.

Kneeling at the water's edge, Jack looked around in every direction. He closed his eyes and listened for any unwanted sounds.

Everything was still. Every blade of grass, every leaf of the bushes. The air around him was taut as his own body.

He pushed the boat into the water and climbed in. The paddles were rough and splintered. *I wonder if this was used by someone to get to America, then abandoned there.*

The rich, vibrant smell of the river enlivened him. He gave the paddles a strong push, nose of the boat pointed downstream. He paddled on one side of the boat to keep from veering too far down the river. His muscles grew tired quickly, but he pushed on with Emma's face at the forefront of his mind.

Jack's heart pounded as he neared the Mexican shore after what seemed like hours. He narrowed his eyes, looking for any movement. Everything was still over here too. When the boat hit sand, Jack exhaled. He climbed out, crouched low, and released the boat down the river again. Resting for a moment among the bushes, he stretched his aching arms.

Jack turned and walked away from the river. He took a swig of his water and another bite of the opened granola bar. He closed his eyes.

Emma and I are in the same country again. We're free. God, I hope Emma made it.

Jack walked until he couldn't see the river any longer. The sun dipped low in the west. Everything was orange and glowing. *Just keep going until you find Emma.*

He meandered through the dark, rugged grasslands. The cool, night air revived him, and he was aware of every noise, every movement of the shrubbery around him. Trillions of brilliant dots spread across the sky above. Jack almost fell over looking at them.

Without the lights of the city, the sky was a giant upside-down bowl, engulfing the land with its velvety vastness.

He walked on.

He couldn't tell where he was going, but it didn't matter. It would've been no different in the daylight.

He sipped on his water little by little and allowed himself to finish one granola bar. As the hours passed, dragging his feet forward one step at a time grew harder and harder. Jack ignored his hunger and thirst, and the cries of his muscles. The cool of the night permeated down to his bones, and he shivered.

He stumbled through bushes, oblivious to the branches tearing at his clothes. Remembering his cell phone, Jack pulled it out of his pocket. It was almost two o'clock in the morning.

A silhouette of deeper black stood a couple hundred yards in front of him. A small house, maybe. Jack's feet shuffled toward the dark mass. As he drew close, he tripped and fell, sprawled out on the ground. It was still warm from the day's heat, like a comforting blanket.

Jack's weighty eyelids slid shut.

Tuesday, June 19th
12:12PM //

"Aaron, you can't do that. What if they find out. We can't jeopardize anything right now." Claire put a hand over her flat belly.

She'd taken a test. She was pregnant.

Aaron put his arms around her waist. "No one will know who's behind it. It's a harmless jab at the Russians."

The air in the apartment was stale. Claire never left and seemed afraid to even open the windows.

"But also, no one will know what it means." Claire laced her fingers around Aaron's neck.

"Exactly."

"So why do it?" Her eyes gave her away.

She liked the idea, but worried about the consequences. She'd given Aaron the same look when he'd told her about the nonprofit he wanted to start.

"Because I think the right people will get it. I'll tell our friends who're still around, and it'll spread. Something like this could bring a lot of hope. My dad sounded pretty hopeless last night. We need to do something to fight back in our own way."

"So, what's your plan?" Claire raised an eyebrow and pulled his head closer to hers.

He dropped a gentle kiss on her lips. "I'm going to tag it on a few walls around the city."

Aaron reached into his back pocket and pulled out a piece of paper. It was Jack's original design for the tattoo he and Emma had gotten. A symbol of freedom and hope.

"Just make sure you aren't seen."

"Oh, believe me, all those years of parkour are going to pay off." Adrenaline pumped through Aaron as he mapped out the city and its remaining vacant walls in his mind.

Claire laughed, her bright, happy laugh. Aaron's heart swelled. He kissed her again.

"I'll be careful. I promise." He put a hand over her stomach, his grin wide.

All afternoon, Aaron walked the streets of Houston with two cans of black spray paint in his backpack. Twice, he found a deserted street and covered large portions of the vacant walls with Jack's design. He noted several other walls he could come back to later.

"Hey Diego. How're you holding up?" Aaron sat on the sidewalk, against a condemned building, next to one of his friends who'd lived in a low-income apartment but was now squatting.

Heat from the pavement seeped through Aaron's shorts. Sweat trickled down the sides of his face.

"So-so." Diego didn't disturb his listless study of the rubble-lined street.

"Hey." Aaron thumped the older man on the arm. "If we give in and give up, we've already accepted defeat. You fought hard to get into this country for the freedom and the opportunities, right?"

"Yeah, see how well that worked out."

"That just means it's time to fight again. They might destroy our city, but they can't take away our freedom or who we are as Americans." Aaron knew his words sounded hollow, and worse, were falling on deaf ears.

"They can sure ruin our lives, and have. Fabian is gone. I can't find him." Diego's voice was strained. He turned away from Aaron.

"I'm sorry, man." More hollow words came to Aaron, but the moment called for silence.

Fabian was Matt's age. *What if Matt was lost to us? What if he is? There's no way of knowing where he, Mom, and Emma are.* It was like a jackhammer chipped away at his heart. *I might never see any of them again.*

Aaron looked at Jack's design. The ink stark black against the white paper. He dropped his head against the side of the building.

"What's that?" Diego looked at the drawing.

"Oh, it's something my sister's fiancé drew. They both got tattoos of it. It's supposed to represent the hope the Russians can't take from us, and that we'll be free again. I've already tagged it on two walls. I plan to do more." Jack's plan was working on Aaron.

Hopelessness faded.

Aaron tested his thoughts out loud. "It'll do no good to stay in our grief or obsess over the uncertainty. We have to move forward and fight back anyway we can."

"I guess." Diego shrugged and closed his eyes.

"Can you spread the word? They're going to start seeing it around and it'll help if we can tell people what it is. Just don't tell anyone it's me. Claire's pregnant. This is already risky enough."

"Wow, man. A new life. I don't know what to tell you about that." Diego shook his head.

"I know. It's not the best timing, but we're excited. If it happens, it's meant to be, right?"

Diego shrugged again.

"Claire's home alone, I'd better head back. Do you need anything?" Aaron pushed against the wall, ready to stand.

"Always need food, man. But you have enough problems already."

"We'll see what we can do." Aaron placed a hand on Diego's shoulder.

"You're a good man. I don't know why, but you are."

"See you later." Aaron chuckled and headed home.

He rounded a corner and the perfect blank wall loomed in front of him. Aaron got out a can of paint and set to work. Footsteps echoed against the brick buildings. Aaron didn't look back but walked forward, unhurried, his heart pounding. The footfalls persisted behind him.

Aaron turned another corner and swung himself up onto the nearest window ledge. He clung to the thin brick window frame. Leaning to his left, he could just reach the rusty fire escape to pull himself higher. Aaron sat on the landing, fifteen feet above the sidewalk. He pressed against the building and waited.

Tuesday 4:34PM //

Jack woke to the warmth of the sunshine pouring over his face. An orange brightness pressed against his eyelids. His body was laid on a soft cushion.

When rich, spicy smells hit his nose, his chin perked up. He eased his eyes open. Blinding light shone through a window. He was laying on a couch in a small, cozy living room. Jack let his body sink further into the cushions. The light and warmth were enough to lull him back to sleep.

Through an arched doorway to the right, a woman worked over the stove in the kitchen. The aromas wafting into the living room engulfed his senses and his stomach grumbled. Jack took in a slow, deep breath.

The woman turned and faced him. She spoke to him in Spanish. "You're awake. How are you feeling? Are you hurt?" She stepped into the living room and stood at his side.

Jack studied her while assessing his limbs. She was probably in her sixties and had sweet, concerned eyes. Jack hurt everywhere.

"Estoy bien." His voice was hoarse. He cleared his throat.

The woman smiled. "Would you like to take a shower? The bathroom is just through there. I can give you some of my son's old clothes." She walked into the small hallway and soon emerged with a stack of clothes in her arms.

Setting them on the counter in the bathroom, she bustled to Jack's side again. "Take your time. When you're done in there, dinner will be ready."

"Where am I? What happened?" Jack sat up. Every muscle stiffening with each movement.

"My husband found you early this morning, lying on the ground outside. He brought you in. You're probably lucky to be alive. My name is Celia."

Jack dropped his head into his hands and rubbed his eyes. *I can't remember anything.*

He looked up at Celia. "Muchas gracias. I'm Jack." He stood and waited for his head to stop spinning.

"Well, Jack, take your time." Celia patted his cheek and turned to the kitchen again.

"Gracias." Jack made his way into the bathroom and locked the door.

An oval mirror hung on the wall. He was covered in dirt. A large, purple and black bruise ran around his right eye. He let out a quiet moan. *The guard at the border with the gun. I walked forever. I don't remember stopping.*

The hot water of the shower was soothing to his aching muscles. Jack stood under the water for a long time, his mind running ahead to Emma. *She's closer. Maybe these people know where the Americans are.*

When Jack entered the tiny, but bright and clean kitchen, Celia wasn't alone. A man sat at the table with his hands around a mug of coffee. The domestic scene was like a balm to his raw spirit.

Jack could have wept but settled for sitting in the chair Celia had pulled out for him at the table.

She loaded a plate with pork, rice, and beans on a fresh tortilla. After placing the steaming plate in front of Jack, she filled a mug with hot coffee.

"Gracias." Jack couldn't trust himself to say anything more.

"Eat up. Please." Celia watched him with pure delight in her worn face, as if he was a long-lost son who'd come home.

"I'm Pedro." The man across the table reached a hand out.

Jack took it, feeling the lines and callouses.

The food was better than anything he'd tasted in months. Maybe ever. Jack slowed his pace after shoveling in the first few bites.

Pedro and Celia dished up plates for themselves and sat with him.

"You came from America, didn't you? What's happening there? How did you escape?" Pedro took a sip of his coffee.

"Yes, tell us everything. We see little bits on the news, but don't know what to believe." Celia took a delicate bite of pork.

Jack chewed and swallowed before lowering his fork. "Well, it's been weeks now since Russia invaded. But I think the government has known about their activity for a while. They moved the president out of the White House one day, and about a week later, Washington DC was levelled by a nuclear bomb. The whole east coast was taken out." Jack closed his eyes as unexpected emotions rose.

"You don't have to talk about it." Celia placed a hand on Jack's arm.

He had a hard time swallowing the next few bites. He took a swig of coffee. "We're from Houston. My fiancée and I. She owns—owned a coffee shop downtown. She worked for years to open it. Then the Russians came and bombed the city. The only reason we didn't get levelled like other cities was because of the oil.

But my fiancée's coffee shop was destroyed. Her home was taken out."

Jack sipped his coffee again, staring at the colorful tablecloth. "So many people fled Houston then. Emma's dad works for the oil refinery, and the Russians held the whole family hostage there. They slept there, ate there. They were forced to clean up the streets. Then they got away. I told Emma I had to go make sure my mom was taken care of. I'd meet her at the border. Why did I leave her?" Jack's neck and cheeks were hot as his voice broke. He shook his head.

Celia's hand still lay on Jack's arm. The silence stretched almost too far. "Mi hijo. Where's your fiancée now?"

Jack took in a deep breath. "I don't know. I think she made it across the border. When I finally got there, the border had closed."

"But you got across?" Pedro leaned back in his chair, his mug held in both hands.

"Yeah. I found an abandoned row boat and came across the Rio. Then I walked until I couldn't walk anymore."

Celia's mouth dropped into a round O. "And you didn't get caught? Or worse, shot?"

Jack looked from Celia to Pedro, who appeared just as surprised as his wife.

"They patrol up and down the river. The news said they shoot Americans who try to cross." Pedro leaned forward against the table, shaking his head in response to Jack's raised eyebrows. "No, amigo, the Mexicans aren't shooting. It must be these Russians."

"They're shooting on Mexican soil? They can't do that, can they?"

"No. From what I've heard, they patrol the US side of the river, but they shoot without discretion. Think of what they did to your land. You think they're worried about abiding by the laws?"

Jack lowered his eyes to the table again.

"You were lucky." Celia patted his arm.

Jack looked up into the eyes of the complete strangers across the table. "Thank you so much, for everything. You've been so kind. I probably would've called the cops if someone looking like me showed up at my house."

Pedro and Celia shared a look.

"You are from Mexico, are you not?" There was humor in Pedro's smile.

"Yes. My mom and I went to America when I was five. How could you tell?"

"You don't have the American accent." Celia chuckled.

Jack grinned, taking in the golden sunlight streaming onto the full kitchen table, the couple sitting with him, talking as though it were a normal Tuesday evening. *If only Emma could be here to share this with me.*

He met Celia's eyes, then Pedro's. "Do you know where the Americans are? Where they've been going once they get across the border?"

Pedro glanced at his wife before meeting Jack's gaze again. "I've heard there's a camp outside Matamoros. I'm sure there are others, but that's the closest one."

"How far is it? Where are we anyway?"

"We're on the Matamoros highway. Not far from La Bartolina. Matamoros is about an hour away." Pedro sipped his coffee.

Jack's stomach dropped. *Emma could be so close.* He stood, sending his chair skittering backwards. "How can I get there? I need to get there."

Wednesday, June 20th
9:35AM //

They didn't have enough food. They'd just returned from getting their refugee IDs where they'd been herded around like cattle. Now Emma was saying they didn't have enough vouchers, and they should save their vouchers for the next day.

Carol looked at her daughter across the tent, her eyes burning to let more tears fall. "How did we run out of food so fast? We barely ate anything yesterday."

"Mom, we just got enough for three people to eat in one day. We didn't stretch it far enough."

Emma's taken charge. She's holding up under the pressure. I need to get a grip. I just wish Joe were here. And Aaron.

Carol couldn't even look in Matt's direction. He was sprawled on top of his sleeping bag, staring at the tent's ceiling.

It's just all too much. Carol took a shuddering breath.

"I'm so sorry." She gave into the fresh tears. "I'm sorry for both of you. I'm sorry I haven't been myself. I just don't understand—I can't—without your dad. I never imagined anything like this would ever happen to us. It's so unbelievable."

Emma sat next to her and put an arm around her shoulders. "I know, Mom. It's hard to believe this is our life now." Emma's voice was thick. "I don't know where Jack is, or if he's okay. I miss Dad too." She took a deep, shaky breath.

"This place is horrible. No one can live like this. They never service the porta-potties or clean the showers. The food is always the same, when we can get it, and it takes hours to cook over a fire. In this stifling heat, it's a wonder we don't all have heat stroke. Everyone is crammed in here like sardines, and we're stuck in these sweltering tents because there's nowhere else to go, and it isn't safe out there." Carol dropped her head into her hands.

"I know, Mom." Emma stroked her hair.

"I'm so hungry I could throw up." Matt moaned on his sleeping bag.

"I'll be back in a while." Emma stood after a few minutes of silence and walked to the entrance of the tent.

"Be careful, Honey." Carol bit her lip as she watched Emma go. "I'm so sorry, Mattie." She could muster no more than a desperate whisper.

Matt clenched his jaw.

Carol curled up on her side, giving in to more tears. Sweat seeped from every pore of her body, and the close stench of body odor turned her stomach.

We can't live like this!

11:32AM //

When Emma returned, she had a bucket full of cooked food in each hand. "Lunch is served."

Carol sat up and nudged Matt who'd fallen asleep. Emma handed each of them a fork and sat on her own sleeping bag. The rice and beans tasted good. Carol's stomach would've accepted anything by that time of day. "Look at us, eating out of buckets."

Carol exchanged a glance with Emma, then Matt.

Matt was staring at his sister with narrowed eyes. "Where've you been? How did you get all this?"

Carol tensed and held her fork halfway to her mouth. *They can't start fighting. Don't start fighting, don't start fighting.*

She opened her mouth to intervene but was stopped by Emma's appearance. Emma shrugged in response to Matt's question. Her eyes were puffy, and a bruise was forming around one eye.

"God, Emma. What happened?" Carol lowered her fork and reached out to touch her daughter's face.

Emma pushed her hand away. "It's nothing. I'm fine."

"Sure you are. What happened?" Matt dropped his fork, his voice full of sarcasm.

"Some bitch punched me in the food line. What are you going to do? At least I got some food." Emma focused on her own plate.

Carol leaned back and picked up her fork again.

"I don't believe you."

Carol looked from Matt, who hadn't taken his eyes off his sister, to Emma.

She looked down at her food. "Just drop it, Matt."

Carol knew she wasn't the most discerning individual, but the tension between her children was palpable as they stared each other down. Tears welled up in Carol's eyes. Her heart broke all over again.

8:03PM //

The heat, always so hot. Always dirty, never clean.

The blackness threatened her vision. Carol's body shook and rocked as she lay on her side.

Mattie. He tried to take a shower. A man. A knife. A knife. He had to run away from a man. With a knife. No one is safe. We can't stay here. Joe. Where's Joe. I need Joe.

All went dark.

Thursday, June 28th

7:37AM //

Matt woke to the suffocating heat of the tent. His stomach roiled in a way that had become familiar, but which was no less uncomfortable. Every inch of his skin was sticky and clammy. He guessed he was probably covered in as much dust and dirt as Mom and Emma were, their features were almost indistinguishable. He wouldn't try to take a shower again anytime soon though.

Matt shuddered at the memory of the evening before. He looked across the tent at Emma, who appeared to be sleeping still.

Where did she go yesterday?

In a dark corner of his mind, Matt suspected the worst, remembering the man who'd called her over when they waited in line for food vouchers, but he wouldn't accept the possibility.

His lungs ached for more air. He rose as quiet as possible and pulled back one flap of the tent's door. No one else had stirred yet.

Many people in the camp slept all day or at least never left their tents. The tragedy that had struck their country, along with learning how to live just to survive had made everyone lazy and incapable of the simplest things.

Down between the rows of tents, a Mexican boy, around his age, was picking up trash and shoving it into a garbage bag.

Matt blinked against the burning in his eyes. He approached the boy and picked up a piece of trash, dropping it into the garbage bag without a word. The boy caught his eye, and though he didn't smile, the look he gave Matt was kind and curious.

They worked side by side for a long time before the boy spoke up. "David." The boy patted his own chest.

"Matt." For the first time since being in Mexico, Matt utilized the Spanish he'd been learning since third grade. "De donde eres? Por qué estás hacienda esto?"

David's face lit up. He responded in Spanish. "I live close by, on the outskirts of town. My father works here almost every day and he told me how bad it is. I thought I'd come help out a little before starting work, now that school's over."

The memory of Matt's last day in school flashed through his mind. "I miss school. They were going to move me up a grade."

David's eyes widened. "You must be really smart. Maybe you can come to my school when it starts again. If you're still here."

Matt shrugged, and squelched the hope rising within him.

"I'd better get going now. I'll see you around." David threw the garbage bag over his shoulder and handed Matt a few empty ones. Then he turned toward the entrance of the camp.

Matt didn't know of any garbage service that came to the camp, so trash was everywhere. The path David had walked already looked better than anywhere else.

Matt opened one of the empty trash bags and shoved the others in his back pocket. He went to work picking up trash around his family's tent.

Rounding the corner of a tent in which someone was snoring loudly, Matt ran into a small group of teenagers. American this time.

"Hey, man. We're going to smoke some weed. We might even get something better than that. Want to come?"

Matt studied the group, all of them looking strung out already. He raised an eyebrow. "That would solve which of our problems? No thanks." Matt bent over to pick up more trash.

A foot hit his backside and he fell forward. The group of guys laughed and walked away. Matt stood and swiped at his dusty jeans. He looked down the line of tents, littered with garbage and sighed.

"Hey Mattie. What are you doing?" Emma's voice behind him made Matt jump.

"Just cleaning up. I have to do something, I guess. Apparently, I can't go anywhere without being attacked."

"What happened this time?" Emma put a hand on his shoulder and looked him up and down for injuries.

"Nothing, I'm fine. A bunch of guys just asked if I wanted to go lose myself in drugs." Matt shrugged, then went on at the concerned look on Emma's face. "I turned them down. What else are they going to do though?"

Emma kept her eyes on him for a moment, then joined him in picking up trash. They worked together in silence for a while.

"We should go see if we can find any firewood outside the camp." Emma looked past the mess of tents with a hand shading her eyes.

"That's a good idea. They said there was never enough in the supply tent." Matt led the way through the maze. Dust was thick in the air and Matt's clothes were soaked in sweat. Every movement was uncomfortable. All he wanted was a cold shower. And a hamburger with French fries.

Outside the boundaries of the camp stretched patches of farmland. They walked around for some time and only came up with a few handfuls of sticks and dry brush.

Out here, with the cluster of tents behind him, Matt could pretend they were back in Texas, playing at someone's farm. The land stretched before him to the cobalt horizon.

We could try to get away. But we would get caught at some point. Or die. Mom's in no state to run anywhere. A sigh escaped Matt's lips.

Emma stopped and gazed over at him. "Mattie, come on." She bent to pick up a stick.

When both their arms were full, Emma and Matt turned back toward the camp. They wound their way to the porta-potties which stood near the supply tent.

The stench stung Matt's nose and he turned away. "I wonder if David's dad can do anything about those."

"What?" Emma held the collar of her t-shirt over her face.

"I met a kid earlier. He gave me the garbage bags. He said his dad works here in the camp. Maybe he could do something about the porta-potties."

"Like what?" Emma raised an eyebrow.

She was always on edge like that now. He watched her defiant face with a sinking heart. He didn't like to see her this way.

"I don't know. Maybe he has connections in town."

Emma's body tensed, and she dropped her eyes. Matt's eyebrows came together. A man had just come out of a porta-potty. The look he gave Emma made the hair stand up on Matt's neck. The man passed very close to Emma, brushing against her shoulder. Emma stood rigid.

"Come on, let's take these to the supply tent, then see if we can get some food." Matt had a strong urge to move Emma away, anywhere else.

They walked in silence to the supply tent where just one volunteer was sorting through donations.

Emma dropped her armload of wood in a corner with the other burnable resources. "I'm going to check on Mom." She handed the food vouchers to Matt and turned away before he could argue.

He made his way to the food distribution tent and got in the long line. In stationary moments like this, Matt couldn't ignore the close smell of body odor and urine. Constant noise assaulted his ears; babies and adults crying, people yelling at each other, and in one corner members of the gang stood looking full and far too happy as they leered at people in line.

Matt's attention was pulled to a young woman, about Emma's age, struggling with five little kids. A baby wailed in her arms, two toddlers clung to the skirt of her summer dress, a five or six-year-old boy looked around wide-eyed with tiny hands on his hips, and a girl of about eight stood with arms crossed over her chest.

Stacked in piles around her were sleeping bags for each of them, a cooking pot, buckets, and utensils. The woman's eyes were red and swollen. Matt couldn't help but notice how pretty she was with light red-blonde hair and freckles framing greenish blue eyes.

Matt gave her a small smile when their eyes met. The woman burst into fresh tears. Matt looked away.

When he reached the front of the line, he handed over the food vouchers and was given two fresh buckets of uncooked beans and rice.

When he reached tent fifty-nine again, Emma had a good fire already going. She was sitting with her legs crossed, staring into the flames. "Mom's asleep." She didn't look up at him.

"I'm here." Mom emerged from the tent and sat next to Emma.

Matt mixed the rice and beans with some water they'd received from the supply tent into their pot and set it over the heat. "There was a woman with five kids at the food tent. She looked lost. Maybe we should go back and see if we can help her."

Emma glanced at him before focusing on the flames again.

Mom gave Matt a tremulous smile. "That's a good idea, Honey."

The food took a long time to cook and there was nothing to season it with. Still, they all devoured it within minutes.

When Matt finished eating, he stood and filled the pot with water from another bucket to clean up. He washed their pot and forks.

"I think I'm going to go find that woman and help her out." Matt looked from Mom to Emma.

"I'll come with you. I can't stay in that tent all day." Emma stood.

They found the woman and her herd of kids in almost the same spot Matt had last seen them.

All the hardness drained from Emma's face and she hurried up to the woman. "I'm Emma, can we help you? This is my brother, Matt."

The woman broke down again. "I'm Georgia. I don't know what to do or where to go. We just got here. My husband was—was killed on the way by the border patrol. My babies are hungry and thirsty."

The baby in her arms cried louder, drowning out his Mama's tears.

"Come on, first, we need to go to the meal voucher table." Emma took charge. "Then we should go to the supply tent and see if we can get some diapers and wipes for this little guy. What's his name?"

"August." Georgia steadied her breathing.

Something in Matt relaxed. Emma was in her element again.

"She has five kids to feed, including herself!" Emma shouted and leaned across the table.

Matt had never seen her so worked up. The man on the other side of the table looked as though he'd heard this same story before but regarded Georgia with sympathy.

"There is nothing I can do." The man shrugged.

Matt wondered if this could be David's dad.

Emma looked at Georgia and her kids for a moment before turning back to the volunteer. "There's something I can do." Emma spoke under her breath as she walked away.

Matt watched her go with a sick feeling in his stomach, then turned back to Georgia holding up the few food vouchers Emma had been able to get for her. "Let's take these to the food line and get what we can."

Georgia had calmed down and spoke into her baby's ear as they got into line again.

"What's your name?" Matt knelt next to the five-year-old.

"Jasper." The boy lifted his chin. "This is Sadie." He shoved a thumb at his older sister.

"Nice to meet you guys. And who are they?" Matt pointed to the twin girls hanging onto Georgia's dress.

"That's Willa and that's Winnie." Sadie supplied the names of the toddlers.

"Hi girls." Matt waved at the twins. "Are you all hungry?"

All four heads bobbed up and down. Sadie's eyes glistened with tears.

"We'll get you some food." A pang stabbed at Matt's heart as he thought of all the food he'd just eaten. He straightened. "Where's your tent?"

"I don't know. I can't find it." Georgia sighed. "It's number fifty-eight."

"Oh, that's right next to ours."

"Really?" Relief flooded Georgia's teal eyes.

"Yeah. I can take you there."

As they waited in the long line, Matt did his best to entertain the kids. The activity livened Sadie up and she took over, leading them in little games.

"You're a good big sister." Matt patted her shoulder.

Sadie beamed up at him.

Georgia tapped him on the arm. They'd reached the front of the line.

"Give her your vouchers." Matt pointed to the girl on the other side of the counter, underneath which stood barrels of rice and beans.

It was the same girl who'd helped them when they'd arrived. Her hair was disheveled, and dark bags had formed under her eyes. "Thanks for all your help." Matt caught the girl's eyes.

Her lower lip quivered, and she spooned up two full buckets for Georgia.

"Thank you so much." Georgia nodded to the server as tears pooled in her eyes again.

Matt led the family back to the tent. He helped the kids settle in the tent to keep them contained while they cooked.

"Our fire is still warm, you can use it." Matt took Georgia's pot to the smoldering embers.

Georgia seemed to be no stranger to cooking over the fire and the food was soon ready. The kids ate with their filthy hands, as though they hadn't eaten in days.

A weight lifted off Matt's heart as he watched them. Emma came back as they fished the last pieces of rice out of the pot, holding a fistful of food vouchers.

"Here." She thrust the wad at Georgia.

Georgia took the vouchers from her and stared up at Emma. "Thanks. Where did you get all these?"

"Ready to go to the supply tent?" Emma took the baby from Georgia's lap. "This one needs a new diaper. And some new clothes."

Matt stared at Emma's back as she led all of them to the tent full of clothes and baby supplies donated by people all over the world. A banner hanging on the outside of the tent proclaimed the United Nations involvement in establishing this tent and getting the supplies to Matamoros.

Emma had brought back a few things from the tent, but none of them had spent a long amount of time in it. There were plastic bins everywhere, on tables, and on the ground, overflowing with clothes. Someone had attempted to keep it organized, but the labels above each table didn't seem to match what was underneath anymore.

Emma took Georgia to an area full of baby's and women's supplies. Matt took Jasper's grimy hand and walked over to the adult clothes. He rifled through the women's shirts until he found a few Mom might like. He even found a pair of shorts that might fit her.

Maybe these will cheer her up. They're clean if nothing else.

Matt moved to the next table and found a new set of clothes that might fit him.

He knelt at Jasper's level. Sadie had followed them too. "Should we look for some new clothes for you guys?"

Again, silent nods. Sadie's face brightened a little. Matt found an area with kids' clothes, and they all dug through the piles. A volunteer was in the nearest corner, doing his best to sort through a cardboard box of items. He looked worn out and about as dirty as any of them living in the camp.

I wonder if this guy's from the UN. If Aaron were here, he'd help these guys. Matt remembered Aaron's bright smile. He thought of Dad, and Jack, and swallowed over the lump in his throat. He coughed and the volunteer looked up.

"Hey, do you guys need help sorting things?" Matt shifted the pile of clothes he'd collected to his other arm.

The guy's eyes widened. "We're here to help you. You don't need to help us." He had a thick Irish accent.

"It'd be better than sitting around in the heat feeling sorry for myself. Are you with the UN?"

The man paused. "I'm a volunteer with the UN, yes. My name's Chris. I see your point. You can always come here and help sort new arrivals. There are never enough people to do it, obviously." Chris looked around the messy tent.

"Cool. Is there anything the UN could do about the porta-potties? They haven't been serviced probably since they were dropped off here. Most of them are unusable."

"I noticed." Chris lifted his eyebrows. "I can talk to somebody, but everything goes so slow with them."

Matt exhaled and refrained from rolling his eyes. "Well, thanks. I'll come by and help when I can. My name's Matt."

"Nice to meet you. Where are you from?"

"Houston, Texas."

"Wow, the Lone Star State." Chris grinned.

His words and tone were like sandpaper to Matt's heart. *Houston's ruined, doesn't he know that?*

Sadie held up a dress for Matt's inspection.

"That's very pretty. Good find. Jasper, what have you found?" Matt turned to the younger boy.

Jasper threw pieces of clothing at Matt one after another.

"Well these will work. Wait, this is too big, my man." Matt held up a t-shirt that had just landed in his arms. It had a picture of Diego from "Dora the Explorer" on it.

"Go Diego go!" Jasper jumped up and down as he shouted.

"He loves Diego." Sadie broke through her timidity to inform Matt of the obvious.

"I guess you could sleep in it. And grow into it. Should we find your mommy?"

Sadie and Jasper nodded, and Jasper hopped to Matt's side, taking his hand again.

They found Georgia and Emma on the other side of the tent. Emma still held baby August in her arms. They'd already put fresh clothes on him. The twin girls stood over their mom, patting her on the head as she sat on the ground, crying. "I can't do this. I can't do this."

Matt looked away.

Thursday 4:56PM //

Aaron rode down streets showing less rubble each day. Sweat traced a path between his shoulder blades as he pushed hard against the pedals. A riot of wildflowers hung over the bucket he'd attached to the bike behind him. His mind turned over the conversation he'd just had with Dad. Aaron had found him out in the oil field, overseeing some Russian workers.

They hadn't talked for long. Dad kept getting the stink-eye from his superior and Aaron didn't want to put him in further danger. Dad was still healing from his last beating. He obsessed over Mom, Emma, and Matt, and whether they'd made it to a safe place.

"You need to get out of here. Go find them. You're going to waste away worrying about them, and you aren't doing anyone any good working here. In fact, you're giving in to what the Russians want. You might as well be fighting on their side." Aaron had spoken as soft as he could. The Russians probably had his dad bugged, for all they knew, but he had to convince Dad to leave.

"I know, but how do I get out of here? I lost my chance when everyone left with Bobby and Marie. Even if I did get out, I couldn't get across the border. I gave them all my money."

Aaron looked around the oil field, thinking. "You know how to fly a helicopter, right? Come up with an excuse to fly one and just take off. You could fly right into Mexico."

Dad stared at the helicopters flying in the distance. He tilted his head to one side. Then Aaron had hugged his dad, told him to hang in there, and that he'd be back tomorrow. Maybe with more money.

Aaron drew in a deep breath. Steering around the next corner, he knew he would see Diego, sitting on the sidewalk, mourning his lost son.

"Hi Dieg—" Aaron's greeting was cut off by the sight of Diego running into the street.

The older man grabbed the bicycle as Aaron stopped. "He's here! Fabian's here. He's alive!"

Aaron lowered his feet to the ground. "You found Fabian?" His heart raced.

"Yes. He's been looking for me ever since we were separated." Diego turned and waved to a young man standing on the sidewalk. "Fabian! Come meet my friend."

Aaron held out a hand. "Nice to meet you, man. I've heard a lot about you. I kept telling your dad he'd find you." The muscles in Aaron's cheeks ached around his smile. It was nice to be sincerely happy for someone else again.

"Nice to meet you too." Fabian gripped Aaron's hand.

"He looks a little worse for the wear, but he's alive." Aaron clapped a hand on Diego's shoulder.

"Si, si." Diego couldn't take his eyes off his son. "I showed Fabian your symbol. You've been busy. Tagging everywhere. Fabian, you love it, don't you?"

Fabian's cheeks turned ruddy. "Yeah, it's spreading. I've heard a lot of people talking about it."

"That's cool. We won't let the Russians get to us."

"Well, don't let us keep you. You're on your way home to Claire?" Diego took a step away from the bike.

"Yep. Found these flowers for her out by the oil refinery."

"Very good. Tell her hello and tell her about Fabian."

"I will. She'll be stoked. You guys have a good night. See you around." Aaron rode on.

Joy spread like a comforting warmth throughout his body. He reached the apartment building and lifted the bicycle up the front steps. He fumbled with the lock while trying to secure the bike to a railing just inside the building. Someone walked in behind him and went to the rows of mailboxes on the opposite wall. Aaron took two steps at a time, clutching the bundle of wildflowers in one hand.

He pulled out his key and shoved it in the door. He knocked four times, their secret signal. Aaron heard the inside lock slide out. Claire opened the door. Aaron rushed in and took her in his arms, drinking her in with a kiss. Her sweet, familiar scent embraced him as her arms wound around his neck. She giggled into his ear as he went after her exposed shoulder. Blood pulsed through his veins. His head was light and giddy.

"Oi!" The harsh voice came from the open doorway and broke the spell.

Aaron's heart dropped, and he pushed Claire behind him. His knees almost gave out. His whole body shook. A man stood in the doorway pointing a gun right at his chest. Aaron's mind sped up as his body seemed to move in slow motion.

"My name is Aaron Smith. This is my wife, Claire. We're going to have a baby. Please don't shoot. I'll do anything." The words rushed out. Aaron backed away with Claire's body pinned against his back. She was shaking violently.

"You've already done enough." The man's Russian accent was thick. "We see you painting that symbol on the walls. We hear the people talking about it. Say goodbye." His finger touched the trigger.

Aaron clasped Claire's hand as the gun went off.

Friday, June 29th
5:35PM //

He hadn't come during lunch. Joe hoped Aaron would show up during dinner. He'd thought all day about escaping in a helicopter. *I can't just leave him like this. I can't leave him and Claire here by themselves.*

The TV on the wall played the "news" as usual. The noise grated on Joe's nerves. He glared at the nearest one. An electric shock coursed through his limbs. Aaron's and Claire's faces showed on the monitor. A clattering sounded in his ears as his fork fell from his hand. Joe stood and walked to the TV.

"A young couple were shot dead in their apartment in downtown Houston yesterday evening. Aaron Smith and his wife Claire were known for stirring up rebellious dissension among the citizens of this fine city." The reporter's accented voice was thick with disapproval.

A new picture appeared on the screen. Joe stumbled backward. Aaron and Claire lay dead, side by side, on the floor of their apartment. Aaron's hand clutched Claire's. Her other hand lay over her belly.

"No, no, no." Joe walked from the cafeteria on legs unready to support him.

In the hallway, he leaned against the wall and groaned. His feet led him back to his room where he collapsed on his bed. He lay for a long time, sobbing. When his tears dried up, he fell into a deep sleep.

Darkness pressed against his eyes when he woke again. His watch read 10:23PM. Joe rose and walked out the door. He strode through the familiar halls without watching for guards, without silencing his footsteps. He wasn't even sure the door to the outside would open, but it did. He had met no one on the way.

The sharp night air revived Joe and he ran out into the oil field. He kept running, farther and farther, the cold air filling his lungs, his muscles eager to pound out the old, familiar pace. Laughter rippled up to his mouth, but he bit it back. He could taste freedom.

The helicopters loomed dark against the night sky just ahead. Joe sprinted to them. He climbed into the pilot's seat of the nearest one and found the key in the ignition. It had been a long time since he'd sat in this seat, but it all came back to him.

Without another thought, Joe started the rotors, then the engine. A few minutes later, he was in the air.

He let his laughter loose as he steered the helicopter south, toward the gulf. If anyone was on the ground shooting at him, Joe was unaware. The lights of the towns sped by, not far below him.

Alone in the air, Joe wished the noise of the helicopter would drown out his pain, but it only left room for the pain to grow. He allowed thoughts of Carol, and Emma, and Matt to surface. Carol's sweet face. Her crystal blue eyes.

How can I tell her our son is gone? Our first grandchild. She didn't even know we were going to have a grandchild. The words formed, unbidden, in his mind.

Tears pooled in his eyes. The deep ache inside him, which had started upon hearing about Aaron, increased. The longing to be with his wife did also. *I don't even know where they could possibly be.*

Joe cleared his throat and turned on the search light long enough to see the gulf coast looming ahead. He checked the fuel gauge and veered west, hugging the shoreline.

Ten minutes later, they appeared out of nowhere. His single-engine heli was no match for their military jets. They would start shooting at any moment, or corner him and lead him back to the refinery. Joe steered his ship over the water, hovered for a moment, unbuckled his harness, and jumped.

Thirty-two Years Earlier //

Carol jumped when Joe brushed the hair off her shoulder. She whipped around to face him. He put a finger to his lips and beckoned for her to follow him.

"When did it start?" Joe raced away from Carol's house, his blood boiling just under the surface.

Carol breathed through a few shuddering sobs. "I don't know. I heard the shouting when I got home, and I didn't go inside. I was trying to see in through the window, to see what was going on, when you came and scared the daylights out of me."

Joe took her hand over the emergency brake. "Sorry about that. Remind me. Why can't you stay in your apartment for the summer?"

Carol looked out the window, avoiding his glances. "I can't afford it, Joe. I need to save money. I—"

"It's not worth that. Nothing is worth that. You won't be able to do your job if this keeps up." Joe loosened his grip on her hand. *The last thing I need to do is scare her more.*

"I wasn't going to go inside this time." Carol lowered her forehead into her free hand.

"It's okay. We'll figure this out."

"Where are you going to take me?" They'd been seeing each other for months, and still the tone of distrust in Carol's voice broke Joe's heart.

"To my parent's house."

"No, Joe. I can't impose on them. It's fine. I'm sure my dad's passed out by now. Just take me home."

Joe forced his tone to be calm. "I'm not taking you back there. My parents will be happy to have you. Lord knows there's plenty of room in that house. You probably won't even see them."

Carol turned to look out the window.

When they pulled up to the Smith's old mansion, Joe caught the same look of awe on Carol's face as when he'd first introduced her to his parents. He swung around the wide fountain in the center of the courtyard and killed the car's engine. Again, he tried to see the mansion with fresh eyes, not like he had the last sixteen years of his life.

The stone house sprawled out in front of them with blue shutters framing the magnificent windows. To the right of the front door, a circular turret rose up, making the house look like a castle.

Joe hurried to the other side of the car and opened Carol's door. He took her hand to help her out.

Her eyes didn't waver from the house as she pulled the straps of her backpack over her shoulders. "How did your parents afford this house?"

"They didn't. They inherited it when I was five years old. My grandfather found gold in the California gold rush, then came home to Houston and bought this house outright. My dad is an engineer. He does all right for himself." Joe shrugged as his cheeks warmed. *Why am I rambling on about this?* "Come on, let's see if they're home."

"You don't even know if they're home?" Carol kept her feet planted.

Joe stopped and shot Carol what he hoped was a reassuring smile. "They're busy people. If they aren't home yet we'll just wait for them."

He led her up the broad stone steps to the large wooden double doors. Mae, the housekeeper, opened the door for them.

"Joe, how nice to see you. Were your parents expecting you? I believe they're still out."

"They're not expecting us. It's not a problem. We'll wait." Joe placed a kiss on the older woman's cheek as he stepped in the door.

Mae had grown up in the old maids' quarters with her mother and father who were the first hired on at Kerriwick Mansion when Joe's grandfather had bought the place. She had been employed by the Smiths since Joe was born, and now lived in Houston with her own family.

"Of course, just come on in. I was about to go home, but if there's anything I can help you with, just say the word. Hello Carol." Mae squeezed Carol's arm.

Carol flinched, and Joe put his arm around her shoulders, careful not to let too much weight fall on them.

He noticed Mae's purse hung over her shoulder. "We'll be fine on our own. You get home to those cute kids."

"Okay then. Bye." Mae waved and walked out the open door.

Joe shut it behind her and turned to face Carol who seemed to be soaking in every detail of the cavernous foyer. The wide-planked wood floor was inlaid with stone. Above the front doors gleamed a colorful, round stained-glass window. Joe looked at his watch. It was almost nine in the evening.

"Come on, let's go scrounge for food. I'm starving." Joe took Carol's hand and wound his way back to the giant kitchen.

"Holy smokes." Carol exhaled and ran her fingers over the granite and stone countertops.

"Guess you didn't see the kitchen the last time you were here." Joe opened one side of the double-door refrigerator. "Aw rad! Pizza." He pulled out an unbaked, homemade pizza, set it on the large island, and walked to the other side of the fridge to turn on one of the four ovens.

Joe took both Carol's hands and waited until she met his eyes. She looked shy, as though she felt out of place. Not like the

Carol he had been getting to know. "Would the lady like some wine?"

Fear flashed in Carol's eyes for a moment. Joe almost missed it. Then her usual determination returned. "Sure."

The oven beeped, and Joe released Carol to slide the pizza inside and set a timer. "Just a glass each. Come on, I'll show you the wine cellar." Joe pulled her along again, down a staircase behind the kitchen.

"This place has a wine cellar?" Carol gasped as they reached the bottom of the stairs and rounded a corner.

The walls were all brick, with a unique chevron pattern of brick in the ceiling. Two of the walls were covered by ancient, built-in wine bottle holders. Joe scanned the wall to the right before picking out an older pinot noir. "You'll love this."

"Are you sure your parents won't mind?" Again, shy Carol made her appearance.

Joe cupped her cheek and stroked it with his thumb. He wanted to make that look on her face disappear for good. "You've met my parents. They're very normal people. They won't care if we open a bottle. They'll probably end up finishing it when they get home. It's no big deal. You can relax here. It's what they would want. And it's definitely what I want."

Joe took his time leaning down, bringing his mouth to meet Carol's soft lips. When he lingered, she sighed, and Joe moved away. "Come on, let's go outside."

With wine glasses in hand, Joe and Carol walked through the dining room, complete with a log fireplace, to the outdoor living area overlooking the pool. Joe sat on the couch and pulled Carol down next to him.

She shook her head as she glanced around. "I can't believe you grew up here. And it's only a few miles from where I grew up." She took a sip of wine and stared at the glass as if it held liquid gold.

"Good, huh?" Joe chuckled and kissed the side of Carol's head.

"You really think your parents would let me stay here?"

"Yeah, why not?" Joe savored a sip of wine. He turned on the couch to face Carol.

Carol looked into her wine glass. "This all just reminds me of how different we are. You grew up with all this. I'm a poor girl from the wrong side of the tracks whose parents barely paid any attention to."

Sorrow swooped through Joe's heart. *That's how she feels?* "Carol Bell, listen to me." Joe put a hand on Carol's neck and lifted her chin with his thumb until she met his eyes again. "This stuff doesn't determine who I am, and your past doesn't define you. I know you, Carol, and you're not a product of a broken life. You've risen above your circumstances and you're building a good life for yourself. We have a lot more in common than you might—"

Carol had shifted forward and grasped the back of his head, bumping her lips against his. After a rough start, Carol persisted, and the sweet kiss intensified. At some point, Carol must have set their wine glasses down. All Joe knew were her lips and the feeling of her skin under his fingers.

"Ahem."

"Oh my."

Joe and Carol jumped apart. Joe caught a twinkle in his dad's eye before he dropped his head into his hands. Heat radiated off his face. *Don't leave Carol to deal with this.* Joe cleared his throat and looked up. "Mom, Dad, you remember Carol."

Dad was only just keeping it together.

Mom was poised and gracious as ever. "Yes, hello Sweet pea. What brings you two here tonight?"

"Oh, come on, Vicki. They must have heard we'd be away and wanted a romantic spot to spend the evening. We pulled a burnt pizza out of the oven for you." Dad winked at Joe.

Joe suppressed a groan. "It's not like that, really. Carol needs a place to stay for a while. Well, at least until school starts again. I told her she could stay here."

"Oh of course you're welcome. As long as you need." Mom sat next to Carol and put an arm around her shoulders.

The heat in Joe's face rose.

"I don't want to be a bother. It's really not necessary." Carol stood and crossed her arms over her chest. Her cheeks were flushed. She was beautiful.

"Nonsense." Dad's tone was easy as always. "If the boy says you need to stay here, that's just fine with us. In fact, there's no one staying in the guest house. You could have that whole place to yourself. Wouldn't bother us a bit."

"That's a wonderful idea, Dear." Mom put a hand on Joe's knee but addressed Carol. "You would be more than welcome to come into the house anytime and use the theater room or the sauna. We just want you to feel right at home. I'll go fetch the pizza for you two, then Joe can help you get settled in the guest house."

As Mom disappeared, Dad pulled out his key ring and took one of the keys off. "Here's the key. Now, let me lay some ground rules. You two aren't to be alone in the guest house together. You can spend time out here together. You understand?"

"Thanks Dad. Understood." Joe took the key.

Mom came back with the pizza, which was only a little dark on the edges, and a few plates. Joe rose and took the pizza from her, setting it down on the coffee table in front of the couch.

"Good night, you two." Dad steered Mom away as she blew a kiss to them.

Carol and Joe sat on the couch again and ate the pizza in silence.

When Carol stood and stacked the plates and pizza tray, Joe caught her arm. "Don't worry about my parents, they're cool."

Carol gave him a faint smile, then turned toward the kitchen. After washing the dishes, Joe took Carol's hand and led her back onto the patio and around the large, in-ground swimming pool. Just on the other side, hidden in some trees, was the guest house.

"It's pretty bare, but it's nice." Joe looked around the near-empty house before his gaze landed on Carol.

"Even this is bigger than our house." Joe had never seen Carol look so nervous. A moment later, she met Joe's eyes with determination. "I can't stay here."

Saturday, June 30th
11:01AM //

We can't stay here. We can't. How do we get out of here? A hand stroked Carol's hair out of her face.

"Joe? Joe?"

"Mom, it's me. Emma. Drink some water."

A water bottle pressed against Carol's lips. She took a few sips.

"Good job." Emma's soft tone and gentle hand brought fresh tears to Carol's eyes.

"Where's Aaron? Is Aaron okay? Is Matt okay? Did he get away from the man with the knife?"

"Matt's fine. That was days ago. He's doing better than any of us. He spends most of his time helping out around camp." Emma's voice had gone dull.

Carol's shakes started again. "He doesn't take showers, does he?"

"No, Mom. He stays away from the showers. We all do. It's okay. We're all okay. Go back to sleep."

Carol trembled, a few moans escaped, until she was able to drift off again.

Saturday 11:14AM //

Joe floated on his back, holding the waist of his pants. As soon as he'd hit the water, he employed an old scout trick. Taking his jeans off, Joe tied the legs together, flung the waist over his head to capture as much air as he could, and put the inflated pant legs around his neck to stay afloat.

It worked better than he anticipated. He'd been in this position, in the waters of the gulf, for hours, watching the course of the sun to ensure he was going south.

It's probably nearing noon. Have I really been out here for nine hours?

Patches of time eluded his memory. At some point, he'd removed his pants, and now floated in his light shirt and boxers. The sun baked his exposed skin, its effects magnified through the water. His fingertips were curdled, and his throat was full of sandpaper. He drew ragged breaths.

If I'm not found soon, or get to land—

Joe tipped up and looked west. His head spun, his stomach lurched. He lay back in the water, angling his body toward land.

Hopefully Mexican land. Have I gone far enough south?

He paddled for another fifteen minutes, eyes closed, sunrays piercing his eyelids with brilliant orange. He straightened again to check for land.

A boat loomed into view. Joe tread water with only his head poking above the surface.

It looks like it's patrolling. Surely the Russians wouldn't be this far south.

Joe stroked toward the boat with caution. *Mexicans.*

He raised an arm to wave and plunged under the water. All strength drained from him. He couldn't bring himself to the surface again. He was sinking. His limbs were so heavy.

Carol's face filled his mind. *I hope she knows how much I love her. I haven't told her in a long time.* Emma. Matt. Aaron.

Will I see Aaron soon? I've never thought much about heaven, or hell in so long. An air bubble floated up from his lips. Darkness clouded his thoughts.

Wednesday, July 4th
1:24PM //

She went through the motions of living, of caring for her family, and for Georgia's family. Emma's cheeks hurt with the effort to smile a lot, to look as though nothing phased her. Maybe nothing did anymore. The blasted sunlight pierced everything.

"How'd you get all this water?" Mom's voice brought her around to the present, in the tent.

Emma was drenched in sweat. "Mom, you should wash yourself. Matt brought you these nice, clean clothes. I think you'd feel a lot better."

Matt and Emma left Mom in the tent alone. They entertained Georgia's kids while Georgia slept. She slept a lot.

When Mom came out, tears surfaced in Emma's eyes. Mom even smiled.

Emma hugged her, savoring the comforting touch. "I'm proud of you. Don't you feel better?"

Mom nodded, though her eyes still held panic.

"Let's make some lunch."

Matt, Emma, and Mom took Georgia's kids to the food tent. Sadie held the twins' hands. Emma kept one eye on the crowds. A pair of disturbed, dark eyes met hers. An arm covered in tattoos rose and beckoned her over.

"I'm going to go help out in the supply tent." Emma walked away, keeping her gaze straight ahead.

She made her way around to the backside of the food tent. Tynan stood with muscular arms across his chest, his legs spread wide.

"You got more food than you deserved. Again. JD says it's my turn. Let's go." Tynan grabbed Emma around the waist.

Emma glanced down at her tattoo of the feathers and set her lips in a straight line. Tynan half-carried her to a cluster of tents set apart, where many of the others in the gang hung around.

The acrid, vinegar smell of what she'd learned was black tar heroin stung her nostrils.

They'd been one of the most dangerous gangs in the States and their reputation followed them into Mexico. They wasted no time getting involved with the local drug scene of Matamoros.

Leers and cat calls followed her as Tynan pushed her into his tent. The usual churning wave of nausea threatened to bring up her meager breakfast. Emma closed her eyes and calmed her breathing. She kept her eyes shut as Tynan's hands traced all over her body, under her clothes. He pressed himself against her.

"Come on, don't act like you ain't loving this." Tynan's hot breath on her neck sent sickening goosebumps all down Emma's spine.

Bile rose in her throat. Tynan grabbed Emma's shoulders and threw her onto his mattress. The smells of sweat and other things Emma didn't want to think about engulfed her when she landed. She swallowed several times.

Tynan stripped out of his white tank top and shorts, and straddled Emma, pulling up her dress. With the dress covering her face, Emma let her tears fall silent, her mind emptied, until it was over. Tynan rolled over and fell asleep.

Emma grabbed a stack of food vouchers as she left the tent and crept back to camp.

"There you are. We came to join you right after lunch, but you weren't here." Matt and Mom were at the supply tent helping the UN employees.

Sadie and Jasper sat nearby folding kids' clothes.

"Yeah, I decided to go lay down for a bit." Emma turned away, so they wouldn't notice her shaking hands. She found another box to sort through and settled on the ground.

Cold sweat trickled down her back. Emma drew in deep breaths. She stood slowly. "Sorry, I'm still not feeling good. I think I'll go lay down again."

She made it to the backside of the porta-potties just as her body heaved and her breakfast made a reappearance.

When she straightened again a woman a little older than herself stood nearby.

"Are you okay?" She had a British accent. Or Irish.

Emma walked away from the porta potties and drew in a fresh breath. The girl followed.

"I'm fine."

"My name's Meg. I know what you've been doing." Her tone wasn't accusatory or judgmental. It was heavy with sadness. "I'm sorry you feel like you have to do that. Can I pray for you?"

Emma's skin crawled. She turned toward the girl. "You think you know about my life? What are you even doing here? Fulfilling your duty to humanity by volunteering with the poor American refugees for a couple hours a week and touring Mexico the rest of the time?"

The girl gave Emma a sympathetic smile. "I'm not here with UNHCR or any of the other organizations. I came on my own. Can I pray for you?"

"I guess. It's a free countr—" Emma turned in the direction of her tent. Her eyes pooled with tears. The old joke had come so naturally to her lips.

"I know you can't put any hope in these organizations or in people. People can only do so much. They're going to let you down. God's with you though. He won't let you down."

Emma stopped and pivoted to face Meg again. "'God won't let me down?' How could God let this happen to me and my family? To my country? Where has God been this whole time?"

"Well, He wasn't behind the Russian attacks. But He's in this, even if you can't see it right now."

"Okay well, good luck with the prayers." Her legs wobbled as she made her way back to the tent.

She lay in the tent with the door flap open, trying to air it out. The air was hot and heavy as always and didn't move. She turned on her side to relieve her sweating back. As if a faucet had been turned on, the tears came in torrents. Sobs wracked Emma's body until she drifted off to sleep.

6:53PM //

Emma was suffocating. She reached out, clutched the edge of her sleeping bag and gasped for air. Her eyes shot open. She pulled herself up and crawled out of the tent. Instead of fresh air she found only the same stagnant heat. The sun was dropping in the west.

Jasper stood nearby, watching her. When Emma met his gaze, he hurried back into his tent.

Emma stood on shaky legs and went into her own tent again, closing the door flap behind her. She stripped out of her clothes, grabbed a few bottles of water, a bar of soap, and scrubbed every inch of her skin. After rinsing the soap off, she stood naked and raw.

She thought of Jack. His voice echoed through her thoughts. She opened her eyes and looked at the tattoo on her arm. *Just because you give them your body, doesn't mean they have rights to your soul.*

A sharp ache stabbed at Emma's heart. She could almost feel Jack's arms around her. A small whimper escaped her lips. Emma shook her head and threw on a fresh sun dress she'd found at the supply tent.

When she left the tent again, Georgia was sitting outside, surrounded by her kids, all except the older two.

"Hi Georgia."

"Emma, you cleaned up. You look beautiful."

Emma turned cold under the compliment. She looked down at the ground.

"Sadie and Jasper are still with your mom and Matt, helping." Georgia smiled at baby August in her lap.

The twins looked bored, sitting in the dirt.

Emma was clean for once, she didn't want to sit in the dirt.

"Do you girls know how to play London Bridge?" Emma glanced from one identical face to the other.

They looked up at her with big, blue, curious eyes. Both shook their heads.

"Come on. I'll teach you." Emma entertained them with London Bridge for a while until Winnie complained of being hungry.

"Do you have more food?" Emma looked at Georgia.

Georgia stood. "Yes. Should we go get the others at the supply tent?"

Emma's stomach lurched. She avoided Georgia's gaze. "Yeah, sure."

She took a twin's hand in each of her own.

When they reached the supply tent, there were people lining up nearby at the food tent. Emma's pulse quickened. Her eyes darted around the crowd. She clung to the kids' hands.

They already had me today. I don't owe them anymore. Emma closed her eyes and took a deep breath. *You'll be just fine.*

They entered the supply tent which was also full of people searching for suitable clothes. Emma left Georgia with her kids by the entrance and snaked through the crowd. She found Mom, Matt, Sadie, and Jasper behind the tables helping people find what they were looking for.

"These are used! Ugh!" A girl of nineteen or twenty tossed a skirt back in Matt's face. She stood with a hand on her hip, glaring at him.

"All of these are used." Matt sounded very diplomatic and patient. "People donated these so we could have clean clothes."

The girl rolled her eyes and snatched the skirt back.

"Come on, let's go make dinner." Emma came up behind Matt and Mom.

"I'm going to apply for asylum in Mexico and try to get us out of here." Mom looked better than she had since they'd left Dad as they walked out of the stuffy supply tent. "One of the UN workers was telling me about the process. It takes a long time, so I need to start now. Maybe by then Dad will be—"

Emma glanced up at Mom. She was looking into the sea of people with an odd expression. Emma tensed. Her stomach dropped. Matt nudged her in the ribs and pointed in the direction Mom was staring.

Emma followed Matt's finger, her heart pounding in her ears. All sound drained away as her gaze locked on familiar, dark eyes. All at once she was home. "Jack."

Her knees shuddered as she rushed to him. Tears ran down her face. Every part of her ached for him. Then his arms were around her, his lips were on her face, in her hair. She breathed him in. Clung to him.

"I found you." Jack's voice was hoarse and broken against her ear. "I can't believe I found you. I would've come sooner, but they made me wait." His tears fell on her neck.

"I was afraid I'd never see you again." The truth Emma hadn't been able to admit before this moment rushed out. Sobs she'd been holding back for weeks cascaded over Jack's shoulder.

I shouldn't even let him touch me. I don't deserve him. I'm filthy. I was saving myself for him and now I've lost it all. Her sobs became uncontrollable. But she couldn't let him go.

"I'll never leave you again." Jack's promise dropped like a salve over her heart.

She didn't know how long they stood there. It was an eternity within an instant. They shared kisses, and they stared into each other's eyes, their foreheads pressed together. His arms around her healed her.

"What happened to you?" Emma broke the sphere of silence around them.

"It's a long story. I'll tell you later."

Matt and Mom came over then, joining in the hugs. Tears glinted in their eyes too.

"Let's go back to the tent and you can tell us all about where you've been, Jack." Mom put an arm around Matt's shoulders and led the way through the maze of tents.

Emma tucked her hand into Jack's and they followed, gazing sidelong into each other's eyes.

Georgia and the kids had already started cooking dinner over a fire. Emma introduced Jack to Georgia. She gave him a wan smile before returning her gaze to the fire.

"How long have you been here? What happened to you? Where's your dad?" Jack faced Emma and held both her hands.

Emma studied his knock-out handsome face, memorizing again the curve of his lips, the way his long lashes made his dark eyes seem bigger, the hair hanging over his forehead.

She took a shaky breath. "I don't know how long we've been here. It feels like it's been forever. I don't even know what day it is."

Jack rubbed his thumb over her cheek. "It's Wednesday, July fourth."

"It's July fourth? Independence Day?" Emma's mind wandered to past fourth of Julys with her family. *All that reason for celebrating was taken away in a minute.*

She cleared her throat. "Anyway, I don't know how long it's been. A week and a half, two weeks. Dad got caught while we were trying to leave the oil refinery. He had to stay behind. I just hope they didn't do anything to punish him or something." Emma looked down at their entwined fingers.

Jack squeezed her hands. "I'm sure he's fine."

"You don't know that. Everything is so unsure." A bubble of panic rose within her and she shivered despite the close heat. "We're hanging by a moment here."

"I know, Em. Remember why we got these?" Jack pulled Emma's arm up.

Emma looked at her tattoo. Despair sickened her. "Where's the freedom here? Where's the hope? We're trapped, and we're at the mercy of what others have to give." She tugged her arm away.

Jack's eyes filled with hurt and confusion. "We're together now. That's all I need."

"Well, I guess I'm not as good a person as you." Emma turned away as more tears formed.

Jack was on her heels.

She ducked into the tent and collapsed on her sleeping bag. Jack lowered himself next to her. He searched her face and took her hand again.

"I couldn't get across the border. It was closed. A guard hit me in the head with the butt of his gun and dragged me into an alley to die."

Emma reached up and touched the bruise around his eye. Tears fell over her nose, down her cheeks. *I don't deserve him. I'm being such a child. He should be with someone better than me.*

"When I woke up I went back to the car and drove east. I thought I'd go to the beach and take a boat, I guess. I don't know what I thought. But then I saw a rowboat along the Rio. I pulled over. I had a warm bottle of water and three granola bars, and no idea where I was going, or which way I should go when I got over to Mexico." Jack sighed and looked down at their hands.

Emma buried her face in her musty pillow.

Jack continued. "There was no one in sight, which turned out to be some kind of miracle. I took the boat across the river, and then I walked. I walked all night. I tried to walk southwest but couldn't really tell where I was going. When the sun started to come up I collapsed."

Emma turned her head to look at him again. His soft, brown hair rested in the palm of one hand as he leaned on his elbow.

An invisible knife twisted in Emma's heart. She winced.

"It was okay, though. I woke up in a nice little house. A man had found me and carried me inside, fireman style. He and his wife were nice. Celia let me take a shower and gave me these clothes. Then she fed me the most amazing meal ever. The kitchen was so clean and warm. But you were all I could think of. I wanted you there so bad. They made me wait a few days to get my strength back. Then Pedro finally agreed to drive me into Matamoros. Now

I'm here, and I'm never leaving you again." Jack kissed the back of her hand, then leaned in and kissed her forehead.

Emma pulled away. "Jack. It's hard here. We've had to do crazy things to just survive. It's changed all of us."

"I know. I can tell. Matt's a different—"

"Please, stop. You don't understand. I don't deserve you."

"What are you talking about? Didn't you hear anything I just said? I'm not leaving you, Em. I don't want to hear you say that again." Jack took a deep breath and ran his fingers through Emma's hair. His tone softened. "What's going on? You know you can tell me anything."

Emma forced a smile. She grabbed the back of his elbow, drawing him closer. "It's fine. You're here now. Everything's going to be fine."

Wednesday 8:23PM //

A white light burned through his eyelids. *I'm dead. Am I about to see heaven? But there's a bed under me. Really uncomfortable too.*

Joe's eyes opened a crack. Everything around him was white, and he was convinced. *Heaven.*

Then a woman approached. "Hola? Hello? Are you awake?"

Joe tried to respond, but only an unintelligible groan came out. He was in a hospital and this was a nurse, not an angel.

"Are you in any pain?" The nurse checked all the monitors surrounding his bed.

Joe assessed the state of his body. Everything ached, but nothing hurt especially. He managed to shake his head.

"Good. Do you remember what happened to you?" The nurse was young and had a sweet face. She reminded him of Emma.

Emma. Carol. Matt. What had happened? Joe closed his eyes as water and sunlight snapped through his mind.

"It's okay, sir. Don't worry about trying to remember everything right now. What's your name?"

Joe cleared his throat, but his voice came out in a raspy whisper. "Joe—Joe Smith. Where am I?"

The nurse smiled down at him. "You're in hospital in Tampico, Tamaulipas."

"I made it. I made it to Mexico."

"You did, Mr. Smith. You're lucky to be alive. You were very dehydrated and malnourished. You've been sleeping for a few days now. It's nice to see you come around." The nurse's eyes were full of sympathy.

"For days? What day is it?"

The girl picked up a clipboard from the foot of his bed and jotted down some notes. "It's Wednesday, July fourth. The Navy picked you up on Saturday. Do you feel hungry?" She met his eyes again.

"A little."

"We'll get some soup for you to try. You'll want to take it easy at first."

"Thank you. What's your name?"

"Rosa. I'll come back with that soup in a little while."

Rosa. I wonder what happened to her, and the Panaderia. Joe closed his eyes again. *Are Carol and the kids close? I don't even know where they are.*

Joe drifted off again.

He woke when he felt a hand on his wrist. Rosa was there, taking his vitals.

"Oh good. I brought you soup. Do you want to try to eat?"

"Sure."

Rosa helped him sit up.

The soup was bland but slid nicely down his raw throat. The small cup only awakened his hunger, but he decided to wait and see how the soup settled.

"Rosa, do you know where the Americans who've been crossing over from Texas might be? I was separated from my family." Joe swallowed around the sudden lump in his throat.

Rosa cocked her head to one side and picked up the empty soup cup. "I heard there is a camp for the Americans in Matamoros. The United Nations set it up there. There are a few along the border. The biggest one is in Tijuana, but the closest one would be Matamoros."

"How far away is that?" Joe clenched the sheets at his side.

"About six hours in a car. Nine to twelve hours by bus." Rosa shot him a remorseful grimace.

Joe dropped his head back and exhaled. The soup churned in his stomach. *We may be farther away than ever, but at least we're in the same country again, assuming they made it. Aaron and Claire. Wherever they are now, the Russians can't hurt them.*

As Rosa left the room again, Joe let his tears fall.

Thursday, July 5th
9:14AM //

Jack cut a box down and stacked it on top of the others behind the supply tent. His eyes bore into Matt's back as he helped a new-comer find some clothes and baby supplies. Emma had complained of a headache and had gone to lay down.

"You sure Emma's okay?" Jack approached Matt from behind as the woman walked away with full arms.

Matt shrugged. "I don't know. She's been on edge for a while. She disappears to the tent a lot. Since Mom's back on her feet, Emma's the one we never see now. It's weird. It's not easy being here though. You can't blame her."

"No, I don't. I'm worried about her."

"Me too."

"You seem to be taking all this okay. You're making things happen. Your mom told me you even arranged a trash pick-up schedule for different areas of the camp."

"Well, UNHCR and the Mexican government are stretched too thin already. We might as well help them help us." Matt sat against one of the tables and crossed his arms.

"From what I've seen just today, it seems like almost everyone spends their time in their tents. Not a lot of people out and about, huh."

"Yeah, we all have to fight the lethargy. And everyone's afraid of the gang."

"What gang?"

Matt's eyes fixed on the ground. "There's a dangerous American gang that has control of the food distribution, they just have their hands in everything. I had to run away from a guy with a knife when I tried to take a shower our second day here."

"What? That's crazy. Do you think Emma's trying to avoid them?"

Matt shrugged, still avoiding Jack's eyes. "Maybe."

"Can't the UN or the government do something about them?" A sick feeling was growing in Jack's stomach.

"Like I said, they're stretched too thin already. Mexico doesn't have the infrastructure to support this many refugees flooding in all at once." Matt stood and clapped a hand on Jack's shoulder. "I'm glad you're here, man."

"I'm going to check on Emma." Jack walked past the reeking porta-potties and through the maze of tents. All the pathways looked the same and he had to backtrack and loop around several times until he found tent fifty-nine.

Emma was huddled on her sleeping bag, her eyes open, staring at the tent wall. Jack sat beside her and put a hand on her shoulder. She jumped and pulled away.

"It's okay. It's me." Jack rubbed his fingers along her arm and watched as goosebumps cropped up under his touch. "What's wrong?"

Emma's shoulders shuddered. He thought she was shrugging, but realized her body was being wracked with silent cries.

Friday, July 6th
9:46AM //

After not being able to keep the soup down, Joe had been put on more IVs to nourish him.

"Rosa, how long do I have to stay here? It's been almost a whole week." Joe caught the nurse's arm before she could leave the room again.

"I know. But as I said when you first woke up, you're very malnourished and dehydrated. These things take time." Rosa graced him with her most sympathetic grin.

"But if you had to guess, how much longer will I have to stay? I've been awake longer today than any other day. I'm getting stronger, I can feel it."

Rosa chuckled. "You are getting stronger, Señor Smith. It's good, but not good enough yet. I make no promises, I'm not a doctor, and they may not decide until you can consistently keep your food down."

Joe sighed and leaned back against his pillows. "Rosa, one more thing. Are there any newspapers in English around I could read? I've been getting false news for weeks."

"False news?" Rosa's eyebrows came together.

"Yeah, Russian propaganda. Things the Russians made up and put on TV as news."

"Oh dear. I will see what I can find for you."

"I don't know what I'd do without you, Rosa."

Rosa shook her head and stopped in the doorway on her way out. "You're just like my papá."

"He sounds like a decent guy."

12:00PM //

At noon Rosa returned with a beat-up laptop. "This is mine. I'm going to let you use it because another nurse told me about a website that reports the real American news. My shift ends at six, you can use it until then."

Joe reached out for the computer. *Maybe I can figure out where most of the Americans have gone. Where Carol and the kids could be.*

Rosa snatched it back from his hands. "If you get tired at all I want you to set it aside and take a nap. I don't want to come back to see your eyes bloodshot and drooping. Promise me."

"I promise. No drooping eyes here." Joe clasped his hands in his lap.

Rosa set the laptop on the table in front of him and rolled her eyes, mumbling under her breath. "Eres como mi papá."

"Thanks. I can translate any website with this."

Joe found the rogue news outlet he'd followed in America. The situation at the refinery had blown out of proportion when he left. It was completely run by the Russians, and only a few Americans were left on the crew. It was reported, if anyone stepped out of line, they were executed on the spot, no questions asked.

Joe dismissed this news after the first article. Nothing was left for him in America. He didn't know just where Carol and the kids had crossed the border, so he searched "where Americans go when fleeing from southeast Texas."

He had to translate every search result into English and found several old, irrelevant articles. He reworded his search to include the current crisis. A major Mexican news outlet was among the first of the results.

"With the help of the Mexican government, the United Nations has set up camps to receive American refugees along various points at the border. Before the borders closed, Mexico welcomed over two hundred thousand Americans fleeing Russian domination. Still more are trickling in, getting around the border by boat."

Joe skimmed down the article until he found a list of cities with camps.

"Camps have been established in Tijuana, Mexicali, Ciudad Juarez, Nuevo Laredo, Reynosa, and Matamoros, the largest being in Tijuana."

A map of northern Mexico filled the screen. Joe's eyes fell on the easternmost city with a star, indicating a camp. *Matamoros. Are they there? Or have they been moved to Reynosa? Or did they even make it to a camp?*

"These camps are stretched thin as there aren't enough employees, volunteers, or money to go around. Most Americans are seeking asylum in Mexico. Some are even looking to Europe to find a new home. This is a long process, and meanwhile, the Americans have to try to assimilate into a culture and language they may not be used to."

How is Carol adjusting? She has a hard time just getting used to a new school and sport schedule every year.

Monday, July 9th
12:53PM //

I haven't had a panic attack in days. And I was able to keep them from the kids. Carol walked to the UN's headquarters.

They had established a cinder block building on the edge of the camp. She was finally scheduled for her first round of interviews for asylum in Mexico.

The sultry air and wide-open farmland around the camp was a welcome contrast to the closed tent she'd sequestered herself in since they'd arrived. She tugged on the clean shirt Matt had brought and pulled the shorts up.

Maybe I've lost weight since being here without even trying. I wish Joe were here. I hope he's not still stuck in Houston. Carol bit her lower lip and stopped the well-worn track of thoughts around Joe and her oldest son.

She wound her way through the people waiting in the lobby and was greeted by the woman behind the desk. "Take a seat. Mr. Hernandez will be with you soon."

She sat on a straight, plastic chair along the cool wall. A fan in the window blew her hair out of her face, but the air did little to cool the mass of bodies.

Carol's eyelids slid shut.

"Mrs. Smith?"

Carol startled awake to see the administrative assistant standing over her, nudging her shoulder. She straightened and reached up to smooth her hair.

"Mr. Hernandez is ready to see you." The woman motioned to an open office door where a man around Carol's age stood in the doorway.

Carol stood, and her arm went to her shoulder to hike up her purse. Finding no purse there, she pretended to swat a bug away.

"Mrs. Smith, thank you for taking the time to fill out these forms." Mr. Hernandez had a thick accent. He leaned forward in his chair and laced his fingers over the desk. "You indicated that you got away without any identification. What happened?"

Carol folded her shaky hands in her lap and took a steadying breath. "My husband works for the oil refinery in Houston, Texas. The Russians took all of us into custody at the refinery. They made us sleep there and eat all our meals there, though they hardly fed us enough to get by. While my husband worked, the Russians forced my two younger kids and I to clean up the rubble out on the streets. All day we were shoveling chunks of concrete and glass."

Mr. Hernandez furrowed his eyebrows but didn't say anything. He typed something on his computer.

"Our house—our house was bombed." Carol looked out the window behind Mr. Hernandez. "We lost everything. When we escaped I left everything, including my purse. I was so nervous. It all happened so fast I didn't have time to think about grabbing my wallet. All our birth certificates, my husband and my wedding certificate, all of it was ruined with our house. I'm sorry. I don't have anything."

"Well, I'm sorry for your loss, Ma'am. We'll see what we can do for you. I saw that you listed a son of fourteen years on your application. Where is he?"

"He's in the camp. He's been helping the volunteers in the supply tent." A smile flickered over Carol's lips.

"Unfortunately, I need him present for the interview. And your daughter, aged twenty-five, she'll need to apply for asylum on her own." Mr. Hernandez glanced at her over his laptop.

"Oh. I'm sorry. I didn't realize." Carol bit her lower lip.

Mr. Hernandez leaned back in his chair. "The fault isn't yours. We'll just have to reschedule." Mr. Hernandez opened a drawer on the side of the desk and pulled out another stack of paperwork. "I'm sorry for the inconvenience. This is the way it has to go. Here's an application for your daughter."

"Okay, thank you." Carol took the application from the desk. "My daughter's fiancé was born here in Mexico. Will he need to apply for asylum?"

"If he was born here and has ID, he's a citizen and doesn't need to apply. This could help your daughter out very much. If they get married sooner than later she could easily get a permanent residency."

Carol sat dumbstruck into silence for a moment. "That would be wonderful."

"Yes. They recently changed the laws so that you have to go outside of Mexico to apply for permanent residency, but given the current crisis I'm sure that will change case by case. Just have both of them come in and I'll talk them through it." Mr. Hernandez stood and held out a hand.

Carol stood as well.

He enveloped her hand with both of his. "We'll figure this out. I can't reschedule until next week unfortunately. But it will give me time to find any information I can on you and your son."

Carol fought tears as he gazed at her with kindness.

He let her hand go and looked at his computer again. "It looks like I have an opening next Tuesday around two o'clock."

"Okay. Thank you for your time."

"I'll do my best to make this easy on you from here on out."

Carol found Jack and Emma in the tent, alone. Emma stared with strange, empty eyes at her as she entered. "Jack, do you have your ID?"

Jack nodded.

"That's good. Apparently, you two should be getting married sooner than later. Once they confirm your citizenship it would help Emma get her residency faster."

"That's awesome! I've been wanting to marry you." Jack's grin was too cheerful as he tagged Emma in the arm.

Carol's eyes trained on Emma. "What's wrong, Honey? I know it's sudden, but why put it off now if it's only going to help you get out of this place?"

Emma lowered her gaze and spoke in a deadpan voice. "Nothing's wrong. That will be great. I can't believe we didn't think of it sooner."

Carol sighed. "Well, the guy who helped today me was very nice. It went better than I'd expected, even though I had to reschedule because Matt wasn't with me." She caught Jack staring at her.

He looked from her to Emma's bent head and back again. A concerned frown clouded his handsome features. Carol cocked her head to one side. *Something's up.*

"Mom, how can I get married without any ID?" Emma broke the tense silence.

"Mr. Hernandez said he would help you figure it out, and not to worry. He wants both of you to go in and talk to him."

"Okay." Emma's tone hinted at her doubts over the UN's ability to push non-existent paperwork through.

"There's not much more we can do than turn in what we can and leave it up to them." Carol put a hand on her hip and dropped the application in front of Emma. "Oh, Honey. It's going to be okay, I promise. We'll be together, no matter what."

Carol knelt beside her daughter. Tears had sprung into Emma's eyes.

Tuesday, July 17th
8:15AM //

"I heard someone say people are starting to go into town for food. They can't keep up with the food demands here. I'd love to go into town and get out of here for a while. It could be good for the kids. And all of us." Georgia looked around the fire at each of their faces.

Emma made a strange movement next to Matt.

"Do you have money?" Matt asked the obvious question when no one else spoke up.

"Yes. My husband made sure we both carried money in case we got separated."

"Georgia, you shouldn't go into town alone. I've heard it's not safe." Mom dipped a spoonful of rice into Willa's mouth.

"Will you come with me?" Georgia looked up from August who was breastfeeding.

An anxious knot twisted in Matt's stomach. "I'll go with you guys."

"We'll go too. Right, Em?" Jack was always smiling, trying too hard to cheer Emma up.

Emma's empty eyes haunted Matt every day. *I'm glad Jack's here, even though she's even more closed off now.*

Emma nodded but didn't look up from her plate. She pushed her food around.

Little of it had disappeared.

"Matt, don't forget I need you to come with me to the interview this afternoon." Mom glanced at him.

"We should all go. We can all see about our asylum processes. Then we could go into town." Jack put a hand on Emma's back. Emma didn't look up.

2:02PM //

The lobby of the UN headquarters was stuffy, the air even heavier than outside, despite several whirring fans. Bodies filed along every inch of the walls. A bulletin board hung by the door where people posted names and some pictures of missing friends and family. The UN also posted the names of people found dead. Matt avoided the board.

All the chairs in the center were filled up, and children sat on the floor. Most were filthy and had the gaunt look of hunger in their eyes.

Matt pressed his back against the cool, cinder block wall. His arm stuck to Emma's and he pulled it away. Winnie and Willa started to cry.

"I'll take them outside." Emma put a hand on each of the twin's heads.

"What if they call you in?" Mom pushed her damp bangs away from her eyes.

"Jack can come get me. We'll be just outside."

"No, I'm going with you." Jack crossed his arms over his chest.

Emma looked down at Sadie who had come to her side. "I'll be fine with the kids. You'd better stay." She left with the twins, tailed by Sadie and Jasper.

August lay limp in Georgia's arms. His blue eyes were dull and listless. Matt had an urge to recoil. *Babies shouldn't look like that.*

An hour, maybe two, passed. Emma came and went with the kids.

Matt and his mom were called in first.

"Mrs. Smith, nice to see you again. This is your son? Matthew?" The man walked around his desk to sit down after giving both their hands a shake.

"Yes, this is Matt." Mom sat in one of the chairs on the other side of the desk.

Matt stood behind her, resting his hands on the back of the chair.

"Nice to meet you. I'm Señor Hernandez." He focused his attention back on Mom with sympathy furrowing his eyebrows. "Mrs. Smith, I've done all I can, but I don't know how to help you without the proper identification."

Mom remained silent. Matt was afraid she would go into another panic attack.

"So, what are we supposed to do?" Matt took a step forward and set both hands flat on the desk. "We can't go back to the US. They held us captive in the oil refinery. We know too much. They'd probably kill us, given the chance. If they haven't already killed my Dad—" Matt spun around, running his hands through his hair.

Mom gasped. Matt whirled around again. Mr. Hernandez was smiling.

"Very good, Matt. I was making sure your stories would add up. What you've said is in line with what your mother already told me. And you have great passion for your family. This is good."

"That was a mean trick." Matt folded his arms.

Mr. Hernandez's face grew serious. "The US has done worse in their interviews with asylum-seekers. But I'm not here to make comparisons. I'm here because I can't imagine having to flee my country under such circumstances and I want to help you."

"Thank you, Mr. Hernandez." Matt sat in the chair next to Mom. "Mom, are you okay?"

Mom turned toward Matt. Her face was white, but she didn't have the crazy glare of an oncoming attack. "I'm okay." She patted Matt's arm.

Matt looked at Mr. Hernandez. "She has panic attacks. I think you almost sent her into one."

"I'm sorry for the trouble. Let's move on." Mr. Hernandez looked at his computer and started shooting questions at them both in turn.

The small office was cooler than the lobby, with a fan in the window blowing into their faces. Matt settled into answering every question imaginable about their family and their history, and Dad's involvement at the refinery. Mr. Hernandez seemed very interested in that.

"It will be difficult to push this through without the proper ID, but not impossible. I would recommend finding a lawyer to help you out. Though, I suppose you don't have money either?" Mr. Hernandez peered around his computer at Mom.

Mom shook her head.

"The coyotes took all our money when we crossed the border. Dad has the rest probably." Matt looked from Mr. Hernandez to Mom.

Mr. Hernandez narrowed his eyes and pursed his lips. "It's a rare situation for a family to escape with nothing. I can recommend a solution that I wouldn't normally endorse, but given the circumstances . . ."

Mom leaned forward in her seat. "We'd be grateful for any help you can give us."

"I just received an email from a friend of mine in Mexico City who told me she's looking for a housekeeper. She would pay a fair price, and you could save up to hire a lawyer. This would all be under the table of course, and you didn't hear it from me."

Mom looked down at her lap for a moment. "I'll think about it."

"She would put you up in the bungalow behind her house, but you'd have to figure out how to get there."

Matt stared at the man, his heart thumping in his ears. His fingers went from hot, to cold, back to hot.

Mom looked at him, her eyes wide. "What do you think?"

"I don't know what to think. This could be a good chance for us. We could get out of here. But what about Emma and Jack? How would Dad ever find us?"

Mom nodded, and her eyes drifted away from his.

"How do we know he's telling the truth?" Matt narrowed his eyes at Mr. Hernandez.

Mr. Hernandez watched him then smiled. "I have a son like you, about your age. David. Passionate and tenacious. There's no real way you can trust me, but I give you my word of honor that I would never lie to you or knowingly send you into a dangerous situation."

"Wait, does David help in the camp sometimes?" Matt gripped the edge of his chair.

"Yes, he does. As much as I try to stop him. I keep telling him it's not safe. Which is why I'm eager to get you out. And why I'm working to get everyone out."

"I met him when we first got here." Matt's cheeks bore up a stiff smile.

"Very good. He's been busy lately, which has kept him away."

"Mr. Hernandez, he mentioned you might be able to do something about the porta-potties. They need to be changed out or serviced, or something. And, there's a man with a knife who hangs around the shower trailer. He's stabbed a few people already, so nobody wants to take a shower. If those two things can be changed at least, things wouldn't be so bad."

And if we had access to more food, it would keep Emma from doing whatever she does.

Mr. Hernandez's eyebrows had risen as Matt spoke. "A man with a knife, huh? I'll see what I can do, but I know better than to make promises. A lot of these things are too much for the local governments to handle. Even the UN's resources are stretched thin."

Matt studied Mom's dazed face. The mention of Matt's run-in with the stabber probably put her on edge again.

She needs to get out of here. Jack and Emma can take care of themselves.

"Of course, you can take a few days to think about my offer." Mr. Hernandez turned back to his computer screen.

"I think we should do it, Mom. Jack probably has a little money for bus tickets. We can always pay him back." Matt took Mom's hand.

She looked at him with clearer eyes. "Okay." The word came out with a shaky breath.

"Great. I think that's the right choice." Mr. Hernandez's eyes crinkled in the corners as he grinned. He grabbed a piece of paper and a pen and woke up his cell phone. "I'll call my friend and let her know you're coming. Here's her address. I'll tell her to expect you in the next couple of days." He slid the piece of paper over to Matt.

"Thank you, sir. Thanks for everything."

"Yes, thank you." Mom extended her hand. "Oh, I'm sorry. Are we done?"

Mr. Hernandez chuckled. "Just about. I have all our conversations on record, so please email me when you do get a lawyer. I wrote my email on that paper too. Then I can forward this information on to him or her."

"Do you have any recommendations for a lawyer in that area?" Mom clasped her hands in her lap.

Mr. Hernandez thought for a moment, then held out his hand for the piece of paper. Matt handed it back over. "Yes, I'll write a few names on here. They may be generous with lowering their fees. Best of luck." Mr. Hernandez stood as he gave Matt the paper.

"Thank you. Thank you." Mom walked around the desk. "Can I just give you a hug? In Texas we like to hug."

There she was. A glimpse of Mom as she giggled and gave Mr. Hernandez an awkward hug. Matt's heart ached as flashes of home, seeing Mom cook in the kitchen, the smells, the French doors opening to the large, green backyard. The taste of sweet tea, with the tang of orange and lemon Mom always added. Even the dull familiarity of school and classes were comforting in his mind.

Matt looked down at the paper and the strange address. *Anything will be better than this place.*

When they entered the stuffy lobby again, Emma was alone. Her eyes were dull as she stared at the ceiling fan. Not quite like August's had been earlier, but the same haunted look she'd had for weeks.

Matt wanted to cheer her up. He stood at her side and held out their ticket to freedom. "We're getting out of here. Mom and I are going to Mexico City. You and Jack should come with us."

Even as the words left his lips, Matt knew it would be harder than that. Their processes would be different. Jack wasn't in with Mr. Hernandez, and who knew how helpful the other case workers would be.

Still, relief washed over Emma's face. "That's good Mattie." Tears pooled in her eyes.

"What's wrong?"

"I wish I could go with you."

Tuesday 2:35PM //

"You kept your breakfast down. That's a good thing. You're looking better every day." Rosa wrote Joe's current vitals in his chart.

"I feel a lot better."

"That's good, Señor. What are you going to do when you leave? Where will you go?" Rosa balanced the clipboard on her hip and studied Joe.

"I really want to take a bus to Matamoros to find my family. But any money I had on me is disintegrating in the gulf."

"Except for this money." Rosa pointed to some bills laid out by the window. "I found these in your shirt pocket and laid them out to dry. It looks like a couple hundred US dollars. If they're worth anything. Your identification is there too. That's lucky. You can't do this plan, though. It takes a whole day to get up there in a bus, doesn't it? You won't be strong enough, even when they decide to discharge you." Concern filled Rosa's large, dark eyes.

"I won't have enough strength to sit on a bus?" Joe bent his head to one side.

"Ugh, señor." She rattled off in rapid Spanish.

Though Joe couldn't understand the words, he did recognize the exasperated tone. He chuckled. "You have enough to worry about with your own family. You don't need to worry about me."

"I'll just have to see if I can hold them off from discharging you then." Rosa hooked his chart on the foot of his bed and raised an eyebrow at him.

"Don't do that now. I'll have to get ornery, and you don't want to see that side of me."

"Like I haven't seen it already?"

Tuesday 3:14PM //

The streets on the outskirts of Matamoros were clean and quiet. It was Versailles compared to the camp they lived in day in and day out. Emma walked along with Jack at her side. Having been born in Mexico, he was a citizen and since he had his wallet and ID, he was told he could get a job.

Emma was relieved the process had been so easy for him.

"No process at all." He'd said when he'd come out of the office.

Emma had been able to get away from Jack only once since he'd arrived to tell JD and his crew she was done. Jack's presence gave her courage, but before she could get a word out, they'd attacked.

"If you don't come back like normal, we will end your little boyfriend." JD had threatened with a perverse grin and a finger across his throat as Emma made her escape.

Outside the camp, her constant tension melted, and her heart rate slowed to a normal pace. Looks of disdain met them from the locals on every street, but no one approached them.

The town had its own drug and crime issues, but they weren't visible in the broad light of day, and they weren't her problems.

"I don't see why you two can't come with us to Mexico City." Mom glanced at Emma and Jack as they made their way down a wide, clean sidewalk.

They'd left Georgia and the kids at a set of swings to find something to eat.

"We didn't get Mr. Nice Guy case worker." Emma stared ahead.

"I just hate to separate. Maybe we should stay." Mom's voice trembled.

Emma stopped. "No, you guys need to go. It would be crazy to pass this up. Jack and I'll be fine. Plus, we can keep helping Georgia and the kids."

"Georgia won't always be able to rely on your help."

Except the only reason she can feed her kids is because of me.

"Maybe you could find a job while we're in town, Jack." Mom looked around as if she would find a "Help Wanted" sign in the next window.

Emma bit her tongue. Heat rushed to her cheeks as her blood boiled. "Mom, he doesn't even have a resume. He can't just saunter into any old place and expect to get hired."

Mom stared at Emma. Her chin might have shuddered. "I'm sorry, Honey. I just want to make sure you're taken care of. You have no idea how impossible it is for me to think of leaving you." Mom brought a hand to her mouth.

The heat drained from Emma's face. She squeezed Jack's hand. "I know. We'll be fine. Jack and I will be together. We'll figure it out."

"I won't leave her again for anything. I promise." Jack put a hand on Mom's shoulder.

Mom looked from Emma to Jack and drew a shaky breath. "You can't promise anything. You never know what will happen. But you can get married. That's a promise you have some control over." Mom eyed a church just ahead, then turned and raised her eyebrows at Emma.

Wednesday, July 18th
7:47 AM //

"I can't go back. I can't go back to that place. I'm not hungry." Emma choked over her words.

She had evaded going back to the food tent ever since Jack came.

Matt looked over from his corner of the tent where he was washing the night's dust off his face. Carol was next door helping Georgia wake the kids up.

"I know, it's awful. I wish I could take you anywhere else in the world to get breakfast. But we don't have a choice." A hollow pit formed inside Jack.

The heat of the day was already building and sweat beaded under his shirt.

Matt stepped out of the tent.

"You don't get it." Emma grabbed Jack's arms. "I can't go back there."

Goosebumps sprang up over Jack's skin. Emma's desperation and the caged-animal look in her eyes turned his blood cold.

"Okay, okay. Come here. It's okay." Jack folded his arms around her. He couldn't meet her eyes, that look, for a second longer. "Just tell me what's wrong."

Wednesday 7:55 AM //

Jack sat down next to her on top of her sleeping bag. Emma tried to calm the sobs rolling up from deep inside. Her strength was dissolving fast.

"I can't tell you, Jack." Emma looked down at her lap.

Jack cupped a hand over her cheek, but she didn't look up at him. "You can tell me anything. I'll try to understand."

Emma's body shook, a cold sweat winding down her back. "I've had to do things for my family just so we can eat and get clean water. Horrible things. But I had no choice. And when Georgia came along, they weren't going to give her enough—"

"Like what things?" Jack's voice was low and hoarse. His hand dropped from her cheek.

Emma experienced an out-of-body detachment. Though she fought against it, the events of that day flashed around her as though they were happening again.

Mom had been a complete mess, lying on her sleeping bag in the tent. Matt looked like a ghost of himself. He'd become skin and bones. They had been malnourished enough at the oil refinery, they couldn't keep going without food.

As soon as Emma knew they wouldn't have enough food to get through another day, let alone the week, she told Mom and Matt she knew what to do. And she did. Emma walked to the food tent. She followed the footsteps of a girl she'd watched on her first day there.

She found JD standing by the food tent, as she had expected, observing the frantic people scrambling for food. Emma's stomach twisted in knots as she walked up to him.

She mastered her features into what she hoped was a blank mask. JD looked her over and seemed to like what he saw.

"You can get food for my whole family?" Emma crossed her arms.

"Depends on what you're willing to do. How many are in your family?"

"Three." Emma looked down at the dust clouding her feet.

"Only if you're willing to do whatever I want." JD licked his lips.

Emma wanted to vomit. She closed her eyes. *It's for Matt. And Mom. We need to eat. There's no other choice.*

She cleared her throat. "I'll do what it takes."

"Good girl." JD grabbed the back of Emma's neck and propelled her forward, behind the food tent.

She had left a half hour later with buckets of food and a cavernous emptiness inside.

Emma heaved in a breath as though awakening from a suffocating dream. She looked around the tent with wide eyes. Jack sat before her.

The story tumbled from her chapped lips. "The food vouchers somehow fell under the control of an American gang before we even got to the camp. I don't know who they paid, or killed to get so much control, but it happened. I've heard of Americans, and probably a few Mexicans, being killed by them—"

"Em."

She'd heard that inflection of finality in Jack's words only once before when they had broken up for a month over a reason Emma couldn't now remember. She shook her head and took his hand, feeling the solidity of it beneath her fingers.

"When we got here we weren't given nearly enough food. I saw how thin Matt had gotten, and I went to the head guy of the gang." Emma closed her eyes.

"No one else knows about it. I've been giving my body to them." She spoke through an onslaught of sobs. "I feel so guilty every time, not just because of what I'm doing, but also because I'm probably taking food away from other families. But Georgia's kids and Mattie need the food. You have no idea what it's like to be faced with a decision like that. But I'm garbage now. I'm ruined. I wanted to save all of myself—" Emma gave in to her cries.

She couldn't see Jack's expression through her tears, but his body tensed. His disgust was palpable.

Thursday, July 19th
7:34AM //

All the air had been sucked out of Jack's lungs, as if he'd taken a strong punch to the gut. He hadn't been able to breathe right since. All he could do when Emma told him the truth was put his arms around her and convince his mind to accept her words, as tears streamed down his cheeks.

She'd never looked so broken, his Emma. In that light dress, her skin brown from the relentless sun. Her hair, so much lighter than it had been, framed her delicate face. She was so beautiful. Jack was afraid she would never look at him the same way again.

Her eyes were always empty and scared, like a hunted animal's.

He couldn't speak to her, couldn't look at her. He had to get away. He hadn't been able to sleep and now stood at the outskirts of the camp.

Golden, pink light seared the eastern sky, revealing the dirt and dust in the air. A haze filtered the farmland surrounding the camp. Jack scuffed his shoe through the dirt.

Just a few weeks ago we were planning our wedding. Living in luxury compared to this. Now we have nothing, we're living here, where everything reeks of feces. And Emma—Emma's had to give herself up just to make sure we all eat. I ate that food. How can I judge her for doing what she's had to do? I should be protecting her and taking care of her. I have to stop this.

Jack buried his face in his hands and groaned around the bile surging up his throat.

"Hey. What the hell's going on, man?"

Jack spun to face Matt. "You scared me."

"You've been avoiding us since yesterday. What's up with Emma, anyway? Every time I try to ask her anything, she bites my head off."

Matt wasn't the sullen teen he'd been in Houston. He looked more alive than Jack had ever seen him.

And I'm being such a baby, pouting in the corner.

"Emma should tell you the reason. But you're right, I shouldn't have run off. Emma deserves better from me. I'm going back now."

They turned toward the camp.

"She's been trading sex for food and water, hasn't she?"

Those words spoken out loud with such bald detachment from Emma's little brother hit Jack like another blow to the stomach. He took a moment to regain his breath. "Yeah, man. I won't let it happen again. Trust me."

"No, it won't happen again. But how else do you suggest we feed ourselves, and help Georgia and her kids get enough food?" Matt glared out of the corner of his eyes.

"We'll figure something out. Anything's better than this."

They found Emma outside the tent with Georgia and the kids. Jack reached a hand down to help her stand. She wiped the dust from her dress.

"Can we walk?" Jack held his hand out again, hoping she'd take it. She did.

They walked away, down the avenue between the rows of tents.

"Em, I'm so sorry for disappearing."

"I understand." Emma's voice was almost inaudible.

"No, listen to me." Jack stopped and faced Emma, putting a hand on each of her arms. "Nothing has changed about the way I feel about you. I love you just as much, if not more." Jack tilted her chin up, making her meet his eyes. "It's my fault, really. You should never have been forced to do anything like that. If I'd been here, if I hadn't tried to find my useless mom, none of this would've happened. I'm so sorry." Jack's vision blurred.

Emma's expression softened. Silent tears flowed down her cheeks. "I didn't know what else to do. I'm ruined now. Our future is ruined."

"No, it isn't. You're still as beautiful and whole to me as you ever were. I'm still going to marry you, even if it takes years of paperwork to get a license. It's going to happen."

Emma fell forward against Jack's chest. He folded his arms around her.

9:16AM //

Jack could breathe outside the camp. He could see glimpses of Emma's laid-back self when they were in town. He shoveled eggs into his mouth. They'd had to walk an hour and a half into the center of Matamoros to find the bus station. But the food was worth it. The morning sunlight glared off their plates in the open-air courtyard. A woman brought out a pot of coffee and refilled their mugs.

"Thanks for breakfast, Jack. This is so nice." Carol almost smiled as she took another bite of her pork.

They ate in silence. When their plates were cleared away they stood from the table and walked two blocks to the bus station. Emma wrapped an arm around her mom's shoulders and held Matt's hand. Jack walked behind the family.

Carol was right. Nothing is guaranteed anymore. Emma knows she might not see her mom or brother again. I might not see them again. Jack cleared his throat as they entered the station.

He approached the ticket counter and greeted the man in Spanish. "Two tickets to Mexico City."

The man printed out the tickets and Jack slid his money across the counter.

He studied the tickets as he got out of the line. "Good. This is a nonstop ride. You won't have to change buses until you get into the city, then you'll have to figure out how to get to the address Mr. Hernandez gave you."

Matt nodded. "I'm sure we can find it."

"Jack, I don't know how to thank you. Are you sure you'll have enough money to take care of you and Emma?" Carol placed her hands over Jack's cheeks.

"I'm sure. I even have some extra for you to hold you over until you get settled there." Jack pulled out a wad of cash from his wallet. "Put it somewhere no one can get to it."

Carol tucked the bills under her shirt then put her arm around Emma again.

Matt stuck his hand out to Jack. "Thanks for everything. Thanks for taking care of Emma."

"We both know Emma can take care of herself." Jack pulled Matt in for a hug.

"Let's go find your ride." Emma swiped at her cheek and looked around the trash-strewn terminal.

When they found the right bus, they all exchanged hugs again. Emma held onto her mom's hand until Carol stepped onto the steps of the bus. Jack's heart ached at the sorrow and fear shadowing Emma's eyes. He put his arm around her shoulder and squeezed.

Then they were gone. As the bus turned out of view, Jack steered Emma back toward the sidewalk. Tears streamed down her cheeks. They spoke only a few words during the long trek back.

When they reached their tent Georgia was sitting outside, surrounded by her kids. She stood when she saw them approaching. A frown creased her forehead.

"Where have you been? We're out of vouchers. The kids are starving." Georgia put her hands on her hips as she glared at Emma.

Emma's breath became shallow, her eyes wide.

Jack pulled her back a little, away from Georgia. His pulse pounded in his temples. "Emma's done everything she can to feed her family and yours. You're the kids' mom, you take care of them for a change!"

Georgia seemed to waver between shouting back and giving way to tears. The tears came first, and she slumped to the ground. Jack rolled his eyes.

"We have a little food left. We can share with them." Emma disappeared inside their tent.

Jack followed her. "Your mom was right, she has to learn that she can't keep relying on you to take care of them."

"What are we going to do about food?" Emma plopped onto her sleeping bag and buried her face in her hands. "I can't just stop, Jack. We have to eat. And they threatened to—they said they would kill you if I stopped coming."

Emma reached out for Jack's hand as she rested her forehead on her knees. "I can't lose you."

"You won't. We'll get someone to go with us and confront them."

"You don't get it. These guys are bad. They'll just kill anyone who gets in their way. How do you think they got so much control in the first place?"

"We have to get out of here." Jack paced the length of the tent in front of Emma. "Where are the clothes you were wearing when you got here?"

"Over there, why?" Emma shoved her thumb at the corner behind her.

Jack stepped over to the small pile of clothes and picked up a pair of shorts. His heart stopped when he felt something hard and rectangular in the back pocket. He froze.

"What is it?" Emma's voice startled Jack.

Without daring to breathe, Jack stuck his fingers into the pocket and drew out the card.

Emma's driver's license.

He turned to face Emma. He met her curious gaze and held the card out to her. Emma's hand flew to her mouth and her eyes grew wide.

Jack's heart jumped as a smile burst over her cheeks. "Baby, this is our ticket to marriage. We can get married, then go anywhere."

Emma ran her fingers through her tangled hair and tried to steady her breathing. "What if my dad comes looking for us?"

"Oh, Em." Jack dropped to his knees in front of her.

"He could still have gotten away. We don't know. Matamoros would be the logical place to look. We could post his picture on that board in the office. Besides, it could still take a long time to get a marriage license and everything."

A muffled cry came from the tent next door.

Jack let out his breath. "Let's go back to the UN office and wait until we can meet with Hernandez. He might be able to help us, if no one else can. Maybe he can speed up the process for us."

"Okay." Emma stood and grabbed her food buckets which held leftover rice and corn.

Jack grabbed her elbow and held up the driver's license. "This is amazing, Em. This will change everything."

Emma's smile was cautious. She nodded.

Jack stayed on her heels as she left the tent and set the food next to the fire pit. Georgia was inside her own tent, but Jasper and Sadie played just outside.

"Let's go."

"Can we come too?" Sadie fell into step with them, reaching for Emma's hand.

"No, you need to stay here. Tell your mom there's food." Emma didn't look down at the girl.

Thursday 11:05AM //

Matt reached up to point the vent at his face. His body melted into the comfortable bus seat as the air conditioner cooled him.

"I'm going to the bathroom." Mom stood and hurried toward the back.

This bus has better bathrooms than we had at camp. And air conditioning. I wish Emma and Jack were here. And Dad. And Aaron. And Claire. These last hazy thoughts lulled Matt to sleep.

7:41PM //

It was getting dark when he woke again. Dim light filled the bus from the light strips along the aisle. Soft breathing mingled with loud snores and the rumble of the bus. Mom's seat was empty. He glanced at his watch—hours had passed.

Matt stood and stretched his arms over his head. Looking up and down the long aisle, he didn't see his mom anywhere. He crept to the back of the bus and found the bathroom occupied. Matt glanced around then knocked on the door.

No answer came. Matt's stomach dropped. He knocked a little harder. Still no answer.

"Mom? Are you in there?" Matt pressed his ear against the door. "Mom?"

He jiggled the handle, but the little door didn't budge. He cleared his throat and ran a hand through his hair. A man loomed behind him.

Matt pivoted. "I'm sorry—"

"Do you need help?" The man's brown eyes were full of concern. His English was broken.

Matt nodded and spoke in Spanish. "I think my mom's in there."

"Ah, si." The man stepped up to the door and pulled hard on the handle. The door swung open.

Matt dropped to his knees. "Mom!" He shook his mom's shoulder, his eyes avoiding the sick mess down her shirt.

"Dios mio." A voice breathed behind Matt.

"Mom wake up." Matt shook her again, clutching at her shoulder.

Mom's eyes blinked once. Her hand twitched.

Matt let out the breath he'd been holding in. Her face was pale and beaded with sweat.

The man had disappeared. The bus was slowing down.

"Why are we stopping?"

"What's going on?"

Murmurs rose around the dark bus. Matt closed his eyes, turned his face away from his mom, and took a deep breath. He jumped when someone tapped his shoulder.

The man stood above him again. "An ambulance is coming. It'll be okay."

"Thanks." Matt stood on shaky legs.

People in the seats nearby stared at him. Scattered lights from the town outside looked like huge stars through the dim light and the foggy windows of the bus.

The driver made his way from the front. He swore and covered his mouth after one look at Matt's mom.

Matt fiddled with the door handle and looked up at the man who'd stopped the bus and called the ambulance. "Where are we?"

"I'm not really sure. I'd guess we're somewhere around Ixmiquilpan." The man looked out the windows then back at Matt. "I'm Louis. What's your name?"

"Matt."

"Did you run away from America?"

Matt looked down at his shoes and nodded. He was choked by tears and fear. He couldn't shake the image of his sick-covered mom lying unconscious just behind him. His eyes caught on red lights flashing outside.

People stood, voices blurred together, as medics came on board. Louis pulled Matt away from his mom as two medics knelt beside her. Matt tugged against Louis's arms. She was lifted onto a backboard. Matt broke free and ran after the medics who left the bus with his mom.

Goosebumps cropped up over his arms at the change in temperature as the heat engulfed him. He jumped into the back of the ambulance behind the medics. Matt sat back as one medic cleaned his mom's face and put an oxygen mask over her mouth. The other medic shoved a huge needle into her arm and attached an IV bag.

Matt's eyes burned under the blaring, white lights. He moved forward until he was at her side. He fought a gag reflex as the smell of vomit filled the small ambulance. Mom blinked, then shut her eyes against the brightness. The siren blared as they rushed away from the bus.

"Mom? You're going to be okay." Matt's hands fumbled along Mom's arm and head. He didn't know where to touch her, how to comfort her. He dropped his head into his hands. Tears leaked out. Silent sobs shook his body. He mumbled a quiet cry into his hands. "We should've stayed with Emma. We should've stayed with Dad."

A groan escaped from beneath the oxygen mask. Matt lowered his hands. Mom's eyes were closed but her hand was searching for his.

He clasped it. "I'm sorry, Mom."

Mom pressed Matt's fingers and shook her head.

"What's wrong with her?" Matt spoke in Spanish to the medic across from him.

The man stared at him for a moment before replying. "She's probably just dehydrated. We'll run some more tests at the hospital. Do you know what happened to her?"

"She went to the bathroom and I went to sleep. I don't know what happened after that." Matt looked at his mom. "Were you in the bathroom that whole time?"

Mom lifted a shoulder and nodded.

Matt raised wide eyes to the medic. "I was asleep for almost eight hours."

"Probably got food poisoning." The medic leaned over Mom. "You'll be just fine."

"You'll still do some tests though, right? Just in case?" Matt leaned forward against his knees.

The medic nodded and crossed his arms over his broad chest.

"All that terrible food in the camp, and we eat out one time and she gets food poisoning." Matt took his mom's hand again.

"Camp? Are you American refugees?" The medic next to Matt spoke up for the first time.

Matt looked from her to the man on the other side of the stretcher. "Yeah."

The emergency responders exchanged a look. "Man, there are a lot of you guys. Does she have a card?"

Matt pointed at his mom's torso. "Just the one she got when we arrived at the camp. I think it's in a pocket of her shorts."

Without hesitation, the man dug into Mom's pockets until he found the laminated card. "We'll make sure she gets taken care of. I can't guarantee anything after that."

"Nothing's guaranteed." Matt dropped his eyes along with his voice.

The ambulance stopped, and the medics jumped up, pushing Matt out of the way. He stumbled out of the back after them and jogged to keep up. The ER was quiet. Everything was bright white. Only curtains separated the hospital beds.

A team of nurses joined the emergency responders and transferred Mom onto a hospital bed. They rushed around, attaching a new IV bag, removing her clothes and dressing her in a gown, taking blood, and administering shots.

Matt stood in the curtained corner. "What are you doing to her?" His voice was weak as he tried to speak to the room at large. No one heard.

Friday, July 20th
7:56AM //

Joe pulled a clean shirt over his head, his muscles raising a complaint with every movement. Rosa had found the shirt and a new pair of shorts in the hospital's lost and found. He picked up his old shirt, ruined by the sun and salt water, and tossed it in the trash. A knock sounded on the door as he collected the money and his license in a neat pile. Rosa entered.

Her bright smile was marred by a hint of sadness.

"You won't miss me, Rosa. There are plenty of people in this hospital who need your help and who won't give you such a hard time."

"You're wrong Señor Smith, I will miss you. And I'm very upset that you think you can just get on a bus and go so far away without anyone to go with you and watch out for you." Rosa placed her hands on her hips.

"Well, I can't thank you enough for all you've done for me. You want to come with me? My family would love to meet you." Joe chuckled.

"Are you crazy? You know I can't do that. You just get going now." Rosa turned away and pulled the blanket off the bed.

Joe touched her arm. "If I can ever do anything to repay you for all you've done for me, please tell me."

"Just go and find your family and don't kick the bucket along the way."

"It's a deal." Joe flashed her one more smile then headed to the front desk with his discharge papers.

He left the hospital ten minutes later with a huge bill and directions to the bus terminal about ten blocks away. On wobbling legs, Joe walked down a street bustling with cars and bicycles. Palm trees swayed in a warm, spicy breeze. Modest, clean houses lined the street.

Joe stopped and closed his eyes. *I'm free.* He stood for a long time savoring his independence. From Russia. From the confines of the hospital. Tension siphoned from his limbs. New, fresh life coursed through his veins. He opened his eyes and continued toward the bus station. *We could start a new life here in Mexico. A good life. Now to find my wife.*

As he eased his way down the sidewalk, Joe had to step into the street to avoid a group of locals who wouldn't move to let him pass.

One man bumped shoulders with him. "Now you gringos know what it's like. Now you want us to just let you run around our country, when you never wanted us in yours."

"Yeah, honky."

Joe paused. Instead of saying anything, he gave them a sad look and continued on.

At the station, Joe exchanged his US dollars for Mexican currency. The exchange rate was abysmal. He approached the ticket booth and bought a one-way to Matamoros. It took a good chunk of his money.

Joe sighed as he settled into the air-conditioned bus and leaned back to sleep through the nine-hour ride. His muscles ached after his walk from the hospital, though he felt stronger than he had in months.

Friday 9:02AM //

Carol opened her eyes by a slit. Rays of morning sun filled the white space around her. Matt sat sleeping in a chair. It calmed her heart to see him there. She was lying on a bed, surrounded by white curtains. An IV was stuck in her arm. Monitors stood around her head. She closed her eyes again and took a deep breath.

The curtain swished as a nurse stalked up to Carol's bed. "How are you feeling?" The young woman spoke in English.

Matt's head swung up and he lunged for Carol's hand. His bleary eyes tried to focus on her face. "Mom are you okay?"

Carol cleared her throat. "I'm alright. What happened?"

"You got food poisoning. We're just making sure you get your fluids." The nurse removed the empty IV bag from the stand.

"Don't you remember?" Matt rubbed his hands through his hair.

We probably both need a shower. "I remember now. I think I'd rather forget it though."

"We're about ready to let you go. All your tests came back normal." The nurse pulled the needle out of Carol's arm in one smooth, painless motion and placed a cotton ball over the area.

"That's good." Relief washed over Matt's face.

Carol wanted to pull him into her arms and assure him everything would be okay, like she did when he was little. "Where are we? Did we make it to Mexico City?" She looked from the nurse to Matt.

Matt shook his head.

"You're in Ixmiquilpan. About two and a half hours from Mexico City. Take your time and come to the front desk when you're ready." The nurse swished past the curtains again.

Matt dropped his head onto the side of the bed.

Carol placed a hand on his head. "Do you know what happened to the cash Jack gave us? It was in my shirt. Where are my clothes?"

Matt exhaled and raised his head again. "I don't know. You won't want them back. Here's some clothes, and here's the money." Matt rose and walked around the bed to a small table on wheels.

The cash was on it, and her refugee card.

"I wish your father were here." Her throat constricted around the words.

"I still have our tickets. Maybe they'll let us get on a bus and finish the ride, since we paid to get to Mexico City."

"Yeah, maybe." Carol pushed herself to a sitting position. She closed her eyes as the room tilted around her.

"We can stay here for however long you need to, Mom."

"What would I do without you, Mattie?" Carol's eyes brimmed with tears. She chuckled and swiped them away.

"Well, don't worry about that."

"You must be starving."

Matt shrugged. "I'm pretty hungry. Are you?"

Carol shook her head. "I'm just glad my stomach has calmed down. It'll probably be a while before I'm ready to eat again. But we should find something for you to eat. The hospital probably has a cafeteria. It might be safer than getting something off the street."

"Yeah. I wonder if Jack or Emma got sick too." Matt stood and stretched his arms over his head.

Carol's mind raced back to when he was four, when he would make himself as big as possible before somersaulting over the arm of the couch onto a pile of cushions. *We can't afford to take any more tumbles right now.*

"I'll wait outside while you change." Matt ducked around the curtain.

Moving slow, she rose from the bed and took the shirt from the table. A fresh set of underclothes lay on top of a pair of shorts. The clothes didn't fit well, but they smelled clean and she was grateful for them.

Carol leaned on Matt as they inched to the front desk. They were discharged by the same nurse who'd unhooked her IV. "We have all the information we need from your refugee card. Here's your bill. Just pay when you can." The nurse slid a piece of paper across the counter to her.

"Thank you so much." Carol looked down at the bill. They'd been given a discounted rate.

For the first time since arriving in Mexico gratitude swelled inside Carol. It was soon hampered by the thought of Emma and Joe and Aaron being so far away from her, away from each other.

Matt's Spanish words caught Carol's attention as he asked the nurse a question.

The nurse smiled and answered him, pointing to her left.

Matt looked down at Carol. *When did he get taller than me?*

"The cafeteria's this way." Matt pivoted to the left and started walking.

Carol watched her youngest son out of the corner of her eye as they ambled down the hall. *He's grown a lot while we've been in*

Mexico and I haven't even realized it. Not only was Matt taller, but something was different in his eyes. A maturity and wisdom that she'd seen glimpses of before, were now etched into every corner of his face.

"Are you okay?" Matt caught her staring at him.

"I'm fine. Still feeling weak. But I'll be fine."

The cafeteria turned out to be a quaint modern café. Matt ordered chips and salsa and tacos. Carol dropped into a chair at a table by a window. Matt joined her carrying four bottles of water.

"Did you drink any water at that restaurant?" He placed two bottles in front of her.

Carol stared through the water bottle at Matt's hands on the other side. "I don't think so."

"Hmm. Well, these should hold us over for a while. You should drink some." Matt pushed one of the bottles closer to her.

Carol tilted her head to one side and grinned. "I miss Aaron. And your dad."

"I know. So do I. Do you think Aaron's okay?" Matt looked out the window.

Carol's gaze wandered out into the sunlight as well. "I have to believe he is, Honey."

One Year Earlier //

"Why'd you bring me here?" Emma raised an eyebrow at Jack.

They stood in the high school parking lot next to her jeep.

Jack's hands were shoved into the pockets of his jeans. He didn't meet her eyes, but looked around, fidgeting. "You've been working nonstop at that coffee shop of yours. I wanted to give you a special day."

"So you brought me to our old high school parking lot?" Emma crossed her arms.

Jack cleared his throat and leveled his gaze at her. His restlessness calmed. "Emma, this is the exact spot I first fell in love with you."

Emma's heart sprinted ahead. Her mouth dried up.

"You've always known exactly what you want, and you've gone after it. You taught me to make decisions and chase dreams. If it weren't for you I don't know where I would be. Probably deep into drugs with no future. Because of you, I have this life. I'm an accountant on my way to a successful career. Because I know that you go after what you want, I've never taken your love for me for granted. Every day I'm amazed you still choose me." Jack stopped and looked at the ground.

Emma's throat constricted, and tears stung her eyes. Renewed love for the man before her brimmed over. She had watched him change from a punk kid into a man. And he had seen her turn from a crazy teenage girl into the woman she was becoming.

"The first good decision I ever made back in high school was that I would marry you someday. Since then, even when we took that weird break, I haven't wavered from that goal." Jack moved closer to Emma.

The tears trickled down her cheeks. Tremors ran up and down her body.

Jack lowered himself to one knee as he pulled something out of his pocket.

All sound faded away. It was just like in the movies, all Emma could see was Jack's radiant face, his tremulous smile.

He opened a small box revealing an exquisite diamond ring. "Emma Jane Smith, will you marry me?"

Emma's hands flew to her lips. "Yes!"

Jack was on his feet, wrapping his arms around her. Emma inhaled his familiar, comforting smell, relished his cheek against hers. *Forever with this guy.*

He stepped back, laughing as tears brightened his dark eyes. He slipped the ring on her finger. "It fits."

"Where did you get this? It's perfect." Emma admired the sunlight sparkling off the diamond and the intricate filigree along the band.

"It was my great-grandmother's. The only thing I have from my family. The only thing my mom didn't pawn off. I took it from her dresser when I left home." Jack shrugged.

Emma took hold of his shirt collar and pulled his lips to hers.

After a kiss that sent chills down Emma's spine, Jack took both her hands in his. "The day is ours, fiancée. We can do whatever you want."

Emma dove into his dreamy brown eyes. "Can we go to the gulf?"

Jack's crooked grin appeared. "Anything you want. Are you hungry? We can get food on the way."

"Yes, and coffee."

"You're addicted." Jack hopped into the passenger's seat of the jeep while Emma slid behind the wheel.

"I am starting my own business. It's bound to happen. Especially when that business revolves around specialty coffee."

Jack leaned over and planted a row of slow kisses on her neck.

"Hey now. You know I'm saving that for the wedding night, not the engagement night."

"I know. But can't a guy kiss his brand-new fiancée?"

Emma flashed a grin. "Of course."

Golden hues and the sparkling gulf drenched their day. The depth of their commitment settled into Emma's heart as they lay on the beach and ran through the water.

"Jack, I'll never forget today. Thank you." Emma dropped her head onto Jack's shoulder as he drove home through the darkness.

He kissed the top of her head. "Thanks for saying yes."

"Whatever happens in the future, I'm glad we'll be together." Emma looped her arm through Jack's and squeezed.

"I think our future together is pretty set. I'll work up the ladder at the accounting firm and you'll own a wildly popular coffee shop. I never thought I would have such a life."

Friday, July 20th
1:21PM //

Hernandez rubbed his hands over his face. Emma sat up straight in her chair, watching. They hadn't gotten in to see him the day before and had waited two hours today until they were let in to his office. Sharp pangs ate at Emma's stomach. Mr. Hernandez removed his hands to reveal a pained, compassionate expression.

"I'm sorry this has been happening to you."

Jack shot up sending his chair skittering backward. "You're sorry? Do you understand the kind of world we're living in when my fiancée has to give herself up just to eat? I don't know how anyone could let this happen. We've got to get her out of here." Jack crossed his arms over his broad chest, his nostrils flaring.

Emma lowered her head and pulled her knees up. No matter how hard she tried though, she couldn't shrink as small as she wanted.

"Look, you somehow by-passed the process for her mom and brother, which we're thankful for." Jack lowered his arms and his voice. "Can you do it again for Emma? If we could just get married, everything would be easier."

Mr. Hernandez met Emma's eyes. "Thousands of people are flooding in every day from the US. I'm sure you've noticed the tents going up as we receive them. People are sleeping in the shade of tents when we don't have enough."

"I thought they closed the borders a long time ago." Emma hardly recognized her own voice.

"They did. Americans have money and Russians want their money. People get across. Matamoros and other towns along the border are filled with wandering, homeless Americans—"

"Why are you telling us this? You can't help us? Just say so." Jack dropped into his chair again.

Mr. Hernandez's eyes didn't stray from Emma's. "There's strength in numbers. One gang can't control all the chaos coming in for long."

Emma lowered her gaze for a moment before looking up at the man across the desk again. "How much longer will it be before we can get married?"

"It usually takes several months under the best circumstances." Mr. Hernandez eyed Jack. "You will have to become financially stable enough to get out of the camp and get an apartment. The government will want to see that you can support both of you. Then you can represent her to the consul to obtain a more permanent visa. While she's here, the UN is responsible for her. Once you get married, she'll be under the Mexican government.

"In the meantime, Emma, you need to make your only form of identification stretch. Normally, you'd need a passport and other identification to get married, but I'll write a letter of recommendation for you to take to the consul, along with your refugee status ID, and they may be more lenient. All they care about is that you're not just marrying to get citizenship."

Jack nodded.

Emma stared at him. "I mean, we are though."

"Yes, but you were planning on getting married long before the Russians invaded your country. That will help your case."

"Thanks, Mr. Hernandez." Jack leaned back in his chair.

Mr. Hernandez took a breath and went on. "Now Jack, we may be able to offer you a job translating. There are people in the local government willing to help process the Americans, but many of them don't know English well enough. Hiring you might help a little."

"Would it pay well? As a citizen, I could get a job in town as an accountant." Jack leaned back in his chair.

"I don't think you'd find many good options in Matamoros."

"I'll take any work you can give me then."

"Tell Luz at the front desk that you need paperwork for an in-camp translator job. She'll get you set up. Bring it back as soon as you can so we can get you working again."

Emma stood and held out her hand to Mr. Hernandez. "Thank you."

"I truly wish I could do more." Mr. Hernandez held her hand between both of his.

"I know." Emma walked out of the stuffy office, through the lobby full of new arrivals and despair, out into the blaring afternoon light. She stood outside the door waiting for Jack.

Jack was at her side moments later with the application in one hand. "That was unexpected. I just have to make some money, maybe get a place in town, then we can work on getting married. It seems more likely at this point than you getting asylum." He turned to face Emma and took one of her hands with his free one. "I've been waiting a long time to marry you. I never could have imagined it would be like this, but the important thing is that we're married."

Emma looked down at the ground and allowed a faint smile to stretch her cheeks. When she looked up again, she pulled his head toward hers, touching her lips to his. Jack returned the kiss with an eagerness that took Emma's breath away. Her smile grew as she pulled away and searched Jack's dark eyes.

After a few moments of silence, the reality of the conversation with Mr. Hernandez dawned on Emma and she cocked her head to the side. "They can't help us with the food situation or the gang. But I think he just told me to start a rebellion. And this time we won't be run out of the country."

Friday 6:03PM //

Joe stretched, looking around the town of Matamoros. As hoped, he'd slept most of the ride here and now energy coursed through his limbs. The maps he'd seen of the camp outside Matamoros showed its location to be just west of town. Joe turned his feet west and started walking.

He walked through an industrial district. His legs grew tired and he sat on a bench in the shade of a building to rest.

"I hope I'm going the right way." Joe sighed.

He sat for several minutes, then stood and walked on.

After a few more blocks, Joe found the end of the industrial buildings. He shaded his eyes. What he had mistaken for clouds of dust, was an expanse of tan-colored tents stretching out as far as he could see. Joe's hand dropped to his mouth and his eyes widened.

His feet shuffled forward. A small cinder block building stood at the entrance to the camp. Joe made his way to it. *Maybe they'll be able to tell me if Carol and the kids are here. And where to find them in this mess.*

"Dad?"

Joe stopped. *I must be more tired than I thought. I could swear that sounded like Emma.*

"Dad? Daddy?" The voice became more hysterical with each cry.

Joe turned just as Emma, his sweet Emma threw herself into his arms. Her tears fell on his shoulder. It was so good to hold her again.

"Emma. I can't believe you're actually here." Joe's voice broke.

Another hand came down on his shoulder.

"Jack! You made it here too?" Joe threw an arm around the young man who was fighting back his own tears.

It seemed none of them could talk for crying. Joe's eyes remained dry, though his insides were bursting, and he couldn't have wiped the smile off his face for anything.

As Emma calmed down, she pulled away from Joe's embrace and looked up into his eyes.

"Dad. I never thought I'd—how did you find me?"

"It's a long story. Can we sit somewhere? I want to hear everything that's happened to you. Where's your mom? And Mattie?" Joe's heart dropped.

"They're fine. They had a chance to get out of here and go to Mexico City, so they took it. Actually, you just missed them. They left yesterday." Emma didn't seem to want to let go of Joe's arm.

His smile widened. *They're alive and they're okay. I know where they are.* Now the tears threatened, knowing his wife was so close, yet again so far away.

"Show me where you've been staying." Joe looked out over the tents again.

Emma exchanged a glance with Jack. "We should get you checked in. See what they say about your situation. We came back here so Jack could return an application." She pulled on his arm and led him into the cinderblock building.

"An application? For what?" Joe held the door open behind Emma.

"Well, this is an application for a job here as a translator. It could help us get some income." Jack held a packet of papers up.

The lobby of the building was quiet and almost empty. Heat from the day hung in the stagnant air.

Joe peered sidelong at Emma.

Emma approached the front desk without stopping. "Is Mr. Hernandez available?"

The woman behind the desk, who appeared to be around Emma's age, sighed. "I think so. One moment." She picked up a landline phone and pressed one button to reach the man Emma had asked for.

After exchanging a few words in Spanish, a man poked his head out of an office to the right. "Emma, Jack. Come in. I didn't expect to see you again so soon."

Emma introduced Joe to the man as he made his way back around his desk. Dark rings circled his eyes.

"My dad just showed up out of nowhere." Emma's voice was thick.

8:27PM //

"You've had to live like this the whole time?" Joe looked around the camp as they made their way to Emma's tent.

Kids played in the dust in front of their "homes." Everyone was covered in dirt and grime. Women held their babies with despondency in their eyes. Teens sat staring like zombies or roving around in tight packs.

Emma exhaled. "Yeah. It's not the best."

"What do you eat?"

Emma exchanged a look with Jack before answering. "Rice and beans mostly."

When they reached the tent, finding it somehow in the maze of identical tents, Joe turned to Emma and pulled her into his arms. Emotion burned behind his eyes. "I'm sorry, Baby. I'm sorry this is your life. I never would've imagined anything like this for you."

Emma shuddered against his chest. Jack kept his eyes on the ground with his hands in his pockets.

"It's not your fault, Dad. Your job is probably what kept us alive, and we wouldn't have gotten out of the country if it weren't for you and Bobby. It's okay. We're doing okay. We're all safe. Right? How are Aaron and Claire?" Emma backed away to meet Joe's eyes.

He couldn't trust himself to speak for several moments. "Honey, Aaron and Claire were—were killed by the Russians."

Emma buried her face in her hands and collapsed. Jack was there, his arms around her before she could hit the ground. Joe lowered himself next to them and they sat for an interminable time as Emma cried.

When will the tears stop?

Monday, July 23rd
7:47AM //

Emma took Jack's hand as they made their way to the food tent. Dad walked on her other side, and Georgia trailed behind them with the kids. Buckets hung at their sides.

Jack released her hand and lifted his bucket, playing a steady rhythm on the bottom like a drum. He gave Emma a sly grin.

With confusion, Emma looked from Jack to the tents around them. Heads poked out of tent flaps. Dad slowed his pace and everyone else followed suit. Trembling, Emma lifted her bucket and banged on its flat surface. A couple of people left their tents and joined the slow parade. Soon they had a mob on their heels.

Emma looked at Jack again. A smile flickered over his face. Her heartbeat pounded loud in her ears mirroring the sound of their drums.

"Is this a normal breakfast time parade?"

Emma jumped when her dad leaned in to whisper in her ear. She shook her head but said nothing. *Dad can't know what's been going on. It might be the last straw.*

When they reached the food tent Emma fell in step behind Jack and Dad. The eyes of the volunteers distributing food grew wide. Emma's pulse jumped. The air was charged and tense with built up hostility. The people behind them pressed forward.

Jack reached the first volunteer and held out his bucket with a smile. The volunteer exhaled, and the tension dissipated. They were given more food than normal, and as everyone passed along the line of volunteers, nothing unusual happened.

"Hernandez was right. There is strength in numbers." Jack murmured as they watched everyone receive buckets full of food without even showing their vouchers.

"Should we go cook some of this?" Dad glanced around as if looking for a stove. "I'm starving."

"Yes, so are the kids." Georgia held her bucket out to Emma as little August slipped in her arms.

He's grown so thin. They all have. Emma touched Georgia's arm. "It's going to be okay now."

Georgia returned her gaze with tears standing in her eyes. She nodded.

Emma carried the two buckets and weaved her way through the loitering crowd. Outside the tent she caught JD's eye. He shook his head and gave her a murderous look.

Emma shivered from head to toe, the rice rattling in her buckets. Jack wrapped his arm around her and guided her away.

As they neared their tents again, yelling drifted from the food distribution area.

Jack set down his bucket and grabbed Emma's arm. Dad stacked wood on the fire pit while Georgia took August into her tent.

"They don't know where you live, right?" Jack's whisper sent pleasant chills down Emma's spine. Something she hadn't felt in a long time.

She shook her head and breathed him in. She couldn't stop shaking.

"You'll be alright."

Emma helped Dad cook the food while Georgia entertained her kids.

"I know you've been eating this for weeks, but I think it's delicious." Dad shoved a large spoonful of rice and beans into his mouth.

Georgia giggled. "Maybe it'll be easier to get enough food now." She met Emma's eyes and smiled.

Emma dropped her gaze. Something gnawed at her gut. *Who knows what happened after we left, but I hope she's right.*

As they cleaned up from the meal, a louder riot of sound came from the direction of the food tent. They all exchanged glances and Emma, Jack, and Dad left the fire pit.

"Has this happened before?" Dad sounded worried.

"No. A lot of fights have broken out, but nothing big." Jack tried to take Emma's hand.

She ran in the direction of the noise.

It was like a scene out of a movie. The Americans and volunteers were attacking the gang members. A mass blur of bodies raged and pulsated closer to them. Food was strewn all over the ground.

Jack rushed ahead to pull an injured woman out of the chaos. Emma joined him in getting other injured people farther away from the fray. After moving three people, Emma heard a loud cry and looked up.

A volunteer jumped onto the food distribution counter with a metal spoon. Tynan jumped up next to him, a knife in his hand, and pulled the volunteer down. Blood splattered everywhere. A mess of people threw themselves on top of Tynan.

Emma shuddered and followed Jack and her dad to another victim. Before she knew what was happening, a strong arm wound itself tight around her neck and a cool blade lay flat against her skin. Her heart jumped up her throat, and JD's foul breath stung her nose.

"Emma!" Jack ran forward but stopped as the knife dug into Emma's neck.

A whimper escaped as the blade sliced into her, but she clamped down on her screams.

Jack held his hands in the air. "Let her go, man. She never did anything to you. Let her go." He spoke in Spanish, perhaps hoping to gain JD's respect.

JD backed away, gripping Emma's neck, not letting up on the knife. "The little bitch is mine now."

Jack looked like he could be sick as he stood, helpless.

Was it the tears brimming in Jack's eyes, the ashen look of defeat on Dad's face, or the thought of being at the mercy of JD? Whatever the cause or motivation, a rush of adrenaline surged through Emma. She let her defenses down for one risky moment and, as she'd hoped, JD's strength slackened also.

Renewed heat washed through her veins and Emma twisted the knife out of JD's hand, slicing deeper into her flesh, and backed into Jack's waiting arms. The gathered crowd rushed in on JD and as Emma sank to the ground with Jack's tears raining over her, the gang was driven out of the camp.

Dad approached on wobbling legs and fell over Jack and Emma, joining their embrace. Emma watched the chaos around them. Her body began to shake more violently than ever before. Blood traced down her shirt from the cut in her neck.

Strength in numbers. Volunteer medics and refugees rushed to help the injured on the ground. As the crowd straggled back from the outskirts of camp tears welled in Emma's eyes. Many coming back toward them held a new light in their smiles.

A medic dropped to her knees in front of their huddle and tended to Emma's neck without asking questions.

"It's over, Em." Jack rubbed her arms as though trying to warm her.

Emma exhaled and closed her eyes. She could breathe.

Monday 12:43PM //

"I can't believe this place, Mattie. I never thought they had such nice places in Mexico."

Matt raised an eyebrow at his mom. "Really?"

"Well, I don't know." Color had come back to her face and energy to her step.

They'd found the bungalow behind a large house in a nice area of Mexico City on Saturday afternoon, with the key hiding under the doormat, waiting for them. It was small, but clean. It was paradise. Matt wouldn't admit this to anyone, but he'd cried himself to sleep the first night for no other reason than having a soft mattress and pillow under him, after scrubbing himself raw in a long, hot shower.

Now they were in the big house getting ready to clean. It was a mansion really, even to American standards. Slatted wood floors, stainless steel in every corner of the kitchen, and a man cave with a wet bar downstairs made the house feel modern.

"This is as nice as Nan and Pop's place was. There's no way you can do all this in one afternoon, Mom." Matt shook his head, peering up at the vaulted ceiling.

"You're right. That's why you're going to help me. If you dust everything, it will save me a lot of time." Mom held out a damp rag to Matt with a rosy-cheeked smile.

"You're loving this." Matt narrowed his eyes.

Mom's face grew serious. "This is the first time I've had something productive to do in months. You and I are taken care of. We've slept in real beds for the past two nights. Don't think I'm not constantly wondering what's happening with Emma and Jack, or where your dad and Aaron are. . ." Her voice trailed off.

"I know. It is really good to be out of that camp."

Mom jumped as a phone rang on the wall in the kitchen. She looked at it as if it might bite her. "Should I answer it?"

Matt shrugged and walked to the nearest side table. He gave it a swipe with the rag as Mom picked up the phone.

She screamed into the receiver. The rag fell from Matt's hand. He ran to her side.

"Joe? Joe, is that really you?" Tears poured down Mom's cheeks. Her eyes were shining.

"That's Dad?" Matt pulled on her arm, his heart pounding in his throat.

Mom nodded, her eyes closed. "Where are you? What's going on?" She moved the phone to her other ear, so Matt could hear.

Matt pushed the button to turn on the speaker phone.

"It's so good to hear your voice." The phone crackled as Dad's voice broke.

"Hi Dad."

"Mattie? How are you doing, Buddy?"

"Good. We have a pretty sweet set-up here."

"Where are you?" Mom interjected and squeezed Matt's arm.

"I'm at the camp in Matamoros with Emma and Jack. I came on a bus on Saturday."

"What? You're in Mexico? How did you escape? How did you get there?" Mom trembled.

"It's a long story, I'll tell you another time." Dad hesitated. He'd never sounded so tired or unsure to Matt. "Hernandez gave me this number and told me where you were. I'm glad you made it there safely."

Mom exchanged a look with Matt. "How's Emma?"

"She's doing fine. There was a huge riot this morning and everyone drove that gang out of the camp. I guess they were controlling the food rations? So, hopefully everyone will get enough food now."

Matt closed his eyes and dropped his head into his hands.

"That's so good to hear." Mom put a hand on Matt's shoulder. "What are you going to do now?"

"Well, I know there are jobs in the oil fields here in Mexico. Hooper was in contact with the operation. Hernandez thinks they might hire someone with my experience. I'm going to apply for asylum here."

"Matt and I will save our money for a lawyer."

"Good. Well, I'd better go for now. I love you both. So much." Dad's voice was hoarse.

"We love you too."

Matt was grateful Mom answered for both of them. He couldn't trust himself to speak.

Mom continued to stare at the phone as the dial tone blared through. Matt pushed the hang up button and cleared his throat.

"We better get to cleaning, huh. We have money to save." Mom placed the phone back on the receiver, her hands still shaking.

Monday 2:43PM //

"You talked to Mom? How is she?" A cold numbness spread over Emma, followed by the warmth of hope.

Dad couldn't hide his smile. "She and Matt are doing well. They sound happy and they have a nice situation down there."

"That's good. Did you tell her about Aaron?" Emma met her dad's gaze before he dropped his eyes. "Dad?"

"No, I didn't. I couldn't do it. She sounded so happy." He rubbed the back of his neck with one hand.

Aaron used to do that too. "She didn't ask?"

Dad shook his head and shrugged.

"You need to tell her. She worries herself sick over Aaron."

"You think this news will help?" Dad's eyes grew stormy and Emma knew to back off.

"I'm glad they're okay." Emma's voice quivered.

Dad pulled her into his arms.

Monday, July 30th
3:23PM //

Joe paced the small office with the phone ringing in his ear. He rubbed the back of his neck as sweat beaded on his forehead. Emma's words echoed in his mind. *'You need to tell her.'*

I've been such a coward.

"Hello?" Carol's voice through the line made Joe jump.

"Hi Carol Bell."

"Joe, it's so good to hear your voice again. You haven't called me that name in a long time." The tenderness in Carol's voice was like a knife to Joe's heart.

"How are you? Where's Mattie?" Joe leaned against Hernandez's desk, then began pacing again.

"I'm fine. He's upstairs dusting for me. How are you? How's Emma?"

"Fine, fine. We're okay. Carol, I have something to tell you. It's about Aaron and Claire."

"What is it? Joe, what's wrong?" Carol's panic rose with each word.

Monday, August 6ᵗʰ
12:05PM //

"Mom come on. We have to go clean." Matt pushed on her shoulder. "She let us have last Wednesday off, but we need the money. We have to go."

Carol stared at the blank wall on one side of her bed. It had been her view for the last several days. "You're right. Of course."

"I can go do it without you, if you want." Matt's voice broke.

Carol rolled over to face him. "No. We'll go together." She put a hand on his soft cheek. "I'm sorry I've let you down this week, Mattie."

"You haven't let me down." Matt sat on the edge of the bed. "I've been sad too. But we need to eat something and go. It will help to have something to do."

Carol sat up and the room spun. She dropped her head into her hands. "You're right again. I can't remember the last time I ate anything."

"Señora Acosta dropped some food off for us the other day. We have eggs and tortillas and stuff."

"That was nice of her." Carol's deep grief chained her to the bed. Getting up, moving on with life, seemed disloyal to Aaron's memory. "I can't believe he's gone." Tears she had thought were dried up trickled down her face. "And Claire."

"I know, Mom." Matt took her hand. "At least they were together."

Carol's body shook with sorrow. *He doesn't know what it's like to lose a child.*

"I think he wouldn't want you to stay down long. He never did. He would want you to keep going and enjoy every part of life you can."

From anyone else, those words would have sounded like empty solace. Carol knew they came from deep in Matt's heart and he knew his brother, and he believed what he said. And he was right. Aaron was full of life. He wouldn't have wanted her to stay down.

"We have to work and save money so we can see Dad and Emma and Jack again." Matt stood and pulled Carol up after him. He let go of her hand and walked out of the room.

Carol looked around the small bedroom. Everything within her wanted to collapse on the floor and wail and pound her fists into the hard wood. But she restrained herself and joined Matt in the kitchen.

He made short order of a few good eggs and poured salsa over them.

Carol's hunger awakened after her first bite. "Thanks." She sacrificed a weak smile for her young son.

When they reached Señora Acosta's house, Matt put on some music before grabbing his dusting rag. Carol took the rest of the cleaning supplies from a closet and suppressed a smile as Matt shook his behind along to the music. To laugh seemed a desecration to her heart.

As Matt dusted, Carol gathered the laundry from all the bedrooms and bathrooms. Aaron's face crowded her mind and she had to sit down several times when the grief was too much. She ran into Matt in the master bedroom.

"Try to focus on the little things you're doing. It helps. In my mind I give myself a play-by-play of what I'm doing. It's seems dumb, but it's makes things easier. See, I'm picking up this lamp. Dusting under the lamp. I wipe the lamp, then I set the lamp down. Like that. I don't know." Matt looked embarrassed at how his strategy sounded.

"I'll try it. Thanks, Sweetie."

The phone by the bed rang and they both jumped. Carol's hands shook as she picked up the phone, the result of her last phone call with Joe seared to the top of her mind. "Hello?"

"Hi Carol." It was Joe. He sounded subdued, apologetic. "How are you? How's Matt?"

The tenderness in his familiar voice was too much for Carol. She pushed through her tears, her words wavering on her tongue. "We're hanging in. It's our first day back to cleaning. Matt's helping me get through it."

"That's good." A long silence settled over the line before Joe spoke again. "I love you, Carol Bell."

"I love you too. When will I get to see you? And Emma?"

"I don't know. We're working our hardest to make that happen as soon as possible, but there are so many unknown variables. I'm doing all I can to get asylum, but it takes time. Jack is working away translating at the camp. Emma is helping where she can."

The vice around Carol's heart relaxed a little as Joe talked of mundane things. "That's good."

"Yeah, you and Matt will be on my asylum application and I'll eventually have to go to Mexico City for the interviews, Hernandez tells me. So I'll get to bunk up with you and Mattie." Joe's tone grew more cheerful. "It will take a lot of paperwork and processing from here before I can make that happen."

"But that's great news." Carol met Matt's questioning eyes.

"Yeah. I just can't wait to be with you again. Be under the same roof, share a bed with you, eat meals together." A longing in Joe's voice broke Carol's heart all over again.

He's grieving too. He's dealing with all this and probably things I don't even know about. When she was able to speak again, her voice was thick, her throat ached with constriction. "It's been way too long, Joe."

Matt walked up beside her and took her hand.

"Way too long." Joe's sigh came loud through the receiver. "I'd better go for now. I'll call you again when I can."

"Okay. Take care of yourself." Carol sniffed. Her body yearned to have Joe's arms around her. In her whole life she'd never felt safer than in his embrace.

"You too, Carol Bell."

Thirty-two Years Earlier //

"Hey, Carol Bell. You ready?" Joe stood in the doorframe of the guesthouse, his grin revealing faint dimples.

A chill from the winter air wafted inside.

"Carol Bell?" Carol twirled to face him as she stuck an earring in her right earlobe.

"You hate it? It's Christmas time, I guess I have carols on my mind. And I always have a certain Carol on my mind." Joe pumped his eyebrows up and down. "Plus, you're pretty as a Christmas card. Look at you." His face grew serious as his eyes traveled over Carol's red dress and black stockinged legs.

Carol couldn't contain her laughter. "Whatever you say. I can't believe you talked me into going to a church Christmas party."

"We met at a church party, and I thought it would be fun to come full circle. Plus, David and Fay will be there. You never get to see Fay since you decided to keep living here."

"Yes, Fay's the real reason I'm going." Carol rifled through her pocketbook to make sure she had everything.

"Whatever it takes, Baby."

She looked up at her boyfriend with a raised eyebrow. "You're in rare form tonight. Are you sure it's safe to take you out? Among other people?"

Joe released a deep belly-laugh. Carol suppressed her own laughter but graced him with a sincere smile.

"I'm glad my parents are letting you stay in the guest house for free. You deserve it." Joe clung to the steering wheel as he drove toward the city.

"What makes you say that?" Carol checked in the mirror to make sure her lipstick was still in place after their quick kiss. She pushed the flap back up.

"You don't see yourself the way I see you. You've been through so much, but you're so strong and beautiful and intelligent. I just hope you know how much I love you."

"You love me?" Carol turned toward Joe. She regretted the doubt lacing the question.

He glanced at her before staring straight ahead. "Yes, I love you." His words were sure and clear.

"You don't even know what you're talking about. Love. How could you love me?"

Joe pulled to the side of the road and let his forehead drop to the steering wheel. When he looked up, Carol saw real heartache in his eyes. "I don't know what to say to make you understand. You've lived your whole life with parents who barely gave you the time of day. You've probably never let yourself feel love before, even though you have some good friends, and you have me."

Carol's body went rigid. Her mind was blank.

"You need to let people love you, and trust that we want the best for you. Carol, I would give my right arm, no—" Joe squeezed his eyes shut and shook his head. "I would give my life for you. That's how much I love you. Wait, don't say anything. Please, let this sink in. I know this is bad timing, because we're going to a party, but I'm tired of your calculated words, I'm tired of the fact that you don't trust me to be sincere."

Carol stared out the front window. Christmas lights on the houses around them lit up the street. Something warm and tangible surrounded her. Her throat closed up and tears threatened to come, but she held them back. *How does he know me so well?*

She felt his eyes on her, felt exposed, like he had x-ray vision. For the first time in her life, she shook off the defenses and let him dig into her soul. She took a deep breath.

"Joe, I will try to understand what you're saying. But you're right, after living my whole life snubbing people's love, it won't be easy."

Joe sounded as though he'd just emerged from cold water. "Oh Carol, that's all I'm asking. Just let me love you."

His hand reached out to gently cup her jawline. He pulled her face toward his.

Later, as they sang Joy to the World, Carol let her tears fall.

Thursday, September 13th
8:43PM //

Emma sat with her back against a pole of the food tent, looking out at the endless farmland around the camp. She closed her eyes for a moment and inhaled deeply. The landscape and the arid smells had become familiar to her. Almost sacred. These were hours she cherished, sitting outside the camp in the quiet.

She didn't know if it was God, or what, but when she sat out here in the silence she felt a Presence. A cool, fresh Someone with her. It always filled her with peace. Since she learned about Aaron's death, she had sought this refuge. The dank darkness of the camp was oppressive, and she had found a small freedom out here.

She had also come to know through this Presence or through instinct that to accept her life as it was now was the only way to peace. Aaron's death acted as the final straw in convincing her that she had no control over what would happen today or tomorrow. There was no way around this mess of her life. No way but through. It's what gripped her and yet freed her. Nothing to anchor to, nothing to be sure of. No promises could be made because none could be kept. This Presence was also rootless and free yet felt more solid than anything else in her life. She clung to it in these moments.

Today this feeling eluded her. The supply tent had been busy and was always understaffed now. People had forgotten them. The camp in Matamoros wasn't a priority, though it was still beyond capacity.

Emma struggled to find peace. She laughed into the passing breeze. Struggle and peace were dichotomous, yet constant companions. *Does any of it matter?* Jack's face filled her mind and peace reigned for the moment in her heart. She hugged her knees to her chest. Laying her cheek on her knees, Emma closed her eyes again as the coolness surrounded her.

Secret American Presidential Hideout
Friday, September 14th
8:07AM //

"What's stopping the Russians from moving into Mexico and Canada?" Richardson looked up from his tablet at the President.

They'd both grown thinner and more haggard. The president's wife lay on the other side of the room, sleeping as usual.

The president shrugged but didn't meet Richardson's gaze. "Maybe they're biding their time. We have been able to overcome some of their forces. Maybe they need to organize again before starting a new campaign."

"Have you spoken with Vaselik lately?" Richardson leaned forward on his knees.

"He's stone-walled me. But I've sent him a new proposition."

Richardson's heart dropped. A sick feeling gnawed in his stomach, having little to do with his lack of any breakfast. "What proposition?"

"Canada and Mexico are joining forces. We may get support from the Allies as well. If we succeed, North America will become a more unified nation. We'll have to if we're ever going to be strong again." The president met Richardson's eyes and sighed. "It's the only way I see to survive this and move forward."

A whimper came from the other side of the room.

Special Thanks //

First, I want to thank Bethany Cetti for opening her heart and mission to me and Zack and allowing me to partner in what she's doing through this book. Thank you for fielding my endless naïve questions and for sharing some of the hardest parts of your experience. For the countless messages back and forth, the phone calls, and for your support of everything going into this novel. This book would not have come to fruition without you! Thanks most of all for giving up all you knew to live among and love refugees.

To my husband, best friend, and believer of in my dreams, thank you! Your view of the world, and your imagination brought so much of this book to life. We make a great team! Hours of banter back and forth over every nuance of this novel! You're amazing. I can't thank you enough for taking the leap of faith with me into the out-of-work writer business. Though it's taken me years to get to this place, you've never wavered in your support and belief that I could do it. Because of you, Jack is faithful and patient, Aaron is adoring, and Joe is steadfast. Because of you I struggle to write men who let their people down. Thank you for believing in me and loving me, and always extending grace. I love you!

To Kirsten Johnson, my other best friend, and graphics designer extraordinaire. You emanate beauty wherever you go, and it shines through your work. Thank you for your excitement and for all the hours you put into this project with me. Thanks for rooting me on every step of the way. You get me.

To my awesome beta readers, Sarah, Alyssa, Fiona, Carly, and Bethany, thanks for all the hours you poured over my shoddy first draft! Thanks for your input and wisdom into things I missed.

Fiona, thank you for meeting with me and believing in me! It's humbling. The experiences you shared with me, and your insights were so appreciated.

Sister Sarah, thanks for your feedback. We've always geeked out over books together, and it's been surreal to geek out over a book I wrote!

Alyssa, your friendship is a rich joy in my life. Thank you for your input and your time, even with all your tiny humans to care for!

Carly, thanks for being a cheerleader from afar and for taking the time to read my book! I'm sad you live so far away, because I think we could be great friends. I appreciate you!

Nothing less than epic team work has brought this book to be what it is. It's taken a village to raise this baby. Special thanks to Joy Richter and friends, Ben, Emily, and Zack for selflessly helping me with the book trailer! Thanks to all the non-profits who partnered with me to make my book launch special.

No Way but Through

Made in the USA
San Bernardino, CA
19 January 2019